ONE
PERFECT
GRAVE

BOOKS BY STACY GREEN

The Girls in the Snow

ONE
PERFECT
GRAVE

STACY GREEN

bookouture

Published by Bookouture in 2021

An imprint of Storyfire Ltd.
Carmelite House
50 Victoria Embankment
London EC4Y 0DZ

www.bookouture.com

ISBN: 978-1-80019-274-4
eBook ISBN: 978-1-80019-273-7

To the law enforcement and private citizens who work tirelessly to find missing children

PROLOGUE

He barreled through the drifts, the snow cascading into his boots. His heavy winter coat flapped in the cold wind. He was so scared.

Had they seen him?

He didn't know what to do or where to go. Maybe he could pretend like everything was normal. He'd always been good at that, even when his mom was passed out and the refrigerator was empty.

He had to go back and get help.

But he was so scared. What if he got caught?

He didn't have a choice.

CHAPTER ONE

Ice pelted Michelle's windshield. Despite the defrost blasting, the wipers struggled to keep the glass clear. She drove slowly along the two-la;/ne road, hoping the headlights warned her of any dangerous patches. She was less than five miles from home, but the most dangerous part of the drive loomed ahead.

Bridges freeze first. Michelle's truck-driver father had practically beaten those words into her brain when she first started driving. With no ground below them, bridges couldn't trap heat the same way a road could. Michelle had to cross the Valley Creek Bridge in order to get home.

Why had she insisted on seeing her boyfriend tonight? The weather reporter had said the storm wouldn't hit until after midnight, but since when were their predictions accurate?

Her cell phone flashed with a text from her nervous mother.

Have you left yet?

Michelle wasn't about to take her hands off the wheel to answer. She should have texted when she left town, but convinced herself that knowing she was on the road would just worry her parents more.

She could swear the ice was coming down faster. The wipers definitely weren't clearing as much space.

Michelle's stomach knotted. Creek Bridge was just ahead. Her heart banged inside her chest, and she slowed to a snail's pace. As long as she drove slowly and didn't slam the brakes, she would be just fine.

She was halfway across now, her foot barely pressing the accelerator as she drove on. Her father had put fresh tires on her car last fall. They had plenty of tread to grip the road.

Michelle wished she hadn't left her coat on. The inside of the car felt like a sauna. Her eyes stung from sweat. She'd almost crossed the bridge. The worst had to be over.

Michelle took one hand off the wheel and rubbed the moisture from her eyes. The car shimmied with her movement, but Michelle held steady and finished crossing the old bridge. She leaned back in her seat and breathed a sigh of relief, her body turning to liquid.

Two miles from home now. She pressed the accelerator, increasing her speed by just a few miles per hour.

She didn't see the patch of black ice until it was too late. The car started to spin, and she pumped the brakes just as she'd been taught, but she hadn't reacted fast enough. Her arms locked, hands clenched on the steering wheel, as the car careened off the road and into a deep gully.

Time seemed to stand still. Michelle jerked the wheel to the right, hoping not to slam into the ground nose-first. The front of the car nosedived into the drifts and then stopped. Michelle's neck whiplashed to the right.

She gasped for breath and peeled her hands off the wheel. Where had her phone ended up? She unlocked her seatbelt and searched for the phone, finding it wedged between the seat and the passenger door, thankfully unharmed.

Her vision momentarily blurred. She shook her head and realized her windshield had been shattered. Phone in hand, she wrenched the door open and collapsed into the snow. She crawled away from the car, following the beam of the headlights. Resting on her knees, she tried to get her bearings, but her head throbbed, and she couldn't quite think straight. Her phone didn't have any bars. She couldn't remember if the emergency call worked with no signal, so she forced her legs to move and stood, holding her phone and praying it picked something up.

She halted, her blood turning cold. Her hands shook, her gaze fixated on the unimaginable thing in front of her. She hit the emergency button.

"9-1-1, what's your emergency?"

"I slid off the road," she choked out. "Down into a ditch."

"Are you injured?"

"No. At least, I don't think so. But there's… there's something here."

"What's your location?"

Michelle shimmied forward, praying her mind was playing tricks on her.

She stared, uncomprehending for a moment.

"Miss, are you there? Where's your location?"

"Just past the Valley Creek Bridge on old Stagecoach Road. I'm down in the gully. I need the police."

"A sheriff's deputy is on his way," the dispatcher said. "Along with paramedics."

A wave of dizziness threatened to overwhelm her. "I think you need more than paramedics. There's a lot of blood and…"

Michelle passed out before she could tell the dispatcher what she saw. Two dead bodies sitting in a lake of blood at the bottom of the old bridge. One a young boy, partially frozen in the ice…

CHAPTER TWO

Led Zeppelin's "Misty Mountain Hop" invaded Nikki's sleep. She peeled her eyes open and rolled over, trying to remember where she'd left her phone. Her searching hands knocked it off the wireless charger. She swore under her breath and got out of bed, her eyes still bleary with sleep. She found the phone on the other side of the nightstand, but it stopped ringing before she could answer the call.

"Damnit." The caller ID read unknown number. Nikki climbed back into bed and waited to see if the caller left a message. Her heavy eyelids closed, and she was starting to drift off again when the phone dinged. She sat back up with a sigh and played the message.

"Agent Hunt, this is Deputy Ron Reynolds with the Washington County Sheriff's office. The boss is on the scene of a real bad accident, and I know you've been helping on the Kellan Rhodes case. I've got two dead bodies here. One looks like a kid, but they're hard to get to and we're waiting on the medical examiner. I was hoping you'd come out to the scene."

The deputy left his cell number, and Nikki quickly called him back.

"Reynolds."

Nikki closed her eyes against the wave of emotion. Nine-year-old Kellan had disappeared after school two days ago. Nikki had found out on the news like everyone else, but as she'd been in town, she'd offered to help search for Kellan. She knew the cops would be overwhelmed—there was so much to be done in the first few moments of a case like this if they had any hope of finding the boy alive. She'd stopped herself from taking over the case entirely—it wasn't her place—but she was already beginning to regret that. "This is Agent Hunt. What do you mean the bodies are hard to get to? Can you see his face?"

"No, ma'am," Reynolds said. "They're down deep in the gully. EMS said they're definitely deceased. Appears to be an adult female and a child, but I'm waiting on the medical examiner before I head down. I'm waiting to hear back from the sheriff, but if the body is Kellan's—"

"What's the location?" Nikki asked. If the other body was a female, then the child was more likely to be Kellan. The past two days had been a blur of long hours spent searching for any sign of Kellan or his mother, Dana. Had Reynolds just found the both of them?

"Valley Creek, the old stone bridge. It's off—"

"Stagecoach Road." Nikki had only recently returned to her hometown of Stillwater, Minnesota, but the old bridge had been a favorite party spot in high school.

"Go south on Stagecoach," Reynolds said. "You won't miss the emergency vehicles. It's still icy out, but I've got a county sand truck en route. You should have some grip."

Nikki thanked the deputy and promised to get to the scene as soon as possible. She debated calling Miller but decided against it in case he was on the road already.

"Maybe it's not them," Nikki whispered out loud. She knew that was a futile hope. What were the odds of another adult female and child being found dead?

Warm fingers trailed down her spine. "What's going on?" Rory's husky voice was thick with sleep. After working nearly two days straight, she'd gone to Rory's place hoping to get a few hours of rest. At least she'd managed to sleep for a couple of hours. That would have to be enough.

"I have to go," Nikki said. "Two bodies have been found, and they might be Kellan and his mother."

Rory sat up, his arm slipping around her waist. "Seriously?"

Her throat tightened, moisture in her eyes. "I don't know, but I've got to get out there."

Nikki flung the covers off and got up, searching for her clothes. She kept a few things at Rory's house, so she grabbed a clean pair of jeans and heavy wool sweater.

"Why don't you let me drive you?" Rory said.

She dragged a brush through her tangled waves. "I can't do that."

Rory pointed to the darkened window. "You hear the sleet hitting the glass? The roads are going to be terrible."

"I can handle it. County's putting sand down."

Nikki flicked on the bathroom light and quickly brushed her teeth. The two hours she'd slept had somehow made her look more exhausted. Her skin was paler, and the circles around her eyes darker.

Rory leaned against the doorframe, his curly hair tousled. "I know you can. I'd just feel better if you let me drive you. Especially since you're so upset."

She wrapped her arms around his muscular waist and kissed the tattoo on his bare chest. "I'll be fine. I can't bring my boyfriend to a crime scene."

His lips twitched into a smirk. "Boyfriend? Is that what I am?"

The past several weeks had been a blur. Nikki had tried to keep her distance from Rory while his brother, the man who'd served twenty years for the murders of her parents—a crime he didn't commit—had acclimated to his freedom. Mark swore that he forgave Nikki for her role in his incarceration, as she'd been a victim as well, but his parents were still angry with her. They'd gone through the roof when Rory told them about seeing Nikki. The last thing she wanted to do was further harm the Todd family, so Nikki had tried to give Rory space. She had a backlog of cases and paperwork that needed to be addressed. But staying away had been harder than she anticipated.

"Maybe." Nikki hadn't introduced Rory to her five-year-old daughter or told her ex-husband she was seeing anyone. "But I need to get going."

He pulled her to his chest and kissed her hard. "Please be careful."

"You forget I grew up in rural Minnesota and learned to drive on icy roads. I'll be fine."

Sleet still fell as Nikki drove slowly down the narrow, old county road. Reynolds had said that the bodies had been found at the bottom of a steep gully near Valley Branch Creek. The area was definitely rural, with several miles between houses, which meant the road had lousy visibility, and the night seemed much darker than she was used to. Many of the rural roads in the area had once been the state's original stagecoach routes, including this one. With the lack of development and light sources, it wasn't hard to imagine the nerve-racking journey of stagecoach travelers, hoping the coach wouldn't be robbed.

The road wasn't as slick as she'd expected, thanks to the heavy layer of sand that allowed tires to get a better grip on ice. Flashing emergency lights stood out in the bleakness, and Nikki's stomach knotted.

Forty-eight hours ago, she'd been trying to watch the evening news while Rory did his best to distract her. Nikki had finally given in when the news anchor announced the amber alert. Their phones had vibrated seconds later. The amber alert had announced that Kellan had been abducted by his biological mother, who'd recently lost custody of him to his aunt and uncle. Nikki had immediately called Miller. Her own daughter was with her father for the weekend, and Nikki had planned to spend time with Rory. Instead, she and Rory had spent the next two days trudging through the snowy woods and fields in search of the little boy. Although

Nikki was a volunteer, Miller had briefed her on the details of Kellan's disappearance.

Dana Rhodes had lost custody of Kellan three years ago because of drug use. Six-year-old Kellan had gone to live with his aunt and uncle, and the Andersons had fought to adopt him. Dana had spent time in rehab and in a sober living house, trying to convince the courts that she was capable of caring for Kellan, but she'd recently failed a drug test, losing her last shot at getting custody back. Nikki knew that Dana had confronted the Andersons multiple times since then, and she'd been spotted in the park outside of Kellan's elementary school twice in the lead-up to his abduction. Dana's old VW Beetle had been spotted near the Anderson home on the day Kellan disappeared, but no one had been able to find the car, even though every cop in a hundred-mile radius was on high alert.

While Nikki wasn't responsible for the case, Miller had still wanted her opinion on Dana's mindset. Dana had never threatened her son's safety as far as Nikki could see. She'd accused her sister and brother-in-law of railroading her, but had never threatened them, and she never carried any kind of weapon. Nothing in her history suggested Dana would intentionally hurt her son, but Nikki had worried that her drug use and impulsivity would cause Kellan to get hurt. Her stomach tightened as she rounded the final curve and the bridge came into view.

The sheriff's department had blocked off the northbound lane for the emergency vehicles.

Nikki parked behind a county sheriff's cruiser. Its headlights had been left on, and they cast an eerie spotlight on the steel railing and steep ravine. She left the engine running to keep the sleet from coating the windshield.

Nikki stepped gingerly onto the gravel. Her winter boots had plenty of traction, but she wasn't going to take any risks. She pulled her red winter hat down over her ears and slowly shuffled toward the steel railing. Dizziness swept over her as she gazed down at the scene. The drop had to be at least twenty feet, and the iced-over creek looked like a thin snake. Crime scene lights had already been set up near the creek, and Nikki could see much of the scene.

Judging from the tire marks, the driver had lost control and slid past the guard rail, plummeting toward the bottom. Hours' worth of sleet left a fine layer of ice that likely accelerated the descent. A large fallen tree had stopped the Toyota Rav in its tracks. Bright yellow evidence markers followed what appeared to be a trail of blood deeper into the gully and out of sight. How in the world was Nikki going to get down there without breaking her neck?

A tall, broad-shouldered deputy raised his hand in greeting. Nikki recognized him from a previous case in Washington County. "Agent Hunt, thanks for coming out."

"No problem." Nikki scanned the bridge. "No one from the ME's office yet?"

Reynolds shook his head. "Short-staff and it's Sunday night. Or Monday morning, I guess."

Before Nikki could say anything more, a second set of headlights flashed behind her. Nikki turned to see Miller's SUV pulling up behind her jeep. He'd been promoted to Acting Washington County Sheriff after the previous sheriff's forced retirement.

Miller got out of the big vehicle and pulled a beanie over his head. Ice pellets freckled across his brown skin. "Agent Hunt, I didn't expect to see you here."

Reynolds cleared his throat. "Sir, I called her after I saw the scene. I assumed you'd be asking for her assistance since she helped search."

Miller nodded and then addressed Nikki. "Is it Kellan?"

"I don't know." She wanted to add that her gut already knew the truth, but she could tell Miller was thinking the same thing as her. "I just got here. Deputy Reynolds?"

"Their faces are obscured, and we haven't touched the bodies," Reynolds said. "I've got another deputy with them. The medical examiner should be here any minute."

"Right," Miller said. "How were they found?"

Reynolds pointed to the smashed white car at the bottom of the deep ravine. "The driver's name is Michelle Chow. She has a concussion and some superficial abrasions. She wasn't driving fast, but she hit the brakes and the ice sent her right into the ravine. There's a blood trail from the car to the area where the bodies are. Michelle saw their feet and called it in." He looked at Miller. "You got any outdoor gear? Getting down is nearly impossible without something to keep you steady."

Miller opened the SUV's hatch. Various outdoor equipment was neatly stored inside. He handed her two trekking poles, which were essentially heavy-duty canes with wider ends that were equipped with special gripping material. The handle looked like a garden hose nozzle, so it was probably adjustable, but Nikki could make them work without fiddling with the height. He grabbed a second pair and shut the hatch.

"It's got to be them, Nikki." His eyes looked bloodshot.

Nikki hadn't known Miller very long, but they'd worked a difficult case together in January. He had kids around Kellan's age, and Nikki knew he would take Kellan's death as an act of failure. She squeezed his arm. "I'm sorry."

"Me, too."

"Reynolds, stay here and wait for the medical examiner. If she doesn't have poles, there's another set in my truck."

Reynolds pointed to the far side of the metal railing. "I put down ice melt over there. It's a little less treacherous. Follow her blood trail. The bodies are about a hundred yards away by the old bridge."

Miller headed down first. "Keep the poles kind of in front of you. Don't worry, they'll support your weight."

Nikki said a quick prayer and started wobbling down the hill. The sticks were made of a strong titanium, but she kept imagining one slipping from her grip and her rolling down after it. She reached the bottom with a sigh of relief. "Lucky you had these."

"My family and I like to do outdoor stuff in the winter." Miller pointed to the smashed car. "She's lucky not to have anything worse than a concussion. Here's the blood trail."

The area around the old bridge had been searched already, and the K-9 hadn't picked up either Kellan or his mother's scent. They walked in silence for a few seconds, pushing through the bushes. The iced-over thorns snapped like twigs as Nikki replayed yesterday's search in her mind. The old stone bridge over Valley Creek was less than a mile from the Andersons' home, and even though it had been closed to traffic for years, kids still liked to play on the decaying structure. Nikki and Miller, along with about ten volunteers, had searched the entire area. They'd seen a few beer bottles and cigarette butts indicative of partying teens, but no sign of Kellan.

The arched stone bridge loomed in the shadow of the Klieg lights like the remains of an old castle. The base could only support foot traffic, and the harsh winters were slowly eating away at that.

Nikki's heart pounded in her chest as two pairs of feet came into view. A small lake of blood surrounded the bodies, and the child was positioned between the woman's legs, curled on his side in the fetal position against her chest. A fine layer of ice covered the blue winter coat that had been placed over the child's upper body and the woman's head, along with his exposed hands.

Nikki's throat ached as she forced the words out. "That's Kellan's coat. His aunt said it's brand new."

The gold swoosh on the bottom of the child's Nikes had probably reflected in the headlights just enough for the driver to realize someone was in the ravine. Nikki could imagine the girl, shaken and possibly concussed, walking to this scene. She'd need years of therapy.

A young, white-faced deputy stood guard, evidence bags tucked under his arms. "Sheriff Miller, Agent Hunt. I didn't want to move the coat until one of you arrived."

Nikki suspected he didn't want to see what was beneath the coat, and she couldn't blame him.

Miller took off his winter gloves and pulled on a latex pair; Nikki did the same.

"Sometimes I really hate this job," Miller murmured as he reached for the coat.

Nikki steeled herself against the wave of emotion, but she could feel the moisture building in her eyes. She almost wished she'd not been part of the search team. She was no stranger to a crime scene, but she felt closer to Kellan. He was only a few years older than her daughter, and he'd gone through so much turmoil in his short life.

From the road, it would have been impossible to see their bodies. They would have been here for weeks if the girl hadn't gone off the road. Dana had wedged herself and Kellan into a small space between a pile of bricks from the bridge and a massive fallen oak. Dana leaned up against the oak, with Kellan between her legs. Her hands lay at her sides, palms up, a bloody utility knife still resting in her left hand. Four-inch vertical slits in both her wrists had caused her to bleed out. Bits of sleet crusted over the wounds. Kellan lay against Dana's chest with a bloody, pink scarf wrapped around his head. Dana's face pressed against the top of his head as though she were giving him a kiss. Blood crusted Kellan's neck.

"The scarf is probably hers," Miller said. "She must have tried to stop the bleeding."

"Some kind of accident, then." Kellan looked so small and cold. He must have been terrified in his final moments. Nikki was glad for the pelting sleet on her cheeks. "This doesn't make sense. If she died by suicide, she's gone to a lot of effort to hide her own body."

"That's a damned understatement." The medical examiner had arrived. Dr. Blanchard dropped her black bag onto the snow and sighed. "Sorry I'm late. I've got two investigators stuck with remains on lousy roads. Miserable night to die."

Dr. Blanchard was Minnesota's first African American medical examiner and exceptional at her job. Her findings had been instrumental in the missing girls case Nikki and Miller had worked, and Nikki knew Blanchard would do everything humanly possible to figure out what happened to Dana and Kellan.

Blanchard snapped on gloves and knelt beside the bodies. She shined a bright penlight on Dana's wounds. "What's the first thing you notice about these cuts?"

"Clean slices," Miller said. "Right down to the artery."

"The radial artery is completely severed," Blanchard confirmed. "She started right at her pulse point and then cut toward the elbow, nearly four inches." Blanchard lifted Dana's slim, still hand.

Nikki knelt next to Blanchard, trying not to look at Kellan. "Not a single hesitation mark. How quickly would she bleed out?"

"With a cut this deep?" Blanchard asked. "Not long, even in the cold weather."

"Most suicide attempts like this fail because the individual doesn't cut deep enough or in the right direction," Nikki noted. "Even if a person really wants to die, survival instinct kicks in."

"She might have been using again," Miller said. "The meth could have made her oblivious to the pain."

Dr. Blanchard touched Dana's cheek. "She doesn't look like she's been using. Her skin is relatively healthy, although there's some scarring from previous sores. She's not emaciated, either. But I'll run a full tox screen."

"Her hair, too," Nikki said. "I want to see if she's been clean since losing custody of Kellan."

"No problem. I'll try to rush the results." Blanchard shifted to the other side of Dana, peering closely at the deep gash. "This one's just as perfect as the other. Meaning she managed to endure the pain of cutting deep enough to sever the artery, without any hesitation. She would have been bleeding profusely and going into shock, but this cut is nearly identical to the other. That's damned near impossible."

"How long do you think she's been dead?" Miller asked.

"Not very long," Blanchard said. "She's been here long enough to get some ice built up, but she's not completely iced over. And her blood hasn't even started to freeze."

Blanchard sighed and mouthed a quick prayer before moving on to Kellan. She gently turned his head, and both Nikki and Miller took a step back.

His eyes were closed, and his skin had a familiar green tint, particularly around the nose and mouth.

"Jesus." Nikki shuddered. "He's been dead a while."

Blanchard nodded, gently manipulating his arms and legs. "Once I get his clothes off and see the extent of the lividity, we'll have a better idea, but he appears to be out of rigor." She brushed off the ice crusting Kellan's clothes. "He's cold but not internally frozen. I'll know more when I get a look inside, but at first glance, it appears he was kept somewhere with a regulated temp for an extended time after death."

Blanchard carefully removed the pink scarf and slipped it into the evidence bag the nervous deputy handed her.

Sleet crystallized on Blanchard's nose as she gently touched the crusted blood on his neck. She shifted his head to get a better look at the side he'd been lying on. "This is preliminary of course, but it looks like he hit his head—or was hit—and died."

"Any idea by what?"

"Not without X-rays."

"Is there any way to tell if he fell and hit it or if someone struck him?" Miller asked.

"We can go through some scenarios," Blanchard said, "but we'd really need to examine the skull to have a clearer idea. Something might show up on X-rays, but I'll have to ask a forensic anthropologist to examine them."

Dana's purse strap was still looped over her shoulder. "Can you check her bag?" Nikki asked.

Blanchard slipped the small bag off Dana's shoulder. "Cell phone and cash. Pack of gum and cigarettes. I don't see a lighter." She passed the bag to Nikki.

Nikki retrieved Dana's cell. She flipped open the old phone and sighed. "Battery's dead."

"We've been pinging that number for activity since Kellan went missing," Miller said. "Those old phones still have GPS. We would've known the minute her phone came on, so it must have been dead since Friday."

Nikki took the evidence bag the deputy offered and slipped the phone inside. "We'll have to find a charger for it." She checked the purse again. "Where are her car keys?"

"Coat pocket," Blanchard said.

"No sign of her car." Miller looked at Nikki. "She had to have come from the trail side, likely sliding down the embankment next to the bridge. We haven't found anything but snowmobile tracks and some footsteps. I'm hoping Courtney will be willing to take a look at them after the sun's up." He rubbed his chin and glanced at Nikki. "Actually, if you and your team have the time, I'd love the help on this one. Reynolds was right to call you."

Miller was an interim sheriff, and he'd told Nikki that he wasn't sure he'd wanted the job at the time. Nikki had been trying to think of a way to offer the FBI's help without making it seem like she didn't think he could handle the case. "Absolutely. I'll call Liam and Courtney and get them out here ASAP."

Special Agent Liam Wilson and lead forensic investigator Courtney Hart rounded out Nikki's team. Both lived in the Minneapolis-Saint Paul area, and the bad roads meant the drive to Washington County would take twice as long.

"My guys will bag the utility knife and contents of her purse for fingerprints," Miller said.

Kellan was an average-sized nine-year-old, but his mother was so petite that she was only a few inches taller than him. "There's no way Dana brought him down here on her own, especially as slick as it is," Nikki said.

The young deputy cleared his throat and pointed to the other side of the bridge. "The embankment is smoother and not as steep. It looks like someone slid down on something."

"Like a sled?" Nikki asked.

"Maybe one of those plastic flat ones," the deputy suggested.

"Did Kellan have one of those?"

"I don't think so," Miller replied. "His uncle's a woodworker, you know. He made him a sled, like the old-school kind. I saw it when we searched the property."

"So it would have left grooves instead of flattening," Nikki said. "Did Reynolds search the old bridge yet?"

"We tried," the deputy said. "I mean, we did the best we could."

"That thing's treacherous enough without adding ice. We'll be able to do a more thorough search in the daylight." Nikki chewed her lower lip as she watched Dr. Blanchard tend to the bodies of Dana Rhodes and her son. She'd worked with Blanchard on enough cases to know she disliked conjecture, but she asked her question anyway. "Dr. Blanchard, I just want to clarify that you don't believe Dana slit her own wrists?"

Blanchard stood and looked at Nikki with grave eyes. "No, I don't think she did."

Nikki didn't need to hear any more. Had Dana convinced someone to get them down here, cut her wrists and help her die, or was she a victim, too?

CHAPTER THREE

Lakeview Hospital had been upgraded multiple times since the current building was opened more than a century ago, but the morgue was still located in the dingy basement. As a Level Three trauma center, the hospital was designed for acute care, and the small morgue consisted of a modest room with a half-a-dozen cold-storage units. Dr. Blanchard would perform the autopsies at her lab in Saint Paul, but she'd brought the bodies to the hospital so the Andersons could make the identification without driving so far in the storm.

Nikki leaned against the wall, typing notes on her phone before sleep deprivation made her forget. Aside from the Andersons, Dana didn't have any family. The only consistent person in Dana's life was her drug counselor, who lived in Minneapolis, Cam Fletcher. He'd told Miller that he hadn't talked to Dana much in the last couple of months, but they had spoken last Monday for a few minutes. She'd sounded scattered and stressed. The counselor had tried to get her to meet because he suspected she was using again, but she'd refused. He hadn't been surprised when Miller told him that both Dana and Kellan were missing but insisted Dana would never hurt Kellan. It still didn't sit right with Nikki. Despite Miller's competence, her inner control freak was relieved to be more involved in the investigation than she'd been over the weekend.

Nikki clicked on the email containing Miller's notes from interviewing the family. Dana had been a surprise baby to doting parents. The fourteen-year age difference between Dana and her sister, Maggie, kept the two of them from being close. Dana had had a typical childhood and excelled in school. She'd received a partial scholarship to the University of Minnesota and made the dean's list all four years. Her father had died shortly after she graduated, and Dana had failed the state's test to get her teaching license. Her drug use had started around the same time.

Despite her sister's history of drug use, Maggie had told Miller this past weekend that she couldn't see Dana hurting Kellan intentionally. There had been no history of violence in her past, and Kellan had told the court he'd never been afraid of his mother hurting him. He was just afraid she would leave him alone again.

According to Miller, both Maggie and the drug counselor feared Dana had become involved with a bad crowd if she were using again and wouldn't be able to keep Kellan safe. If his death had been brought on by some kind of negligence, Dana's suicide might make sense. But Nikki was certain she hadn't killed herself.

Nikki was anxious to get her team here. Perhaps their fresh eyes would see something that Miller's team hadn't. Nikki had called them on the way to the hospital, but between the weather and traffic, they were probably still an hour out.

Miller poked his head around the corner. "The Andersons want to speak with you."

Nikki had expected as much. They were here to ID both bodies, and she knew she was about to face a wave of emotion.

Her chest tightened as she entered the morgue. Dana's and Kellan's bodies lay side by side in the small room, with only their faces exposed. In the harsh light, the green tinge of decomposition was even more noticeable on Kellan.

Joe and Maggie stood next to Kellan, tears on their faces. Ice pellets still dotted Joe Anderson's bald head. He was a barrel of a man, but Maggie was several inches taller than her sister and much stockier.

Maggie's face was pale and streaked with tears. She stared down at her nephew, as though she were in a trance. Yesterday afternoon, after hours of searching in the cold, Maggie had been ready to give up hope. She had looked so lost and tired that Nikki had made it a point to tell her that she was confident Kellan would be found alive. She knew better than to make that sort of guarantee, but her ego had gotten the better of Nikki.

"Mr. and Mrs. Anderson, I'm so sorry for your loss," Nikki said.

Joe nodded, tears wetting his thick mustache. "Thank you."

"You're thanking her?" Grief layered Maggie's soft voice. She glared at Nikki, tears stinging her eyes. "You said she wouldn't hurt him."

"Mrs. Anderson, I'm still not certain that she did. We're investigating all possibilities here, but I promise you we will find the truth."

"You're not certain? Look at his head," Maggie replied, gesturing towards Kellan's body. "She killed him."

"Mrs. Anderson, we don't know—" Dr. Blanchard started.

"It doesn't matter." Maggie rounded the table and pointed her shaking finger at Nikki. "Kellan died in Dana's care. Whether he fell or hit his head, whether she did something or not, she didn't keep him safe. He was with her, and now he's dead. I know my sister. She's never taken responsibility for anything in her life, including her son."

Nikki resisted the urge to remind Maggie that she'd also said Dana wouldn't hurt her son. Right now, Maggie needed a target for her grief, and nothing would dissuade her. "I promise I'm going to do everything—"

"Don't use that word with me," Maggie said. "You're a liar. I don't know why I expected anything different from a selfish woman who let an innocent man sit in prison for twenty years."

"Mags," Joe choked out. "That's not right."

"No, what's not right is that Kellan is dead. I fought so hard to keep him safe, and now he's just gone." She advanced on Nikki, her eyes wild with grief. "You promised you would find him alive."

Miller moved to step between them, but Nikki motioned for him to stand down. "Because I believed she wouldn't hurt him. I'm so sorry I was wrong."

Maggie moved like a bullet toward Nikki.

Miller reached for Maggie, but Joe beat him to it. "Mags, stop." He put a hand around her waist. He looked at Nikki with pleading eyes. "She's not herself."

"There's no need to apologize," Nikki said. "Mrs. Anderson—"

"I want you to leave," Maggie said. "I can't look at you right now."

Nikki's pride stung, but she nodded. She would respect the family's wishes, and Miller was likely going to get more information without Nikki in the room. "Chief Miller, I'll let you finish here. I'll meet you at the command center."

Miller nodded, clearly stunned at Maggie's actions.

Nikki looked at the small woman who was now effectively pinned against her husband's chest, heaving with sobs. "I'm so sorry. But I will do everything I can to get answers."

She left the room before Maggie could respond.

A second round of ice dripped from the sky, and Nikki nearly fell, walking to her jeep. She managed to wrench the door open despite the thin layer of ice that covered it. She started the vehicle and turned the defrost on high. Her throat ached from fighting her emotions. Maggie's aggression wasn't the issue—Nikki had endured worse as a field agent. As a profiler, she trusted her instincts. Miller had asked Nikki to go over Dana's file, and she'd been confident that Dana wouldn't physically harm her son, but if the kidnapping somehow went south, Nikki worried that Dana wouldn't be able to handle the consequences. After seeing his body and Dana's deep wounds, Nikki feared she'd been right. Kellan had died, and Dana couldn't live with that pain. Still, she hadn't cut her own wrists. Someone else had to be involved.

Nikki rubbed her stinging eyes, wishing she could call her ex-husband and ask to speak to Lacey. The two of them shared custody and got along better as friends than they had during their marriage. But it was barely 4 a.m., and Lacey would sleep for at least another two hours.

Nikki's cell phone vibrated, and she felt comforted when she saw Rory's text. He ran a successful construction business and was usually up around five. Nikki hit the call button and turned up her volume, anxious to hear his voice.

"Hey." Rory sounded sleepy. "I wasn't sure when you'd see my text. What's going on?"

"Bad things," Nikki said. "I'm meeting Miller at the command center."

"Shouldn't you try to sleep?"

"I don't know if I can," Nikki replied. "I'm taking over the case, Rory."

"You OK?"

The concern in his voice made the lump in her throat ache. "I have to be. That's my job."

"You can do your job and not be OK at the same time," he said. "In fact, you kind of excel at it."

"I guess I do."

"Are you staying at my place again tonight?"

The longing in his voice made Nikki want to drive back to Rory's house and curl up with him in bed. "It's my night with Lacey."

She hadn't introduced her daughter to Rory yet. Nikki hadn't even told Lacey about him, but she knew her ex-husband suspected she was seeing someone. As amicable as their split had been, Tyler still loved her and wouldn't take the news very well.

"Right, I forgot. Are you going to stay in town while you're working the case like you did before? It's nearly an hour's drive between here and Saint Paul during rush hour. And I can save you money on a hotel room."

"Probably. I'll know more later in the day. Are you still working in the new development?"

"Yeah, and thanks to the ice, we're behind," Rory said. "It's supposed to warm up a bit today so it should melt. I'll probably be there late."

"I'll try to stop by before I leave town, if that's all right."

"It's always all right for you to stop by. You don't have to ask."

Warmth spread through her and she smiled. "Thank you."

Nikki ended the call. This case was going to be far more complex than she imagined. Time to get to work.

CHAPTER FOUR

The Washington County Sheriff's office main campus was located in downtown Stillwater as part of a large campus of county government. When Nikki had worked a missing girls case with Miller several weeks ago, they'd set up in the county's government center, but Miller had set up a command center in a conference room at the sheriff's office. The single location enabled him to keep track of volunteers and tips, and Nikki preferred it to the larger government center. She showed her credentials to the desk sergeant, who buzzed her in.

She passed by Miller's locked office and said a silent thank you that Hardin had retired after his involvement in railroading Mark Todd into prison for the murders of Nikki's parents. For two decades, Nikki had believed the man who destroyed her life was locked away in prison while the real killer lived happily ever after, thanks to Hardin. Eventually, Nikki had put the real killer in prison, and Mark Todd was finally free. While she knew that Maggie's comments were driven by her own grief, their reality still stung. Nikki had testified against Mark.

Rory's voice played in her head. *And when you realized you were wrong, you helped get him out. You were a victim, too.*

The one person who should have resented Nikki had done just the opposite, and Nikki would be forever grateful.

She turned on the lights in the command room and sat down. The room wasn't large, but since the sheriff's office building was fairly new, it was outfitted with modern equipment, including semi-comfortable chairs. Nikki found her notes and spread them out in front of her, even though she had the details memorized.

The Andersons lived in Afton, a small town on the St. Croix River, about twenty minutes from Stillwater. Kellan and Dana had been found around a mile from the Andersons' home. Kellan attended Afton Elementary, and the school had an early out this past Friday. Kellan's bus driver had dropped him off at approximately 1:22 p.m. Since the Andersons' house was a quarter-mile back from the road, Kellan had to walk down the driveway for a few minutes. The house was protected by a swath of snow-covered trees, making it easy for someone to hide in wait. Nikki's own house growing up had also been a significant distance from the road, but without the swath of trees. But her parents' place had been surrounded by cornfields, and Nikki had hated walking all the way to and from the bus stop at the end of the long drive. As kids, Nikki and her friends always pretended the creepy scarecrows in the fields might come to life. It was supposed to be in good fun, especially in the chilly fall weather when everything was dying, but Nikki had secretly been afraid that something might really be lurking in the cornfields.

Her phone's ring blasted through the silence, and Nikki jumped, her notes falling on the floor. She searched for the phone in her bag and then scowled when she saw Caitlin Newport's name on the screen. The reporter had played a pivotal role in clearing Mark Todd's name, and she'd been hounding Nikki for a sit-down interview for her documentary ever since he was released from prison. Nikki would eventually get to the interview, but Caitlin's persistence was annoying. She was one of the most single-minded people Nikki had ever met, and she didn't have the energy for Caitlin's questions today. Nikki sent the call to voicemail and gathered her notes again.

She found the satellite image Miller had printed from Google Earth. The wooded area in front of the Andersons' house was probably as wide as it was long, which meant Kellan had plenty of places to explore. A former high school running back, Miller had converted the distance to the length of four and a half football fields and noted that it would have taken Kellan around five minutes to get to the house at a normal pace. Joe Anderson ran a successful woodworking business out of the large building behind the house, so he was always there when Kellan arrived home from school around 4 p.m.

Joe had forgotten about the early out and gone to consult with a client thirty miles away about building a custom cabinet. He'd stopped to fill up with gas on the way home, and the receipt confirmed he was at least ten miles away when Kellan got off the school bus. According to Joe, the walk through the snowy woods made Kellan nervous. Joe always met him at the bus and walked him back to the house, but this time, Kellan had no choice but to make the long walk alone.

Joe had returned home before 4 p.m. and was surprised to see Kellan's backpack in the kitchen. He'd checked the calendar and realized his mistake. Part of Joe's woodworking shop doubled as a man cave, complete with a large flat-screen television and a state-of-the-art gaming system. He'd assumed Kellan had gone to the shop thinking Joe was there and decided to settle in and watch television. He'd searched there, then the rest of the property, including the woods in front of the house, and found no sign of Kellan. He'd called his wife around 4:45, and the police had been called shortly after.

Deputies had searched the Andersons' property and found footprints near the house and wood shop that measured around a women's size six—the same size Dana wore. Despite an exhaustive search of the Andersons' property and surrounding area, deputies hadn't found Dana's car. Miller had issued an APB for Dana's VW Bug, but no sightings had been reported.

Maggie had no idea where her sister currently lived. Until a few months ago, Dana had lived at the halfway house, but she'd moved out after the adoption hearing, and Miller hadn't been able to find her current residence. Judging from the clothes on her body, Nikki was sure Dana hadn't been living on the streets. She was either living with someone or paying cash. That wasn't uncommon for someone trying to get back on their feet, and Minneapolis had its share of low-income rentals. It likely wouldn't have been hard to find a landlord to give her a break.

Nikki rested her head on the table and closed her eyes, hoping a few minutes of quiet would clear her head. The crime scene played through her dream like a movie reel. She saw herself crouched in front of Dana's and Kellan's bodies. Blanchard was telling Miller that Dana hadn't been dead long. She touched Dana's skin, feeling warmth, as though her blood was still flowing. Then she looked up at Dana, and the woman's eyes were open, staring at Nikki. Fresh blood spurted from her wrists as she grabbed Nikki's arm. "You could have saved us."

Nikki wrenched her arm free, and some part of her consciousness told her this was a dream. She needed to wake up. *Wake up, Nikki.*

"Nikki, wake up." Someone was gently shaking her shoulder. Nikki recognized Courtney's hand lotion and forced her eyes to open. Courtney held up a large coffee cup. "I brought you a fresh Americano. Five shots."

"And that's why you're my best friend." Nikki sat up, instantly fully awake, and greedily took the coffee.

Courtney laughed softly. "I heard what happened at the hospital. Miller thought she would have hit you if her husband hadn't stopped her."

"It's nothing. The woman's devastated."

"Yet another reason I couldn't be a cop," Courtney said. "My natural instinct to fight back would override common sense."

Nikki had first met Courtney when she returned to Minnesota from the FBI's Behavioral Analysis Unit—the BAU—at Quantico to start the Criminal Profiling Unit in Saint Paul. She'd hand-picked Courtney from a stable of highly skilled forensic specialists because of her obsessive attention to detail and outgoing personality. Courtney was one of the best forensic investigators Nikki had worked with, and they'd become close friends over the past few years.

Courtney sat down, clinging to a large cup of sugar mixed with a little bit of coffee. Nikki marveled at the way her friend consumed sweets and never seemed to gain a pound.

"I talked to Blanchard," Courtney said. "She's going to send all of Kellan's and Dana's effects to the FBI lab, along with anything she finds during the autopsy. Miller already fingerprinted the utility knife and it's clean."

"Did she tell you about the scene?"

Courtney nodded solemnly. "I'm glad I wasn't with you. But at least the Andersons have closure. The not knowing and being chained to hope would be the worst." Courtney shook her head. "I read an article about missing kids the other day. There are so many unsolved, so many parents still holding out hope."

"I'm not surprised. I don't think I would be able to give up hope if something happened to Lacey." Nikki's hands trembled at the thought. A missing child was every parent's nightmare, but Nikki had seen the worst humanity had to offer. If she allowed herself to think about all the things that could happen to Lacey, she'd never be able to leave her daughter's side.

Courtney sucked down the rest of her Frappuccino. "I've told you this before, but there's a special place in hell for people who hurt kids."

"It's called the general prison population," Nikki said dryly. "They make child-killers' lives worse than hell. Where's Liam?"

"With Miller, getting up to speed. By the way, Blanchard said there was a lot of blood. It will be frozen by now, which isn't a bad thing. If there's any tangible evidence nearby, the ice might preserve it."

"We need to look for footprints." Nikki sipped her coffee. "Blanchard is confident Dana didn't cut her own wrists. And even if she was involved in Kellan's death, I have a hard time believing a mother would leave her son's body in some ditch where it could be torn apart by scavengers, or never found. It's cruel. It's inhumane.

It's not what a mother would do. So, someone else had to have been at the scene. Dana wasn't much bigger than you. Her footprints will be easy to differentiate from someone else's."

Courtney looked down at her drink and sighed. "Blanchard said Kellan's death might have been an accident."

Nikki clasped her hands behind her back, stretching her neck and shoulders. "If she's right about the cause of death being blunt force trauma, it's definitely possible, especially since it looks like he might have been dead since Friday. I'm thinking this person was supposed to help Dana take Kellan, but something went wrong, and Kellan died. The other person could have killed Dana to cover their tracks. There's also the possibility that this person simply murdered them both. Staged Kellan's death to look like an accident, and staged Dana's to look like suicide."

"What about the Andersons? Aren't the closest relatives the usual suspects?"

Nikki told her about Joe's mistake Friday afternoon. "Miller said his deputies discreetly searched the Anderson property for the vehicle or any sign of Dana. Maggie works second shift for the county's emergency dispatch, so she's accounted for right up until Joe called her around 4:45 p.m. when he discovered Kellan was missing. Joe's alibi is solid as well." Nikki sighed.

"I bet that poor guy's never going to forgive himself," Courtney said.

She was probably right. Nikki knew from experience that some mistakes could haunt your life forever. She would never forgive herself for her part in Mark's wrongful conviction. The rational side of her knew that anyone else would have done what she did, but the emotional side refused to cut her any slack. Rory and Mark's forgiveness almost made it worse at times.

Liam and Miller entered the conference room. Liam always dressed business casual, but this morning he wore jeans and a Vikings sweatshirt that had seen better days. Liam had joined her profiling team a few years ago, and he was one of the most solid agents she'd worked with in more than a decade at the FBI.

"Where did you come from?" Nikki asked.

"Sorry?"

She gestured to his outfit. "Clearly you didn't have your usual attire on hand. Which means you must have come from someone else's place."

His fair skin reddened. "I was at a friend's."

Courtney snickered. "A special friend. You should have nicer clothes at her place."

Liam rolled his eyes and sat down across from Nikki. "Sheriff Miller brought me up to speed. This is a terrible shitshow."

"Acting sheriff." Miller trudged into the room. His skin was ashy, his eyes bloodshot from lack of sleep. "And that analogy sums things up perfectly."

"How did it go after I left?" Nikki asked.

"About like you'd expect," he said. "Maggie's fourteen years older than Dana. They were never close, and the past few years have made it even worse. She's so angry, and she doesn't know anything about Dana's personal life."

"Fourteen years?" Courtney asked.

"Their parents had Maggie young and then thought they couldn't have any more children. Dana's the surprise change-of-life baby."

"Wow," Courtney said. "My brother's five years older than I am, and I thought our relationship was messy."

"Both of their parents are gone?" Liam asked.

"Yes, and it's clear that Maggie blames Dana for their mother's stroke several years ago." Miller opened the file he'd brought in. "I briefed Nikki on some of the family background. Dana didn't get into drugs until after she graduated college. But once she did, the meth took over her life. When she got pregnant with Kellan, she came home to her mom and got clean. She stayed clean for a while after he was born, but it didn't last. Kellan would have gone into the foster system if they hadn't been living with Dana's mother."

"What happened after the mother died?" Liam asked.

"Maggie wouldn't let Dana stay in the house. She said Dana and her friends would just trash it. They sold it, and per the mom's will, almost everything went into a trust for Kellan that he couldn't access until he was an adult. Dana received a quarterly check for interest and, according to Maggie and the court records, spent most of it on drugs. When Kellan was six, Dana went on a bender and left him alone for two days in her studio apartment. Kellan got scared and finally called his aunt. Maggie and Joe were granted emergency custody, and then the fight began."

"It took her three years, but Dana did get clean," Nikki said. "At least for a while. But she failed her last drug test, and the judge had enough. That was two months ago. The Andersons were moving forward with the formal adoption, and Dana wasn't having it. Police were called at least three different times because she harassed her sister, including going to the Anderson home."

"One of my deputies responded to that scene," Miller said. "Legally, Dana wasn't supposed to have contact with Kellan. But she came to the Anderson home and demanded to be let in. She and Maggie got into a screaming match. Kellan called the cops. Deputy Reynolds heard Dana say that she would get her son back one way or another."

"Did the Andersons get a restraining order?" Liam asked.

"After that, yes." Miller rubbed his eyes. "But you can see why everything adds up to her snatching him."

"We have a statewide alert for her car," Nikki said. "If she did have an accomplice and they're dumb enough to drive around in that, they'll be caught." Nikki didn't think that would happen. "What about her cell phone?"

Miller held up the bagged Nokia. "It's a pay as you go, and none of the chargers around here work. I'm going to call the cell stores and see if they have one, but I've got a mound of paperwork and the mayor to deal with first."

"We can take the phone and try to find a charger. I'd like to read through her texts anyway." Nikki looked at Miller. "But this is still technically your case. Tell us what you need us to do."

"I'd like all of us to go to the scene now that it's light out. I've got deputies keeping it secure. And then I want you two to talk to Maggie and Joe."

"You think that's a good idea?" Liam asked. "If she went after Agent Hunt in the hospital—"

"I've seen you guys in interviews," Miller said. "You know how to get through to people in the worst situations. And the Andersons are sick of my face. If the two of you go, maybe we'll get some new information."

"All right," Nikki said. "I want to talk to Cam Fletcher, the drug counselor, and see if I can get him to come to town for an interview. He's alibied, but if anyone knows about Dana's plans, it's him."

Nikki heard a quick knock on the door and then the front desk sergeant poked her head into the room. "Agent Hunt, I'm sorry, but Caitlin Newport is here. She says it's urgent."

Liam stood. "I'll talk to her. Agent Hunt doesn't need to deal with her right now."

"It's all right," Nikki said. "She's already called once, and she won't be satisfied until she talks to me. Besides, if she sees you in your old, stained sweater and wrinkled jeans, she'll probably do a report about how unprofessional my team is. I have the excuse of being out until all hours at the scene."

Liam flushed and sat back down. "You're probably right. Good luck."

Nikki smoothed her hair and popped a couple of mints in her mouth. Although she'd started out as a beat reporter, Newport had gained notoriety as a documentary filmmaker over the past several years. Nikki suspected that she was banking on the Mark Todd documentary to be her launching pad to notoriety. Because of her time in front of the camera, Newport always looked perfectly put-together, even in casual attire. Nikki would never speak the words out loud, but she always felt like the frumpy mom around Caitlin.

Nikki stopped short at the sight of Caitlin pacing in the lobby. She'd never seen Caitlin without any makeup. She wore jeans and sneakers and a long black puffer coat, her blonde hair in a high ponytail.

"I've never seen you looking so casual," Nikki remarked.

Caitlin stopped pacing, but her nervous energy was palpable. "I tried to call. You didn't answer."

Nikki sighed. "I've been a little busy. If this is about the documentary—"

"It's not," Caitlin said. "It's about another missing boy."

"In Washington County? You should be talking to Miller."

Caitlin shook her head. "Chisago. A twelve-year-old boy went for a joyride on his grandparents' snowmobile Friday morning and hasn't been seen since."

Chisago County was north of Stillwater, and Nikki hadn't worked any cases in that area since she returned to lead the profiling unit five years ago. "No one from the sheriff's office has asked for our assistance."

Caitlin's expression darkened. "Because the sheriff thinks Zach rode the snowmobile across the St. Croix River and the ice broke. They think he drowned. The family contacted me early this morning. They asked me to speak with you."

"How do you know the family?" Nikki asked.

"I know a lot of people," Caitlin said shortly. "Zach lives with his grandparents. They know that I have a relationship with you and wanted me to speak with you about it."

Nikki raised her eyebrows. "A relationship is stretching it."

Caitlin shook her head. "His grandparents don't think Zach would have ridden the snowmobile over the water. He was terrified of it. The sheriff refuses to look at any other options, even though the divers haven't found the snowmobile or Zach."

Nikki sighed. "I'm still not sure what you want me to do. I can't just waltz in and tell a county sheriff he's wrong."

"Zach's only a few years older than Kellan Rhodes, and he was involved in a custody battle when he was little. Both boys ended up with family members because of parental issues. Don't you think it's a little odd they both disappeared on the same day?"

Caitlin talked so fast Nikki barely kept up with her. "How much coffee have you had this morning?"

"Not enough," Caitlin replied. "I didn't get much sleep last night. I'd planned to take the day off and catch up on some things when Zach's grandparents called me. I promised them I would speak to you as soon as possible."

"Right," Nikki said. "Based on what you're telling me, I don't see a solid reason to believe they were taken by the same person. Kellan was taken by his mother."

"And she's dead," Caitlin said. "I know it's a stretch, but I promised them I would speak with you. Could you just look into it?"

Nikki sighed. She looked at Caitlin and could see the desperation in her face. If she and her team were going to find out what happened to Kellan, they needed to be able to focus. But why was Caitlin trusting her with this? Caitlin had been the first person to criticize Nikki's career, to tell her that she had settled for the truth too soon when it came to Mark Todd. Nikki could see Caitlin's nerves were on edge; she noted the bags under her eyes. She sighed, already regretting her decision. "All I can do right now is talk to Miller and have him do some digging."

Caitlin looked up from her shoes, relief on her face.

"If I go poking around without speaking with the county sheriff, they'll be furious and won't share any information."

"Thank you," Caitlin said. "Call me on my cell as soon as you know anything."

CHAPTER FIVE

Nikki fought back a yawn as she cradled her coffee. The cup's warmth helped her focus on something other than sleepiness and the memory of Kellan's and Dana's bodies in the cold morgue. "I could have driven."

"Your head is chicken bobbing," Liam said.

"You just like driving my jeep instead of your little wind-up car."

"That, too, especially out here."

The sleet had stopped in the few hours they'd been at the station. Although the roads had improved thanks to the county's efforts, ice still covered the trees and shrubs, the rising sun making each piece look as delicate as crystal.

"What did Caitlin want?" Liam asked.

Nikki had already given the information to Miller, and he'd promised to check in with the Chisago County Sheriff. Like Nikki, he didn't think the cases were related, but they'd both experienced Caitlin's relentless pursuit of justice, and they knew she wouldn't stop hounding them until they'd done as she asked. "A twelve-year-old boy in the county north of here disappeared Friday morning after he borrowed his grandparents' snowmobile. Police believe he rode across the river and went through the ice, but Caitlin seems to think the case could be connected to Kellan's."

Liam drummed his fingers on the steering wheel. "How?"

"Apparently, he was involved in a custody battle, too. But that's the only commonality. She knows the family and told them she'd speak to me about it. I'm sure she hurried right over there for a scoop when she heard about the case. God help that family if she's in their business. I don't know if she's trying to drum up more publicity for herself or if she really believes the theory."

"You think she'd stoop that low?" Liam asked. "Seems like a stretch."

Nikki shrugged. "I'm not sure. I will say she didn't seem like herself, but if she knew the family, she's probably shaken up. Miller's going to contact the Chisago County Sheriff today, but this happens nearly every year. People think the ice is thick enough and try to cross the rivers. The ice breaks, and they don't have a chance."

"Jesus," Liam said. "What that family must be going through. Did she say how she knew them?"

"No," Nikki replied. "It's a terrible situation, but I don't think it's anything we can or should help with, unless Miller finds additional evidence."

They rode in silence for a few minutes, Nikki struggling to keep her eyes open.

"Are these country roads really old stagecoach routes?" Liam asked.

"Yes, at least parts of them. I think they became dirt roads after the railroad put the stagecoach out of business, and I'm sure they've been altered over the years, but plenty of the routes are still used as paved roads." Nikki gazed out the window at the frozen trees and sheets of ice on the rooftops. Her father had been a history buff and very proud of Stillwater's claim as the birthplace of Minnesota. He'd been full of historical facts and trivia that bored most people but always fascinated Nikki. She was grateful to have paid such attention to those moments.

"Weren't you out here for the weekend already?"

"I was visiting Rory. He helped with the search this weekend. I was so sure Dana and Kellan would be found safe in Minneapolis."

"They should have been," Liam said. "Something went wrong. We'll find out what it was. We always do."

"Did you check up on our old friend?" Nikki and her team had been searching for a killer known as Frost for the past five years.

Like clockwork, at the height of winter, he left a perfectly frozen woman in a public space. He took one victim a year and appeared to keep them alive for a while. All of his victims had been left in either Wisconsin or Minnesota, where the cold weather stretched well into spring. Frost had never left a victim later than Valentine's Day. But February had come and gone without a body. Liam had been searching for missing women or unsolved murders in surrounding states, but so far nothing matched Frost's preferences.

"Nothing new," Liam said. "I called the Canadian authorities, too. They're searching along their borders. Maybe we'll get lucky and he's in jail for something else."

"Unlikely." Nikki knew Frost better than anyone, and he was too smart to get caught for some dumb infraction. "But he could be injured or dead."

"From your lips to God's ears. Is that sign actually warning us to watch out for snowmobiles?"

Nikki laughed. "You're a city boy. Snowmobiles are all over the place out here. You have to watch out for them just like bicyclists because they're always crossing the roads. The place is just around the bend," Nikki said. "Don't brake hard because this is a tight curve and there's probably black ice. Miller's got one lane blocked for emergency vehicles. Just park behind him."

Liam guided her jeep behind Miller's SUV and killed the engine. "I'll help Courtney with her stuff. It weighs more than her, and we don't need her falling down and breaking something."

Nikki nodded, draining her coffee. She zipped her coat to her chin and pulled on the winter beanie she'd swiped from Rory's. She felt silly, because she had plenty of winter gear, but the hat smelled like him, and wearing it brought a sense of calm that Nikki needed.

Miller was already getting the snow poles out of his SUV. He looked up at Nikki as she approached. "Good thing I have two kids. I've got enough stuff for all of us."

"Courtney's the size of a child, so that works."

"I heard that." Courtney's red parka stood out like a flame in the snow-covered landscape. She shuffled in front of Liam, who carried her bag of crime scene equipment. If she wasn't so tired, Nikki would have smiled. Courtney and Liam bickered like siblings, but they loved working together.

Miller handed Nikki the snow poles. "I talked to Cam Fletcher. He's a wreck, but he agreed to talk. He's going to meet us later."

Deputy Reynolds emerged from his patrol car parked on the side of the road. "Chief, Agent Hunt."

"Deputy Reynolds, this is Agent Liam Wilson and our head forensic examiner, Courtney Hart."

Reynolds shook hands with Liam and Courtney, fighting back a yawn.

"Reynolds was first on the scene last night," Nikki said. "And you overheard Dana's threat to take her son a few days ago, right?"

Reynolds closed his eyes. "I swear to God, if I'd known she was serious—"

"Don't do that to yourself," Nikki said. "You did your job just fine. Have you found anything new down in the gully in the daylight?"

Reynolds held up an evidence bag. "Found a fiber on one of the thorn bushes. Looks like it tore someone's jacket. Matching it will be tough. We tried not to mess around much down there since we knew your forensics team was coming."

"I'll take it." Courtney took the evidence bag from his hand.

"We're certain that Dana and Kellan arrived here via the trail over there." Miller turned to Reynolds. "Did you guys find anything searching the area?"

"Starnes said there's some footprints at the edge of the trail, but most of them are ruined by snowmobile tracks since the trail's used regularly. But there's no reason anyone should have stopped there in the last few days, so any fresh tracks are likely to have been made by someone present at our crime scene," Reynolds explained.

"I'd love to take a look at those prints," Courtney said.

Reynolds pointed across the gully. "They're on that side. Go down the road a bit and you'll see the trail entrance. Starnes is there, too. We've put down ice melt, but it's still a bit slick."

"We'll all go," Miller said. "Thanks for staying, Reynolds. Go home and get some rest." Reynolds yawned loudly in response and headed toward his car.

Valley Creek trail had several entrances, but the one with access to the stone bridge was only a few hundred yards down the road.

"The trail isn't big enough to drive on," Miller explained. "There are no security cameras."

"This is a snowmobiler's dream." Nikki pointed to the long, narrow tracks. She hadn't been on a snowmobile in years until two weekends ago, when Rory took her out for a twenty-mile ride. She'd forgotten how fun they were—and how dangerous they could be. Rory had let her drive and she'd turned too sharply. They'd almost hit a tree. They were both fine, but Nikki had endured his teasing ever since.

"Especially the ditches, even though they're not supposed to be riding in them."

Nikki suppressed a smile. She had been one of those rule-breakers as a teenager. In fact, it was easier to count the rules she hadn't broken than the ones she'd kept.

Miller waved at the deputy coming from the opposite direction. The deputy's face was partially covered by a scarf. "Starnes, anything new?"

"Lots of tracks," Starnes replied. "Too many to make sense of. But you can't miss where Michelle went down the bank."

Miller wanted to brief with Starnes, so Nikki, Liam and Courtney went ahead, following the trail into the woods. Courtney had been right about the ice. It had effectively preserved the entire scene, but there were so many tracks it was impossible to tell which ones had been made last night.

A large red sign from the DNR warned the bridge was dangerous. A pair of roadblocks on both ends of the bridge had been moved out of the way, and judging from the tracks, it didn't look like the snowmobilers were worried about the bridge collapsing.

"How old is this bridge?" Liam asked.

"Old," Nikki said. "I think it was used only a few years before the railroad came in. It eventually became obsolete and dangerous. It was off limits when I was a kid."

"And did that stop you?" Courtney asked.

"No," Nikki replied. "But I've only been out here a few times, mostly at night. It's pretty freaky in the summer, because the trees are overgrown and the branches kind of go everywhere. Plus all the wildflowers and weeds. I remember it being dense back here. You couldn't see at night without flashlights, and from the looks of things, it's even worse now."

Courtney retrieved her camera from the bag Liam still carried. "Places like this fascinate me. It's like they're frozen in time when everything else evolves. It's amazing how they get left behind when just a few miles down the road is a big town."

Tangled thorn bushes and vines covered the ground, but the ice continued to work in their favor. Just before the bridge was a small opening in the vegetation that led down to the creek.

Courtney took several pictures of the mangled vines. "These have been cut with a knife or an axe."

"Or a sharp utility knife," Nikki suggested.

"That would work."

Instead of footprints down the gully, a narrow indentation was clearly visible in the snow. "They slid down."

"Plastic sled?" Liam asked.

"I don't know. The width is less than twelve inches. That's a damn small sled." Courtney grabbed Liam's arm and crouched down to get a closer look. She got on all fours, turning her head to the side until her cheek almost touched the frozen ground.

"Are you searching for something under the bed?" Liam snickered.

"There's butt marks."

"You're kidding." Nikki dropped to her knees and mirrored Courtney. She had to get at just the right angle, but the dip in the snow was visible, preserved by the ice. "She's right. There's a dip. Someone sat down and slid."

"I'll be damned," Liam said. "Given how packed down the snow's been, it's hard to believe someone Dana's size would make that indent."

Courtney stood, holding her arms out for balance. "But if Kellan was on her lap, that's another what, fifty, sixty pounds of weight?"

"She wasn't down here by herself." Nikki reminded them what Blanchard had said about Dana's wounds. She'd hoped to see footprints leading back up the gully, but there weren't any in sight. "Even if they both came down this way, someone must have found another way out. The ice should have preserved those prints just as well. Let's go down."

"Don't use this path," Courtney said. "I might be able to get fibers out of the ice, and it's supposed to warm up to thirty-four today. This stuff will start to melt."

They walked across the bridge, searching for another route down, but found nothing. Nikki and Liam left Courtney searching for her trace evidence and retraced their steps on the trail. Miller was headed their way, and Nikki filled him in on what they'd found.

"She found butt indentations?" he asked incredulously.

"She's like a hunting dog," Nikki said. "She won't stop until she gets what she wants. She's looking for evidence, so let's go down the same way you and I did last night."

The sun had already started loosening the ice, but Nikki still clung to the poles as the three of them descended.

Despite her bright red coat, Nikki could barely spot Courtney through the trees. Crime scene tape roped off the area where Dana had bled out. The blood had frozen relatively solid, and a fine white powder covered several of the bricks.

"Did your guys find prints on the stones?" Nikki asked.

Miller shook his head. "No, but if you want to take some into the lab and have Courtney test, go ahead."

Liam pointed to the right, where the gully narrowed and then seemed engulfed by more weeds. "What's on the other side?"

"Believe it or not, private property. Reynolds spoke to the homeowners this morning. They didn't see or hear anything."

"Is it just me or does the snow look unnatural in places? Like something was brushed across?" Liam asked.

Nikki squinted. "Maybe. We'll have Courtney look."

Liam walked toward the end of the gully and peered into the tangled mass. "It looks like this is all vines and weeds, but there's a fallen tree." He edged forward, pushing the bushes out of his way.

"Watch out," Nikki said. "Thorn trees."

"Yeah, one already got me. Come see this."

Nikki's adrenaline spiked as she and Miller walked to Liam. She could see more of the flat spots that looked like the snow had been filled in and flattened. Liam held the branches aside and motioned for Nikki to step in front of him. Preserved on the fallen tree was a single boot print.

Nikki stood on her tiptoes but still couldn't see over the brush pile. She craned her neck to look at Liam. At more than six feet tall, he had an advantage.

"There's another print that leads to the chain-link fence at the end of the private property."

"So, our suspect comes through this brush and scales the fence, and then either fights his way through the eastern side of the gully, up the bank, where there's so much tangled brush his footprint are hidden," Miller said, "or he scales and walks through the private property onto the road."

"He thought this out," Liam added. "If Blanchard's right and Kellan died on Friday, that means Dana and her accomplice—if she had one—had two days to figure out what to do. Plenty of time for the accomplice to decide their best option was to get rid of Dana and how."

Nikki agreed, but they were no closer to identifying the mystery person. "Courtney needs to see these prints before they melt."

"I know the property owner," Miller said. "I'll see if they'll let me look around the back."

"I think it's time we talk to the Andersons," Nikki said.

CHAPTER SIX

The Andersons lived on several acres of land, with the house set back off the road and hidden by a small forest of trees. The area reminded Nikki of northern Minnesota, where forests and large tracts of game land and lakes dominated the landscape, with a log home or tiny gas station popping up every once in a while. The woods had scared her as a kid when they'd gone up to the lake. Nikki wondered if they were as thick and imposing as they had been when she was young, or if time and humans had thinned the trees out.

"Lots of places for someone to hide in these little woods," Liam said.

"I was thinking the same thing." She hadn't been part of the first search team to walk through the woods, and she hoped that she and Liam would find something the first team had missed.

"How big is this wooded area in front of the house?" Liam asked.

"Miller did the math. It's roughly the size of four football fields."

Liam nodded. "Enough evergreen trees to break up a person's line of sight."

Nikki rounded the driveway, and the Anderson home came into view. It was a large split-level, with an updated brick exterior and a three-car garage. Joe Anderson's GMC pickup was parked in the driveway.

A winter's worth of plowed snow sat at the far end of the driveway, standing at least twice Liam's height. Nikki could see impressions in the ice from small feet and what looked like a sled. She'd grown up in the country, and every year her father had made a massive mound with the plowed snow.

A pang of sadness went through her. Her parents' murders had finally been solved, but the sharp pain of that loss never really went away.

Nikki pointed. "Dana Rhodes hid behind that mound a couple of weeks ago waiting for her sister to come home."

"Did Maggie file a police report?"

She nodded. "And got a restraining order. Until Kellan disappeared on Friday, things had calmed down." Nikki walked slowly down the sidewalk, trying to think of how to respond if Maggie became aggressive again.

The door to the house flew open, and Nikki braced herself for a fresh onslaught of Maggie's anger. Instead, she stepped out onto the front porch. "Agent Hunt, I am so sorry for my behavior earlier." Maggie Anderson still wore the same clothes, and her hollowed-out face indicated she hadn't gotten much sleep since leaving the hospital.

Nikki exhaled. "You have nothing to apologize for."

"No, you're an officer of the law," Maggie said. "I've worked for the Washington County police since I was twenty, and I know better than to act like that to a law enforcement officer. Please, come in."

Nikki sensed that fixating on her actions was probably helping Maggie avoid some of the grief of losing Kellan. "This is my partner, Special Agent Wilson."

Nikki and Liam left their shoes in the entryway and then followed Maggie up the short flight of stairs to the main floor. The house smelled of linen and cleaning products, and Nikki noticed there wasn't a speck of dust on the stair railing or furniture.

"I'm a compulsive cleaner." Maggie seemed to read her mind. "When I get upset, it's one of the few things that helps calm me down."

Joe Anderson sat at the kitchen table, staring at a cup of coffee. "Hey, Agent Hunt."

Nikki introduced Liam, and they both sat down with Joe and Maggie.

"This table is impressive," Liam said. "Is it one of yours?"

Joe nodded. "One of the first things I made in the new shop."

Nikki knew that Joe Anderson had inherited a small dairy farm and eventually sold out to a major producer. They'd purchased their current home and acres shortly after, and Joe had started his woodworking business.

"I've seen your products in a couple of high-end stores in the Cities," Liam said. "You're very talented."

"Joe's business has just grown like wildfire. He started out of the garage several years ago, and now he's got a big, fancy shop." Maggie's eyes misted. "I wish my parents were here to see it."

"I'm sure they would be proud," Nikki said. She could tell that talking about trivial things was distracting them, but their sadness and grief was still written on their faces.

Joe shook his head, and anger flashed in Maggie's eyes. "They never liked Joe because he married me. Dana could date any guy and that was great, but my parents nitpicked every single one of my boyfriends. Nothing Joe did changed that, even when he sold the dairy farm for a very large amount of money. I told my mother we were millionaires, and she tells me about her big plans for Dana's college graduation."

Bitterness dripped from Maggie's tone. Nikki was an only child, and though stories like this should have made her glad she didn't have a sibling to fight with, they simply made her sad that she had no one to share things with.

"I would imagine you two grew up very differently," Nikki said, remembering the age gap.

"That's putting it lightly," Maggie replied. "My parents couldn't afford to send me to college, so I had to go to beauty school, which I hated. But they were much more financially stable when Dana was growing up. She had no idea how easy she had it."

"How so?" Liam asked.

"My parents spoiled her rotten," Maggie said. "Mom did everything for her. Do you know that when she was sixteen years old, Dana still didn't know how to make scrambled eggs? She didn't want to learn to cook so Mom never made her. I was making my own lunch by the time I was ten."

"What about your father?" Liam asked.

Some of the hard lines in Maggie's face softened. "He was a good man who worked hard. He retired at Goodyear after thirty years. He had a heart attack less than a year later, not long after Dana graduated from college. They were close, and she started using around then."

Nikki looked at Joe. "Given their age difference, I assume Dana was still young when you and Maggie started dating. Did you get along?"

"Sure. I mostly saw her at family events and holidays. She was a nice kid. Spoiled, like Maggie said, and naive. She thought she'd go to college and become a big-time journalist."

"I thought she wanted to be a teacher?" Nikki asked.

"After she found out journalism wasn't a walk in the park." Maggie smirked. "But then she couldn't pass the Minnesota teacher licensure test. She blamed it on grief, but when I look back, I think she was already using then."

Nikki knew part of what happened once Dana started using, but she wanted to hear it from Maggie's perspective. "I'm sure that was hard on your mother, being a widower."

"She threw herself into helping Dana," Maggie said. "I don't think she ever let herself grieve for Dad. Dana came home and mooched off her and did drugs. Then she got pregnant." Maggie's jaw hardened, her eyes bright with anger. "I couldn't get pregnant, but she's a drug addict with no clue who the father is."

Nikki wondered if Maggie had ever talked to her mother about any of this. Holding on to all of that anger was exhausting.

"But she got clean, didn't she?" Liam asked.

"My mother made her. She was two months pregnant with Kellan when she found out, and she'd been using that whole time, so everyone was worried he would have issues. But other than being small, he was fine." Maggie's jaw trembled. "I loved him from the start. I even made amends with Dana. I was proud of her for staying clean. And she started out a very good mother."

"Then she started using again," Joe said sadly. "I really thought she'd keep her act together."

"Mom took charge. She made sure that Dana didn't have a big inheritance to blow through and that Kellan had something when he grew up. Dana threw a fit when she found out, of course."

"She was completely cut off?" Nikki asked.

"She received the interest off Kellan's trust to help with living expenses. It's around seven hundred a month, depending on the market."

"Was she still receiving it?"

"It was going to her expenses at the sober living place, but they were to cease if she didn't stay clean. That was the agreement. I notified the bank when I found out she failed that drug test, but I don't know if they stopped sending checks."

"Would you be able to give us the name of the bank?" Liam asked. "We might be able to get her new address from them."

"First State Bank and Trust, but that's one of the first places we checked when Kellan went missing. Her forwarding address was a post office box."

Nikki perked up. "Do you happen to remember it?"

Maggie shook her head. "I'm sorry. I can call and ask."

"Don't worry about it," Liam said. "I'll stop by the bank later today."

"Miller mentioned that you tried to reconcile with Dana after your mother died, is that right?" Nikki asked.

Maggie looked down at her hands. "I sat her down and told her that we were all each other had. Mom had made me promise to look out for her. And when you lose both your parents, you start to realize how fast life goes. Dana was all for it. I know I sound like a bitter shrew. I do love my sister. I know she loved Kellan, but she had demons she couldn't control. I begged her to let me raise Kellan, at least until she was truly on her feet, but she wouldn't have it. I even invited her to live with us."

Nikki had heard so many similar stories from families throughout her career, and addiction didn't discriminate. Whether the drug of choice was prescription painkillers or cheaply made methamphetamine, drugs tore families apart. "Fast-forward to the last several months. You've had Kellan for a long time, and Dana has been working on being healthy enough to get her son back. Dana's drug counselor told the family court she was clean and working steadily over a six-month time period. She had supervised visitation. How did those go?"

"Fine, as far as we know. Dana wanted the social services woman to supervise and didn't want Joe or me in the room. We agreed, because Kellan wanted the same thing."

"And no issues?" Liam asked.

"No," Joe said. "The social worker was impressed by her. Honestly, all signs pointed to her getting him back. I was shocked when she failed the drug test."

"Do you know if Dana ever brought anyone with her to the visits?" Nikki asked.

Both Andersons shook their heads. "Absolutely not. That wasn't allowed."

"I read the trial notes," Nikki said. "Her drug counselor spoke on her behalf, as well as the woman who ran the halfway house. We're going to talk to both of them, but we need you to think about anyone else Dana might have trusted."

"We'll do our best, but she didn't exactly confide in us," Joe said.

Nikki had been debating whether to tell the Andersons what they'd found, especially without an official ruling from Dr. Blanchard. "We found some evidence that suggests that someone else was at the crime scene."

"But I saw that Dana's wrists were cut," Maggie said. "She clearly killed Kellan and took her own life."

Nikki bristled. She knew this was the easiest explanation for Maggie. "We think Kellan's death could have been an accident—we haven't determined that yet. Dana's wrists were cut; it's possible she did commit suicide. We're just considering every possibility."

Several beats of silence passed before Joe finally spoke. "You think they might have been murdered?"

"There's certainly a possibility that Dana was murdered, yes," Nikki said. "I have reason to believe that someone else could have been involved. It's still possible that this was all Dana, but I need to be able to eliminate all other theories."

"Good God," Joe said. "If that's true… What do you need from us?"

"I know Chief Miller and his deputies searched your property, but I'd like to do a walk-through. Now that we know what happened, we might see something important that was missed before."

"Such as?" Maggie asked.

"I won't know until I see it," Nikki said. "You'd be surprised at the things that break a case. May I see Kellan's room?"

"I don't understand," Maggie replied. "There's no sign anything happened in his room."

"It's possible Dana had communication with Kellan that you didn't know about. Perhaps something was planned."

"No," Maggie said. "He didn't have a computer or phone. No social media. And he didn't want to go back to her."

Nikki could tell that Maggie was becoming defensive, but she needed to push on. "I'll just be quick."

"Mags, let them do their job," Joe said. "Go on and take her to his room, and then I'll show them the rest of the property."

"Thank you."

Maggie stood, her posture rigid, but she relented. "His room is upstairs."

Nikki and Liam had discussed their approach with the Andersons on the drive over. Nikki hoped getting Maggie alone would give her time to earn her trust and learn more about the family. They walked in silence up the stairs.

"His room is across the hall from ours."

Nikki was surprised. The Andersons' house had at least four bedrooms, so putting Kellan at the other end of the hall would have allowed for more privacy. "Did Kellan have issues with nightmares or being afraid at night?"

"No, why?"

"Just wondering why he was so close to you in this big house."

"This is the room he liked best." Maggie opened the door and looked at Nikki. "I just can't be in here."

"I understand."

"Please don't take long."

Nikki nodded and went inside. An unmade double bed with superhero sheets was in the center of the room, across from a heavy-looking chest of drawers made of oak, with flowers etched in the center of each drawer. "Is this handmade, too?"

Maggie paused in the doorway. "One of Joe's first projects. We always kept it in the guest room. I'll leave you to it."

Once Maggie was out of sight, Nikki used the flashlight function on her phone and examined the hard edges of the dresser and bed. It was unlikely anything had happened in Kellan's room, but she didn't want to miss anything.

His window faced the large backyard, with a view of the wood shop. A sheet of ice covered a prefab swing set, and Nikki could make out several attempts at snow angels, along with a half-finished snowman. She didn't see anything that resembled the marks a flat, plastic sled would have made.

Books and handheld game devices covered most of the desk. A nightlight in the shape of the Incredible Hulk was plugged in next to the bed. She checked the dresser drawers, finding them neatly organized. She'd have to ask if that was Kellan or Maggie's doing. The walk-in closet was similar. Hockey skates and a stick, as well as baseball equipment, took up part of the space. Nikki examined anything that could have been used as a weapon and snapped some photos, but everything was as she'd expected it.

Her phone vibrated with a text from Caitlin, asking for an update and a chance to sit down and talk.

Nikki swore under her breath. Was she really using her friend's missing grandson as an excuse to get Nikki talking? Caitlin had seemed genuinely upset this morning, but she'd fooled Nikki before.

Nikki fired off a text letting her know she'd given the information to Miller and was currently waiting for an update.

Can we talk? Caitlin replied.

I'm working. I will call you if I have information.

Nikki muted the conversation in her alerts and turned her attention back to Kellan's room. She was surprised there were no photos of Dana. Even though Kellan had told the court he wanted to stay with his aunt and uncle, he surely loved his mother. He didn't have a computer or tablet, so he wouldn't have them saved electronically.

Nikki checked the top nightstand drawer and found birthday cards for the past three years, all with personal notes about how much his mother loved and missed him. No pictures, but the cards might prove more valuable to their investigation. These were the only things Nikki had seen in Dana's own words. Nikki took pictures of them before she left the room.

She found the Andersons in the great room, talking with Liam about Joe's woodworking business.

"Thanks for allowing me to look in his room. I hope you don't mind, but I took pictures of the birthday cards Dana had sent him."

Joe didn't seem surprised, but Maggie's face turned pink. "I didn't know he'd even seen those."

"Why wouldn't he have seen them?" Nikki asked. "The envelopes all have this address on them."

"I just assumed he didn't want to read them and threw them away."

Nikki could tell from Liam's expression that he wasn't buying her story, either. She decided to let it slide. "Mr. Anderson, would you mind giving us a tour of the rest of the property?"

"Of course. Just let me get my boots and coat."

Liam stood. "We'll wait outside."

"Mrs. Anderson, thank you for your time. Please take care of yourself. I'm sure we'll speak again soon." Nikki followed Liam outside, making sure to shut the front door.

"She thought Kellan didn't get those cards," Liam said flatly.

"I know. Why on earth would she want to keep them from him? I know she and Dana had issues, but still. That's very petty."

Liam shrugged. "Siblings are complicated. Even in healthy families, they spend plenty of time at each other's throats, especially growing up. Some of that stuff's hard to let go."

Nikki remembered that Liam was the youngest of three brothers. "Is that how it is in your family?"

"Kind of," he said. "My oldest brother and I have a good relationship. But things between my middle brother and me are always shaky. We got into a lot of fights as teenagers. He holds a grudge."

Nikki wished she had siblings to talk about or lean on when her parents had been killed. "Do you think Maggie's bitterness makes sense, then?"

"From what we've heard. That's a big age gap. There's always a pecking order, anyway. Parents don't say it—at least most don't—but they do have favorites. Some are better at hiding it than others. But it makes it hard for the sibling who feels left out. Add in all of their issues, and I'm not surprised Maggie's so bitter."

"Seems like part of it is about her parents."

"Absolutely. Unresolved issues she can't let go of, so Dana becomes a scapegoat of sorts."

Joe came out of the house then in a heavy work coat with a skullcap over his bald head. "Sorry to take so long. Maggie's just a wreck. I'm trying to be there for her."

"We understand," Nikki said. "Whatever the situation was between her and Dana, she lost her sister as well as Kellan. It's a lot to deal with."

Joe nodded gruffly. "So, where to start." He pointed to the big snow mound. "There's Mt. Rocky Road. Kellan always named the snow piles. Different one every winter. He helped me drive the plow this year." Joe cleared his throat. "Let me show you the garage."

He walked to the attached three-car garage and punched in a code on the security pad. The first door opened, revealing his work truck. Maggie's SUV was parked next to it. The far end of the garage housed lawnmowers and other equipment.

"That is an impressive sled." Liam walked over to the storage side of the garage, where a handmade sled was propped up against the wall. It looked like some of the vintage sleds Nikki had seen growing up. A red rope was attached to the bar across the front for steering.

"I made it for Kellan's first Christmas with us," Joe said. "It's a flyer. Fast, too."

"I always wanted to ride on one of those. My parents always bought the plastic ones."

Joe made a face. "Yeah, the saucers are fun, but not fast like this is. I say if you're going to sled, you have to do it right."

Nikki was impressed at Liam's subtlety. She wandered around the garage, casually looking at the gardening tools hung on the wall and the snow shovels stacked near the sled. Nothing out of the ordinary, although they could have been cleaned. Still, she didn't see anything that made her want to run out and get a warrant. And she didn't see any plastic sled tucked away.

"Can we see the shop?" Liam said. "I'm fascinated with the stuff you can make."

Joe puffed a little bit. "Sure. Just go on out that side door. I keep a shoveled path to the shop."

"Kellan really liked playing in the snow, didn't he?" Nikki asked. The wood shop was maybe a hundred yards behind the house. "I noticed his work from his bedroom window."

"He'd stay out until he just couldn't stand the cold any longer. Always building snow forts and stuff."

"How far back does your property go?"

"See the tree line a little ways back? That's the end of our property. I've been planning on putting up a fence to keep some of the wildlife out, but Maggie's fine with the deer chewing on the garden as long as she can enjoy watching them."

A shoveled, sanded path led across the large backyard to the massive metal building that served as Joe's wood shop. As Nikki walked along, she marveled at the size of it.

"This is impressive," Nikki said. "Is this building new?"

"It replaced my original shop a few years ago. I'm proud to say I outgrew it. And I went all in with this one. It doubles as my man cave." He unlocked the door and motioned for Nikki and Liam to go inside. "I try to keep it tidy, but it smells like sawdust."

"We don't mind."

Much of the shop was full of tools and different-sized worktables. An impressive shelving unit filled the west wall. Miller's team had already gone through the shop, but Nikki didn't think they were looking for blood. The tools looked cared for but used. Many of them were stationary, used for cutting patterns or larger objects. Several had sharp corners.

"Mr. Anderson, can I be blunt?" Nikki said. She had been hoping to get a moment alone with Joe. "I know Maggie has taken some offense to our questioning, and I understand, but we have to ask the family members the same questions we would a suspect. Statistically, crimes against kids are usually done by family members, and even if we don't see you and your wife as suspects, I have to thoroughly investigate. If we skip any steps, a good defense attorney can find loopholes you wouldn't believe."

Joe nodded. "I assumed that was the deal. You can look at anything you want."

"Since Kellan was killed by blunt force trauma, Liam and I have to make sure there's nothing in your shop that could have been used." She looked around and smiled. "There's a lot of stuff in here."

"Do what you need to. If someone else was involved, I want them held responsible," Joe replied.

"Thank you."

Nikki and Liam walked around the equipment. Nikki paid special attention to the corners of the big tables, including checking underneath. If Kellan had hit his head on one of them, she might find some kind of residue.

She glanced at Liam, who shook his head. So far, so good.

Nikki pointed to the shelves that contained the handheld equipment. "Custom-built, I assume?"

"First project for this shop," Joe said. "I planned to sell it, but it was too perfect for the building."

"No doors," Liam noted. "With all this expensive equipment, I'd think you want these locked up."

Joe grinned and walked to the opposite side of the shelving unit. He grabbed the old china doorknob that had been attached to what Nikki assumed was just the frame. Instead, a wooden panel emerged. "I can slide this over the entire shelving unit and lock it."

"Wow," Liam said. "That's cool."

"Why the china knob?"

Joe's cheeks reddened. "It's from my parents' old place. A memento."

"So you did the single panel instead of a bunch of individual doors. That's a timesaver."

"It is, but I'm also terrible at organizing and remembering where I put tools. This way, I can see them and it doesn't matter if they're in the wrong place."

Nikki could see why Joe's work was in high demand. "Where do you store the wood?"

"Actually, I only keep what I need on hand. I get an order and then pick up the wood from various mills. That way it stays premium, and my overheads are lower. I don't have a lot of waste."

They walked toward the back of the shop, where a flat-screen television hung on the wall, far away from the tools. A thick area rug provided a cushion against the concrete floor, and a cozy sectional couch and an armchair surrounded it, along with a hand-carved end table.

A half-built toy log house sat on the floor in the middle of the rug. Nikki felt a pang of sadness. She'd loved Lincoln logs as a kid, and she and her father spent hours on the weekend building all sorts of things. Laccy had never really liked playing with them. But these didn't look store-bought. "Is this a custom set?"

Joe's thick mustache twitched, his eyes misting. "I made it for him right after he came to live with us. It started out as your basic house, but then we kept making more things. That plastic tote over there has about a hundred more pieces." Joe sat down on the sofa and stared at the toys. "I can't believe this happened."

Nikki looked at Liam, knowing he'd understand.

"Joe, mind if I look at the rest of the place?"

"Go ahead. Bathroom and utility rooms are about all that's left. My office is in the house."

Liam nodded and Nikki sat down in the chair across from the big man. Despite his pro wrestler bulk, he had a teddy bear quality. "Joe, how long have you known the family?"

"Well, me and Mags have been married twenty-five years. We dated for about a year."

"So Dana would have been, what, seven?"

"About there, yeah." He cleared his throat. "I know Maggie seems bitter. But she did love her sister. Both she and her mom tried for a long time to help Dana. When their mom died, Maggie couldn't deal with it anymore."

"Did Dana tell anyone why she started using? She graduated and planned to get her teaching license, right?"

"Dean's list every semester, too. She was smart. I don't know if she ever did tell anyone the specific reason, but she and their dad were really close. He died just a couple of months later. I always assumed that had a lot to do with it. She'd already paid to take the test, and she wasn't ready. I think failing pushed her over the edge. She wasn't used to that."

"I don't have any siblings, so it's a little hard for me to understand the sisters' dynamic. I can't imagine my parents having a surprise baby when I was teenager." She tried to sound lighthearted, but the words fell flat. Her parents hadn't even seen Nikki graduate.

"Maggie was a little jealous, I think. But that's human nature, right?"

"It definitely is. Was Dana that spoiled, or did Maggie's feelings kind of color her opinion?"

"Oh, she was spoiled. And when she was little, sometimes a little bratty. She knew how to get her mom to give in. But she had a big heart, and she didn't get into a lot of trouble. Dana seemed like one of those kids that was on the right path: college, job, family, good life. Maggie's mom said it was almost like a switch flipped, and Dana became a different person."

"Did anyone ask her why?"

Joe shrugged. "She always said stress and none of our business."

Liam returned. "All good, as expected. Joe, thanks for cooperating so we can scratch the shop off our list."

"No problem. Least I can do." He jammed his meaty hands into his pockets, his broad shoulders sagging. "This is my fault. I forgot the early out. If I'd been here—"

"Beating yourself up isn't going to help you or Maggie get through this," Nikki said. "Everyone makes mistakes."

Joe grunted. Nikki knew he'd carry the guilt for a long time. He led them outside and locked the door. "You need anything else, call me."

CHAPTER SEVEN

Instead of going back to the station to regroup, Nikki and Liam went to the small coffee shop near the interstate where Dana's drug counselor had agreed to meet them. Nikki and Liam both ordered large coffees and then found a table at the back. Nikki added cream and sugar to her coffee while Liam went over his notes from this morning.

"Let's get a warrant for the bank," Nikki said.

Liam nodded. "What time are we due at the elementary school?"

Liam had called the school on the way to the coffee shop. Nikki wasn't sure how much they'd get from the staff, but they needed to confirm some details with Kellan's teacher.

"One o'clock. That gives us time to talk with Kellan's teacher and the bus driver before he leaves on the afternoon route."

"What about talking with his friends?"

"That's more delicate," Nikki said. "These are young kids. Miller told me that school counselors are speaking to Kellan's class, including his small circle of friends. I'm going to ask his teacher if she thinks there are any friends we should talk to, but we have to tread carefully. It's traumatizing enough for them to hear that Kellan is dead."

Nikki sensed the atmosphere in the cafe change. Her stomach flipped when she realized why some of the patrons had suddenly turned to stare at her.

Mark Todd had entered the shop. He kept his head down as he made his way to the counter to order. He'd no doubt picked up the habit in prison: keep your head down and don't draw attention to yourself, and hopefully no one bothers you. A pair of middle-aged women sat in the corner and openly stared as Mark walked by and then started whispering to each other. There was no denying Mark's innocence. There was DNA evidence and a confession from the real killer, but the stigma of being in prison for twenty years would follow Mark everywhere.

One of the women stood and smoothed her coat. She said something to her friend and then marched toward Mark.

Nikki stood as well. She wasn't going to allow the woman to harass Mark. "I'll be right back."

Nikki scurried around tables, but the woman had already started talking to him. He seemed surprised by whatever she had said, his pale cheeks reddening.

"Is there a problem?" Nikki asked.

Mark and the woman turned around to look at her. The woman looked Nikki up and down, recognition shining in her dark eyes. "There is now. Leave him alone."

"Excuse me?"

"He's got a record because of you," the woman spat.

"Actually, my record's been expunged, Linda," Mark said softly. "Thanks to Nikki."

"You lost twenty years of your life—"

"Stop." Mark looked at Nikki apologetically. "This is my cousin, Linda," he told Nikki, turning to the woman. "Nikki is my friend," he reassured her.

That's why she looked so familiar. Nikki must have seen Linda in the family reunion photos that Rory had shown her.

"Then why is she bothering us?"

Nikki flushed. "I assumed you were going to tell him to leave."

"Because he was in prison? I know he's not a criminal, Agent Hunt. Apparently, you still see him as one. Does Rory know that?"

"Linda." Mark's soft voice was stern. "You know she spoke on my behalf."

"After the DNA exonerated you."

Nikki wanted to sink into the ground. "I'm sorry to have bothered you."

"You didn't," Mark said. "Linda, go sit down, and I'll join you in a minute."

Linda glared daggers at Nikki, but she did as her cousin asked.

"I'm sorry about her."

"Don't be," Nikki said. "I should have minded my own business."

He smiled. "You were going to stand up for me."

"She's right. I assumed something I shouldn't have."

"Because you know how mean people can be. Can I buy you a cup of coffee?"

"Oh, uh." Nikki hooked her thumb over her shoulder. "I'm here with my partner. We're discussing a case."

He nodded. "No problem. Maybe another time."

Nikki had only seen Mark a couple of times since his release. His parents wanted nothing to do with her, and Nikki had no idea what to say to Mark. They'd known each other since they were kids, but her parents' murders had sent them on two very different paths. Nikki still blamed herself, and she couldn't assuage the guilt she felt every time she looked at him.

"Definitely," she said. "Have a good day."

Mark nodded, and Nikki turned back to Liam. She was surprised to see a man she assumed was Fletcher had joined him. She'd been so focused on Mark that she hadn't noticed anyone enter the coffee shop.

She shook off her conversation with Mark and his cousin and headed back to the table. The man sensed her presence and stood up. He was tall, with dark blond hair, and his lightweight sweater hugged muscular shoulders. With his khakis and blue sweater vest matching his checkered shirt, he looked like he'd just come from a J. Crew photo shoot.

"Cam Fletcher?"

He stood and extended his hand. "Yes. Agent Hunt, I recognize you from the news." His eyes were red-rimmed and swollen.

Nikki smiled tightly and took her seat. "I'm very sorry about Dana."

"I just can't believe it," Cam said. "I've been doing this for ten years, and she's one of the few people I thought would actually stay sober."

"We don't have the tox reports back," Nikki explained. "You're a licensed addiction counselor, right?"

Cam nodded. "Someone helped me get clean, and I wanted to help other people. So I went back to school."

"That's very admirable," she replied. "I assume you met Dana for the first time when she arrived at your program?"

"Yes. She was sent to New Hope for rehab. Our residential recovery program is an extension of New Hope."

"This wasn't her first time in rehab," Liam said. "What was your initial impression of her?"

"Sad and alone," Cam replied. "She didn't trust anyone. That's not unusual for addicts. Most don't start using or drinking because of a happy life. It took a long time to earn her trust, but once I did, she seemed to turn a corner."

"Why didn't she trust you initially?" Nikki sipped her coffee.

"She'd been burned—her words—by other counselors. She felt like her sister and the court system were working against her. Given her meth addiction, I initially chalked things up to drug-induced paranoia."

"What changed your mind?"

Cam was silent for a moment. "It's hard to explain. She started passing drug tests and we knew she was clean, but the belief that her sister was undermining her persisted. Dana believed that Maggie had resented her all of her life and that it got worse after Kellan was born. I guess Maggie can't have children."

"Their age difference created a difficult dynamic," Nikki said. "Did Maggie or Joe ever visit her in rehab?"

"Maggie did, a couple of times. But Dana was always so agitated after, we asked her to stop coming for a while. Dana did have regular, supervised visits with Kellan." Cam stared at the table. "He was such a good kid. He loved seeing his mom and was so proud she was getting better."

"Did he talk about living with her again?" The Andersons had said Kellan didn't want to go back to Dana.

"Absolutely," Cam said. "Her last visit with him was a week before the custody trial. She had over a year of sobriety and was glowing. She'd been saving money for an apartment, and since Kellan was in school in Afton, Dana hoped to find a place nearby, so he didn't have to switch schools."

"She was living at the Gateway Center by then?"

Cam nodded. "Yes, once a person successfully completes the rehab program, they're eligible to apply for our sober living program."

Nikki had heard of the program. It was located in a residential area of Minneapolis not far from the Mall of America. "Is that nonprofit?"

"We just have a small monthly program fee. Residents need to be able to work or be in school. I'm sure you know Minnesota has one of the strongest programs for helping recovering addicts transition and succeed. Dana's college degree made it a little easier for her to find work. She wanted to get her teaching license eventually. She worked at an inbound call center for Central Alarms. She had to pass a monthly drug test."

"But she no longer worked there," Liam said. "We were told that she was fired after she failed the court administered drug test."

Cam's mouth tightened. "I can't believe I'm saying this, but…" He paused. "I'm certain Dana didn't fail that test. As soon as I found out about it, I was sure there was some kind of mix-up."

"I'm sure it's hard when someone falls off the wagon," Nikki said. "But it sadly happens more often than not. I know you want to believe—"

"I'm not naive, A gent," Cam replied. "Gateway is strict about maintaining sobriety. We run bimonthly tests, and Dana passed every one for six straight months, including the last one a few days before the court-ordered test. I probably don't have to tell you that using again after that many months would have greatly affected her behavior. She was very paranoid and angry when she was using. Twitchy. She wouldn't have been able to hide that. I've dealt with enough addicts to know when someone's high. Dana wasn't. She fully expected to get her son back that day, and she should have. Instead, she loses him, and Gateway kicked her out. I tried to plead her case, but they have a strict no-tolerance policy and retesting was out of the question."

"Where did she go?" Liam asked. "We haven't been able to find out where she's been living."

Cam looked down at the table, the tops of his ears pink. "Over the course of her treatment, Dana and I became friends. I have a spare room."

"Isn't that a conflict of interest?"

"As long as the relationship isn't personal, no, it's not."

"Was it personal?"

He blanched. "Not in that way, no. I would never disrupt someone's recovery with a complicated physical relationship, and that's why she moved out after a few weeks. She knew that I loved my job and didn't want to get me in trouble. I told her it was fine since we weren't involved, and she gave me this look like…"

"She had feelings for you," Nikki guessed.

"I tried to talk to her, but she clammed up and went on packing her things. She called a few days later and said she was staying at the women's shelter off Kellogg Boulevard."

"You didn't mention this when you spoke to Miller on the phone Friday evening," Liam said.

"I know. I was at a family function, and I didn't want to get into it if I didn't have to."

"But you weren't surprised that Dana tried to take Kellan?"

Cam sighed. "Yes and no. During the first few months I knew her, when she was still trying to get sober, she talked about taking him from her sister if she wouldn't give him back. Every time, I would tell her all the ways it could go wrong and she'd lose any chance at an appeal. When she called me from the shelter, she promised me she wouldn't lose her cool and take him."

"But when Chief Miller called Friday, you assumed she was using again?"

"I'm not proud of it, but yes. Kellan was Dana's entire motivation for getting clean. Losing him crushed her. On top of that, she lost much of her support system when she was kicked out of Gateway."

Nikki wished she had her notes on hand, but she was certain Cam had told Miller he'd gone to a friend's wedding. "I thought you were gone for the weekend at a friend's wedding."

"Yes, that's right." He looked confused.

"I'm just clarifying, because you mentioned a family function."

"Ah." He smiled sadly. "Being an addict burns bridges. My friends are my family."

"I understand. So the last time you spoke with her was when she called from the shelter?"

"No," Cam said. "She called me out of the blue last week and wanted a counseling session. She wouldn't say if she'd fallen off the wagon, but I suspected it. We set up a time, but she never showed."

"Where did you meet?" Liam asked. "Gateway?"

"She refused to meet me there. I couldn't blame her. I asked her to meet me at a little hole-in-the-wall breakfast place in downtown Minneapolis that I knew she liked. She didn't show."

"Which place?" Liam asked. "I'm always on the lookout for good breakfast places."

"Al's," Cam said.

Liam snapped his fingers. "Bacon waffles, right?"

Cam nodded sadly. "Dana always got those."

"Did you try calling her again after that?" Nikki asked.

Cam nodded. "She never answered. I didn't know where she was staying, so I couldn't track her down."

"She wasn't at the shelter?"

"She said she'd only stayed there a week or so and then found a place. Honestly, I worried she'd fallen in with the wrong people. She was in a fragile state after losing Kellan."

"Do you remember what she said about the Andersons when the drug test came back positive?"

Cam's jaw tightened. "She lunged at Maggie, right over the court chairs. I caught her before she could do anything to get in trouble. Dana was certain Maggie had something to do with her failing the test."

"Did you or Gateway look into it?"

"Dana had lost all faith in the system at that point." Bitterness colored Cam's voice. "When she first came to stay with me, all she talked about was how stupid she'd been to believe her sister wouldn't continue to meddle after Maggie convinced the court to move the custody case to Washington County. I suggested trying to find an outside attorney, and she said she'd think about it. I don't know if she ever contacted one. She believed everyone was against her. And I don't think she was wrong about that."

"Hold up." Liam looked up from his notes. "When did Maggie do this?"

"Before I knew Dana," he said. "I think within the first few months of Joe and Maggie having temporary custody. Dana was in and out of rehab at the time with no permanent address. Maggie convinced the Hennepin County judge to move the case to Washington County since Kellan was living with them, and Dana was unstable."

"That's not entirely unusual," Nikki reminded him. "The family courts are overrun. Anytime they can shift a case to another district, they're happy to do so."

"I know, but Dana thought it was because Maggie was friendly with the family court judge. There are only two in Washington County who handle family court. Dana didn't realize it at first, but she figured out that Judge Frasier went to high school with Maggie."

"Stillwater has a huge high school," Nikki said. "That's not exactly being friendly, especially since they had to have graduated in the early nineties. Did she have proof they were in current contact?"

"Not that I know of," Cam replied. "But Dana wholeheartedly believed that her sister wanted to take Kellan from her for good."

"Maggie didn't think Dana would stay sober," Liam said. "She wanted to protect Kellan."

"That's what I told her." Cam shook his head. "Dana believed it was all about keeping her in her place. Maggie wanted total control of her life. She's the one who talked their mother into changing her will."

"To keep Dana from going through the inheritance," Nikki suggested.

"There were no stipulations," Cam said. "Dana was just cut out, and that wasn't like her mother."

Nikki checked her notes. "She was getting money every month from the interest, though. What happened to that after she lost Kellan?"

"Maggie had to agree that it went to Dana's rehab bills."

"Then why was Dana so sure Maggie didn't want her to get better?"

"Control. Dana believed that Maggie's resentment of her drove her actions."

"Because Dana was so much younger, and their parents were able to do more for her?" Nikki asked.

"I guess so."

Liam looked unconvinced. "Do you know if there were any incidents when they were younger? Anything specifically?"

Cam drummed his fingers on the table. "Well, when Dana was seventeen, Maggie and their mother got into a huge fight over Dana's prom dress. It was expensive and nicer than anything Maggie ever had. Dana said that fight kind of pulled the lid off Maggie's anger, and their mom kicked her out of the house. They eventually smoothed things over, but there were many family arguments after that, and most of them were about how their parents helped Dana and did nothing for Maggie. Of course, I only know Dana's perspective. She said her mother told her that they'd helped Maggie as much as they could."

"Do you know if there are any extended friends or family that might be able to give us more information?"

"Dana talked about a cousin in Iowa. Second cousin, I think. I might have her name in my records. I'll look as soon as I'm back on my laptop. Sorry, but I need to run. I have a meeting with a client."

"Of course. Thanks for coming out." Nikki turned to Liam as Cam left. "What do you think?"

"I'm not sure," Liam said. "He definitely believed Dana's accusations about Maggie. If he was the person closest to her, he seems the most likely person she'd ask for help to get Kellan back."

Nikki nodded. "His alibi's fairly solid, but it doesn't mean he didn't help Dana in some way." She sighed and yanked her phone out of her purse, noticing Caitlin Newport's number lighting it up again. Nikki stood to leave, checking her watch. "We need to hurry if we're going to make the meeting with the teacher."

Hearing Cam's account of Dana's troubled life made Nikki wonder how stable Dana had been when she'd taken Kellan. If he'd refused to leave his aunt and uncle to live with her, could she have snapped and hurt her own son?

CHAPTER EIGHT

Nikki followed the GPS toward Kellan's elementary school while Liam took notes. She hadn't gotten a bad vibe from Cam, but she wanted to be able to cross his name off the suspect list. "Listen, make sure you run a full background check on Cam Fletcher. See if you can drum up any associates that he might have sent Dana to for help."

Miller's caller ID flashed on the jeep's touchscreen.

"So fancy," Liam teased.

Nikki rolled her eyes. "Hey, Chief Miller. We just finished talking to Cam Fletcher," Nikki said. "Dana swore up and down that Maggie was out to get her and that she somehow had the drug test falsified."

"Meth makes people paranoid," Miller replied shortly.

"That was my initial thought, but Dana told her drug counselor that Maggie would take Kellan from her early on, and she never wavered from that, even when she was clean. We were out at the Andersons' this morning. The family history was intense."

"You mean the bad blood between Dana and Maggie," Miller said. "Speaking of which, I just got a call from Maggie Anderson fuming because you told her husband they were suspects."

Nikki and Liam looked at each other. She'd never heard Miller sound so irritated. "We told Joe we had to do a standard investigation. He understood and told us to look wherever. We went through the house and wood shop and found nothing."

"Maggie seemed a bit defensive the entire time," Liam added. "I think she's dealing with her grief by being angry at everyone else."

"If we're stepping on your toes—" Nikki started.

"No, no, no," Miller said. "That all came out wrong. I'm so mad, I can't think straight. I followed up on Caitlin Newport's information with the Chisago County Sheriff for you, and the conversation I had with him has riled me up. He got all offended and said I was questioning his judgment. I reminded him that he should have notified surrounding counties to help search, and he accused me of trying to stir up another sensational case to bolster my chances at staying sheriff. He's got no tolerance for Newport, so that didn't help matters."

"Did he give you any information?" Nikki asked.

"Not much more than you already know," Miller replied. "Zach Reeves lives with his grandparents. According to the sheriff, he snuck out on the snowmobile sometime before his grandpa woke up, around 7 a.m. The grandparents thought he'd eventually come home, but when he didn't show up by lunchtime, they started searching. Police were notified late that afternoon. A couple of neighbors reported seeing him riding near the river that morning."

"What's the ice cover like?" Nikki asked. Riding snowmobiles across the frozen lakes was common winter fun, but taking one out on the water in early March was risky. Fooling around with the St. Croix River was flat-out stupid.

"Patchy, like most years at this time," Miller replied. "They searched the area and found the kid's stocking hat near the shore."

Liam had his cell phone out and pulled up a local map. "The hat wasn't found anywhere near the bridge where Kellan and Dana were, was it?"

"No," Miller said. "They found it about ten miles from Zach's house. But I should have been informed since the damn river flows south and the current is usually still moving at a good clip beneath the ice."

Nikki understood Miller's agitation over not being informed, but she doubted his involvement would have made much of a difference. "Do you think the sheriff is right about what happened to Zach?"

"Probably. But finding the hat's kind of convenient, don't you think?" Miller asked. "It wasn't frozen, and the ice doesn't get patchy until a couple hundred yards offshore. Maybe it's just the fact that the sheriff is a politician without a lot of investigative experience and had the balls not to tell me about Zach. The sheriff says he knew I was busy looking for Kellan and saw no reason the two disappearances were related since Kellan was believed to have been taken by his mother."

"That's a reasonable theory, though," Liam said. "Especially with Zach taking the snowmobile."

"I know," Miller agreed. "Danny Braintree and I have never seen eye to eye. My judgment's probably clouded."

"When was the last time you slept?" Nikki knew Miller had been working around the clock with little rest since Kellan disappeared.

"I took a nap."

"Go home and get some real sleep. Liam and I are going to talk with Kellan's teacher. We'll keep you in the loop. As for Zach, do you want us to poke around?"

Miller snorted. "Braintree would have a fit at the idea. He's old-school and friendly with Hardin. You can imagine what he thinks about that situation. I sent a deputy to help with the search and see what else he can find out."

Nikki had no desire to deal with Braintree, especially if he supported Hardin, the ex-sheriff who'd been partially responsible for Mark Todd's wrongful imprisonment, but she knew Miller was stretched thin. "Let me know if you change your mind. Now go home and sleep in your own bed."

"Hey, I'm the acting sheriff," Miller said. "I'm not letting some FBI suit boss me around."

Nikki laughed. "Go home, Kent." She ended the call and punched in Caitlin's number.

Her anxious voice boomed through the Bluetooth system. "What did you find out?"

"Miller spoke with Braintree, and I'm sorry, but despite his poor attitude, there's just no solid reason to think these two cases are connected or that Zach didn't go through the ice. And Braintree definitely doesn't want me involved."

"Please, Nicole," Caitlin said. "If you just sit down with me—"

"I'm not doing the interview about Mark until after this case is finished."

"That's not why I want to talk to you," Caitlin snapped. "I promised Zach's grandparents that you would help."

Liam cleared his throat. "Caitlin, I heard the call with Miller. Nikki's right; there's no reason for us to barge in. And going over Braintree's head would make everything worse. Let them do their job and get the family some closure."

"By fishing his body out of the river, you mean." Caitlin's voice rose. "He did not drown. He's out there somewhere, and the same person who hurt Kellan could have hurt Zach."

"I'm sorry this isn't what you want to hear, but we're good at our jobs," Liam said icily. "Please let us do them."

"I didn't ask for your help, did I? I want Nikki's."

"Caitlin, we're knee-deep in this investigation." Nikki tried to keep her irritation out of her voice. "Miller has a deputy keeping track of Zach's search. I promise you if I hear about any shred of evidence supporting your theory, I will look into it."

The call abruptly ended, and Nikki sighed.

"She really hung up on me."

"She obviously has some emotional investment," Liam said.

"That's why I'm trying to be nice. But you know as well as I do that if we go barging in, all it's going to do is annoy Braintree and delay the recovery of Zach's body."

Caitlin was a good reporter, and she knew how an investigation worked. If she could take a step back and look at things rationally, she would see that Nikki was right. Still, the odds of two kids going missing on the same day in a small town like Stillwater were slim.

But Zach must have gone through the ice, she reminded herself. It was the only logical explanation.

Nikki made a sharp turn into the elementary school's parking lot. "Sorry about that," she said, noticing a drop in the mood in the car.

Liam didn't respond.

Nikki glanced at the passenger seat to see him texting furiously, his mouth pinched in concentration. "Liam?"

He looked up in confusion. "Sorry. Just dealing with a friend of mine." He slipped the phone back into his pocket and stared out of the window.

"Is everything OK?" Nikki asked.

"It's fine." Liam sounded uncharacteristically on edge. "I've got the junior agent in the office running Cam's background check."

"Is this friend the same woman you spent last night with?"

He rolled his eyes. "Who said it was a woman?"

Nikki snorted. "You're not seriously asking me that, are you?" She paused. "Do you want to talk about it?"

Liam sighed. "Thanks, but no. It's not a big deal. Let's just focus on interviewing Kellan's teacher."

Kellan's teacher, Cara Knopp, looked to be in her mid-twenties, with short, wavy dark hair and a bright smile. She knotted her sweater around her small waist and sat down at the round table, motioning for Nikki and Liam to do the same.

The small plastic chairs were child-sized, and Nikki sat carefully, hoping she didn't topple over. Liam's knees nearly touched his chin. Nikki focused on Cara, who looked like she might still be in shock from the news.

"I'm sorry for your loss," Nikki said. "It must be so hard to explain what happened to Kellan to your students. I hope the counselors have been helpful. If you need any additional resources for them, we can help."

Cara dabbed her eyes with a tissue. "Thank you. I still can't believe this has happened."

"I know," Nikki said gently. "Was Kellan a good student?" she asked.

"Yes, he was a sweetheart. Very hard-working. Mrs. Anderson said he'd never been to school when he first came to them, and she'd tutored him so he could join first grade. He was very bright and a quick learner."

"Did he play with a lot of kids?" Nikki inquired.

"No, he was very shy. He liked to be on the sidelines. Sometimes I think he'd learned to blend in because of all he's been through with his biological mother. He was nice to the other kids but reserved. The counselors spoke with all of them already."

"Don't worry, we're not going to push the kids. I just want to know if he had any friends he might have confided in."

Cara thought about it for a minute. "He and Lindsey Sutton liked to walk the school track together. But he was mostly in groups."

"Is she here today?"

"No," Cara said. "All the kids are shaken up. Her parents called her in sick today."

Nikki made a mental note to ask for the parents' information. If Lindsey had stayed home today, maybe she had been close enough to Kellan to know some of his secrets. "Can you think of anything unusual happening in the last few weeks. Did Kellan seem different? Distracted?"

"No," Cara replied. "Everything was normal. He was ahead in class, so I'd given him some higher-level books. He was proud of that and often stayed in at recess to read."

Nikki and Liam glanced at each other. "Did he seem afraid of being outside with the other kids?"

"Oh no, I don't think so. The winter's been so cold we've had several recesses in the gym. He sometimes went and played with the others and seemed fine, but he just really loved reading."

Nikki wasn't sure what she'd hoped to find out at the school, but disappointment washed through her. So far, everything in Kellan's day-to-day life appeared normal.

After Nikki dropped Liam off at his car and then purchased a charger that worked with Dana's phone, she decided to stop and see Rory before she headed home. He had a large crew on a new build on the west side of town. Several new houses had already been built, but it wasn't hard to find his worksite. He'd told her it was one of the largest homes he'd designed to date, and Nikki believed it. She guessed it was at least 6,000 square feet, plus a three-stall garage.

A couple of work trucks were parked behind Rory's, and Nikki's nerves flared. They hadn't gone out on many dates in town because of gossip, and she'd never visited him on site. Even though she knew she'd see him tomorrow, she really needed to see him before she left town.

The front door stood open a couple of inches, and a radio blared classic rock. Nikki knocked even though she doubted anyone would hear her over the music. She hadn't seen the blueprints for the house, but the large open foyer was impressive. She followed the music to a kitchen Martha Stewart would envy. It was as large as a five-star restaurant's with stainless-steel appliances, a gas range with a double oven and a center island twice the size of the one in Nikki's own kitchen. A protective cloth was draped over the large island.

Rory stood on a ladder working on the cabinets. His jeans were splattered with paint stains, but they hung just right on his narrow hips, and the old T-shirt was so thin she could see the dragon tattoo on his shoulder.

"Hey."

He looked over his shoulder and smiled. "Hey, you. I wasn't sure I'd see you again today." Rory climbed down from the ladder.

"I'm glad you stopped by." His gentle voice and familiar scent were a respite from the long day.

"I needed to see you."

Rory drew her into his arms, and she buried her face in his chest. He was tall enough to rest his chin on the top of her head. "I can't even imagine. The Andersons have closure, at least."

"Right."

He kissed the top of her head. "I guess you won't be back in town until the next time Lacey's at her dad's."

Nikki stepped back and looked up at him. "Why do you say that?"

"I just assumed the case was basically closed. Word around town is that Dana committed suicide and had something to do with poor Kellan's death."

"Word around town?" Nikki said. "Who told you that?"

"One of my guys. He heard it from a friend. You know how small towns are, Nik."

"Full of people spreading rumors instead of minding their own business." She crossed her arms over her chest and leaned against the counter. "The medical examiner hasn't finished the autopsies yet. But, sure, let's gossip about a dead little boy and his mother."

Hurt flashed in Rory's eyes. "I'm not gossiping. My guys know we're together and mentioned what they'd heard. I just wanted to get an idea of when I'd see you next."

Shame washed through Nikki. "I'm sorry. I can't get into details, but there's a good chance Dana didn't do this," Nikki said.

"You're kidding."

"I can't say any more, and we're waiting for Blanchard to make it official. But someone else was clearly involved and they're still out there. That poor little kid." Her voice caught. "He was so small and helpless."

"Jesus." He hugged her tightly. "No wonder you want to get home and see Lacey."

"Thank you for understanding." Nikki composed herself and leaned back so she could look into his eyes. "That makes things easier."

"I'm glad," he said. "Your job is miserable enough."

She laughed and stepped back, wiping her eyes. "It's not always bad. It's pretty awesome when we catch the bastard."

He pushed a lock of hair out of her eyes. "I bet it is."

"So, this place is impressive. This kitchen makes me weep."

He grinned. "Wait until you see the final product. They bought every possible bell and whistle."

"Are you going to be able to get back on schedule?"

"Oh yeah," Rory said. "That's the construction business. You're either behind or not busy enough. I'll take too much work any day."

She wanted to tell him about what happened at the coffee shop, but she didn't want to drive any bigger wedge between Rory and his family. "I saw Mark this morning. He looks good."

"Where?"

"The coffee shop near the I-10. He said he was going into work."

"He's working on a rehab project for me not far from there. Did you guys talk?"

"A bit. I never know what to say, and I had to work. I'm glad he's doing so well."

"He's been talking to my parents about you. They'll come around."

"That's nice of him, but I don't want to be the cause of tension. They just got him back."

Rory kissed the top of her head. "Thanks to you."

"You're the one who didn't give up on him and made me see the truth."

"We'll both take credit, then." He kissed her softly, and warmth spread through her system.

Her phone interrupted them. "It's the medical examiner. I have to take it."

Rory nodded. "Want me to walk you out?"

"No, you need to finish here so you can go home and rest. And I've got to get on the road." She answered the call before it dropped. "Hi, Dr. Blanchard."

"Text me when you're home," Rory mouthed. "I miss you already."

She smiled at him before she went outside. "Sorry, Dr. Blanchard. I was just wrapping up with someone."

"That's fine," she said. "I have both autopsies finished, pending toxicology reports. Kellan died from blunt force trauma by what appears to be a round object. I still can't tell if it was an accident or intentional. I sent X-rays to the forensic anthropologist. I'm hoping he can tell how much force was used and the direction the blow came from. Going by his stomach contents, he died around six to eight hours after his school lunch. Good news is there's no sign of sexual assault."

"Did you find any signs Dana was currently using? I've seen a couple of pictures of her when she was, and she was rail-thin and had some sores on her face."

"No," Blanchard said. "She was normal weight. Her skin has some scarring, but nothing recent. That's not to say she didn't just start again. We won't know for sure until toxicology gets back. You should also know that by the time I got her on the table, postmortem bruising was visible on her exterior hand and palm, consistent with being held tightly."

"Can you tell time of death from that?"

"Deep bruising usually takes at least twelve hours to appear. I had a late start today and then did Kellan's autopsy first. I didn't start Dana's until close to noon, putting time of death around midnight Sunday. And that's consistent with the state her corpse was in when we arrived this morning. She also has some yellowed bruises on her arms that are probably a week old or so."

"Could you tell anything about the cuts on her wrists?"

"Yes, and that's part of the reason I waited to do her autopsy, because I wanted my assistant M.E.'s opinion. The cuts were made top to bottom rather than starting at the wrist. I can tell you I've never seen a suicide where someone cut from their forearm down. Most start at the wrists, and most don't know how much it takes to be successful."

"Just to make sure I'm understanding this, you're saying that someone held Dana's hand tightly enough to leave bruises and then cut her wrists with a downward motion instead of up as you'd expect."

"Correct. The bruising is on her right hand. My guess is that's the first wrist that was cut."

"She had to be drugged," Nikki said. "Or there would be more signs of a fight."

"I'm expecting to find some form of sedative or benzodiazepine."

"You mean Rohypnol."

"Yes," Blanchard said.

When Nikki found out who'd really killed her parents, she also discovered that she'd been drugged that night and nearly raped. She appreciated Blanchard's word choice, but the medical examiner didn't have to sugarcoat things for Nikki. "Was she raped?"

"Not that I can see. But I'm comfortable ruling hers as a homicide."

"And Kellan?"

"At this point, it's undetermined. I want to see what the bone doctor says first."

Nikki was relieved to hear that her instincts had been correct, but the grim reality sent a wave of sadness through her. Dana had been murdered.

CHAPTER NINE

"We're going to hatch butterflies in the spring." Lacey grinned, pizza sauce on her chin. She'd talked non-stop since Nikki had picked her up from her dad's house. Her nearly six-year-old daughter had an endless supply of energy. She talked with her hands, sometimes speaking so quickly Nikki could barely understand her. On days like this, Nikki wanted to grab Lacey in her arms and not let go. Life was too fragile.

"That's very exciting, honey." Nikki handed her daughter a napkin. "Wipe your chin. Do you know what kind of butterflies?"

Lacey's little nose scrunched. "Um... pretty ones."

Nikki laughed. "I hope your teacher takes lots of pictures."

"She said you can grow butterflies at home, too. Can we get some?"

Nikki didn't know much about butterfly gardens, but Lacey had been begging for a pet for months. Maybe the butterflies would satisfy her for a while. "I will definitely check it out."

Lacey bounced in her chair and then reached for another piece of pizza. She picked the pepperoni off first, each piece separately. Then she started in on the slice.

"You're going to be staying with Daddy the rest of the week," Nikki said. "Mommy has to work."

Lacey sagged in her seat. "Why can't you work from here?"

Nikki tried to be as honest as possible with her daughter about her job without giving her too many details. Her ex-husband was also an FBI agent, but he worked in white-collar crimes and his schedule was more consistent than Nikki's. Thankfully, Tyler was flexible, and they were able to share custody without either feeling shortchanged, although Nikki's responsibilities at work often cut into her time with Lacey. "Well, a little boy was hurt, and I have to find out who did it."

"Is he going to be OK?"

"No, honey, he isn't. That's why Mommy is going to be working long hours and it will be easier for me to stay in the same town."

"Are you going to stay in a hotel? With a pool? Me and Daddy can come and swim if you are!" Her cheeks flushed, her eyes lighting up.

Nikki tried not to flinch. She hated lying to her daughter, but she wasn't sure now was the time to talk about even more change in her life. "No, there isn't a pool. But you and Daddy always have fun."

Lacey rested her face on her hands and pouted. "I guess."

"I know it stinks," Nikki said. "But the case will be over before we know it."

Nikki wished she believed that.

After she tucked Lacey into bed, Nikki sat down with Dana's now-charged phone. It had only about three weeks' worth of calls and texts, which lined up with Cam's information about her getting a new phone. Nikki didn't see the Andersons' landline or cell phone numbers on the call log. Dana's last four calls had come from four different unknown numbers in rapid succession on Friday evening. She hadn't answered any of them.

Nikki punched in #69 on Dana's phone to call back the last number. It was already disconnected, meaning it was probably a burner number. Those were usually hard to trace because temporary numbers were constantly being used, so the chances of tracking down Dana's murderer this way were slim.

Nikki checked the text messages. There were a couple of obvious telemarketing texts, but the other four texts were all from different numbers and had been sent in the last several days before Dana died.

Nikki read through the messages. She was surprised to see that they sounded more like threats than a conversation about coordinating a kidnapping. What had Dana got herself into?

I'm watching you.

You know what I can do. Will be worse next time.

Don't forget what I told you.

If I have to come back, you'll be sorry.

The last text had been sent a few nights before Dana and Kellan disappeared. All four sounded like they were coming from the same person. The second text seemed like a reminder of the person hurting her. Blanchard thought the yellow bruises on Dana's upper arms were roughly a week old at the time she was murdered, so whoever had hurt her was probably the same person who sent the threatening texts.

Nikki knew there were burner apps that touted total privacy for the user, allowing them to purchase several temporary numbers. She went to the app store on her phone. A search for "burner number" returned dozens of apps. Some stated in the fine print that they kept a call log should law enforcement require records, and each of them required the user's phone number and email address. A few others offered total anonymity, allowing the user to pay for as many numbers as they wanted with zero records kept by the company.

Nikki would need a warrant to make any of the app creators give up their records, but if the call had used one claiming total anonymity, she was likely at a dead end.

She opened the pictures she'd taken of the birthday cards Dana had sent Kellan. Dana's handwritten notes were upbeat; she was reminding Kellan that she loved him, and they would be together soon. Kellan had turned nine shortly before the final custody hearing, and Dana's note made it clear she expected to get him back. She even talked about finding a place to live close to the Andersons' and Kellan's school so he didn't have to switch.

She'd sounded so full of hope and it made Nikki question whether she fell off the wagon. Maybe Dana had sabotaged herself because of a deep-seated fear that she couldn't stay sober and take care of Kellan. Had Maggie convinced her of that? Was it really possible the test results had been falsified? If they had and Dana was snooping around, their suspect list needed to be a lot longer.

Nikki had an appointment with the sober living house's executive director in the morning. She hoped he could shed more light on Dana's state of mind, but for now, she'd try to get to know Dana the best way she knew how—by creating a solid profile.

She thought back to the conversation with Cam earlier in the day. He'd mentioned that Dana was easily influenced by her friends and she'd had to cut ties. Is that how she'd been in college? Nikki wondered if Maggie had any contact information for Dana's college roommates.

Exhaustion overtook Nikki. She made a note to check with Cam and Maggie about the college friends and then crawled into bed. Tomorrow would be another long day.

CHAPTER TEN

Nikki dropped Lacey off at school with the promise to FaceTime her tonight, and then headed toward the sober living facility Dana had lived at for the past year. Nikki hated driving anywhere in Minneapolis during morning rush hour. Getting to the FBI office from home or Lacey's school was essentially a straight shot up Interstate 94. It was always busy, but getting into the downtown areas took more patience than she had on a normal day, let alone today. She'd barely slept last night and hadn't had time to check in with her team. She was eager to meet up with them after meeting with the facility's director and catch up on their leads.

Gateway wasn't far from the Sculpture Garden, and it was within walking distance of two nice parks. The building looked like a regular apartment building—three stories and well-maintained, but not flashy. According to their website, Gateway had a weight room, two common areas, as well as a reading and music room, along with conference rooms for group therapy.

Unfortunately, Nikki had to park on the street, and by the time she found a place and then walked the two blocks to Gateway, she was five minutes late for her appointment. She smoothed her hair and hurried into the building, bypassing the mailboxes and a vending machine. The door with the keyless entry next to the administrative desk must be how the residents and visitors accessed the living area.

Nikki knocked on the front office's open door.

A man in his mid-twenties smiled warmly at her. "Can I help you?"

"I have an appointment with Dr. Randall." Nikki held up her badge.

His face fell. "About Dana. We're all heartbroken."

Nikki offered him a sympathetic smile. "I'm sorry for your loss." She glanced at his nameplate. "Drew, right? How well did you know her?"

"Not well, really. But that door's the only way into the residences, so I spoke to her just about every day. She was nice. I'll page Dr. Randall."

"Thank you. Have you worked here long?"

"A couple of years," Drew said. "It's a good place to work."

"No issues with residents not getting along or having problems with following the rules?"

"Occasionally," he replied. "But Dr. Randall is usually around to work with everyone."

"Is he the only therapist?"

"He's the only full-time therapist, along with being the director. We have a part-time therapist and a few drug counselors. Cam Fletcher worked with Dana. Have you spoken with him?"

"We have," Nikki said. "He's pretty upset."

"They were close, I think. Cam's that kind of guy though. Everyone likes him."

The door buzzed and opened, and a man who looked more like Santa than any mall Santa smiled at her. His thick, white hair matched his beard, and his waistline would definitely fill Santa's suit. Nikki swore his eyes twinkled, too. "I'm Dr. Jake Randall."

"Special Agent Nikki Hunt." She shook his extended hand and smiled. "Thank you for meeting with me."

"We're just sick about Dana." He led her into the common area decorated with cozy Ikea furniture and soothing colors.

"This is very nice."

"We pride ourselves on routine and normalcy, but comfort is important, too. Being an addict doesn't mean a person should be regulated to lousy living conditions."

"How many residents do you have?"

"Our capacity is sixteen right now." He motioned for her to follow him down the hall. "We're working on funding for a secondary location. Our entertainment room is on the left. In addition to the books and card games, we have a piano and some very talented residents. The weight room's farther down the hall. As you can see, the lower floor is for administrative and daily use. We've got two conference rooms as well. The residents live on the second and third floors."

"How long does a resident usually stay?"

"It varies." Dr. Randall sounded a little out of breath as he ushered her into his office. "I hope you don't mind if I leave the door open. We try to be accessible at all times."

"That's fine." Nikki slipped her coat off and folded it over her lap.

"Can I get you anything to drink? We have water and coffee, although I probably need to make a fresh pot. To answer your question, residents are welcome to stay as long as they stay sober and maintain work. Our goal is to make sure a client is truly ready to be on their own."

"Did you think Dana was ready?"

Dr. Randall's pleasant expression turned to sadness. "She failed the drug test. Our board of directors is zero tolerance. I was as shocked as anyone. Have you spoken with Cam, her drug counselor?"

"Yes, I have." Nikki recounted what Cam Fletcher had told them yesterday, minus the personal information.

"Everything he said is accurate. She passed the last test here and, like Cam said, I didn't see any behaviors that I would expect to see if someone is on meth. The other therapists agreed with me, and that's why I went to the board on her behalf. It's rare, but mistakes do happen in the court system. But they wouldn't budge."

"I assume your lab and the court's chosen lab screen for multiple drugs?"

"Oh yes, although you probably know that meth users rarely find something else that will do what they need, unless it's heroin. And that's a totally different behavior. Dana's court-ordered test was positive for meth."

"Can you tell me about your treatment process?"

"Of course," Dr. Randall said. "We have four counselors, including Cam. They each have four residents and handle day-to-day counseling along with any court-ordered tasks. Each resident has a forty-five-minute therapy session with me once a week."

"So you're a licensed therapist?"

"Specializing in addiction, yes. I'm not a psychiatrist or a medical doctor, so any patient who needs medication of any kind gets those outside of here."

"I understand. What can you tell me about Dana's sessions?"

Dr. Randall smiled. "I'm sure you know Minnesota privacy laws prevent me from giving that information without a warrant or the executor of the patient's will. Dana didn't have a will, but Maggie Anderson is her next of kin and de facto executor. If she agrees—"

Nikki had expected as much. She handed him the warrant that had arrived this morning.

"You come prepared, I see. I like that. I'll have Drew email you my notes. As for Dana's sessions, she was a tough nut to crack. Her primary objective was getting her son back, and she was afraid therapy revelations might be a roadblock."

"Is that a typical fear of the people you see?"

"Yes, but unless someone is a danger to themselves or others, it's not an issue when it comes to child custody. The patient's rights are protected."

"Did you think Dana was a danger to herself or Kellan?"

"Not at all," Dr. Randall replied. "She circled around her issues during much of therapy, but she did everything she was supposed to do for the court. And her attitude improved as time went on. She seemed happy and confident during our last session."

"Did you ever get anything significant out of her in terms of her personal life and the issues that led to her addiction?"

"Bits and pieces. She talked a lot about her sister's jealousy and its impact on her. But during her last few sessions, she began to open up more. She had started taking uppers to study, and then her addiction sprang from there. However, when I asked about her life outside of college during that time, she clammed up. Our last session, I thought we were having a breakthrough because she tried to talk about something that happened when she was younger. She started talking about her parents going to see *Fargo*, and she went somewhere else. I thought we would have a breakthrough, but unfortunately, it triggered a panic attack."

Nikki leaned forward. Traumatic events in childhood were often a catalyst for addiction and self-destructive behavior. "What do you think she was trying to say?"

"I think something very traumatic likely happened to her, possibly as a kid or as a young adult in college. We never got deep enough for me to know anything more."

"How did she speak about her parents and immediate family?"

"She loved her parents dearly. She longed for Maggie to love her."

"What about Joe?"

"She didn't have anything bad to say about him. I don't think she spent much time with them since he and Maggie are so much older. And my impression was that Maggie was in the driver's seat in terms of the interaction with Dana."

"Did Dana spend time with any other residents?"

"Here and there," Dr. Randall said. "She worked as many hours as her employer allowed and attended all her counseling sessions, but she did visit the common areas a few times. She played the piano very well. She spent much of her free time in the entertainment room. I can see if anyone is available to talk to you."

"Thank you."

"Head into the entertainment area, and I'll see who I can rummage up." He shuffled away.

Nikki could see why the residents usually did well at Gateway. Dr. Randall was kind and compassionate, and he seemed genuinely sad about not being able to keep Dana in the house. She headed into the cozy-looking room and laid her coat over the back of a chair. A bay window overlooked what was likely a very pretty garden in the summer. A pair of cardinals flitted around a bird feeder. Her mother used to say that seeing a cardinal meant that someone you love who's passed on is nearby.

The lump in her throat took her by surprise. Her parents had been gone for more than half her life, and the pain of losing them could still take her breath away. She tried to tell herself that recent events had made things worse, but deep down she knew that all she'd done was tear a scab off a wound that had festered and never fully been allowed to heal. Maybe Rory was right, and she should go to therapy. She'd gone for a few years during college, but work and life had eventually given her an excuse to quit going.

"Agent Hunt, I've found two ladies who are happy to talk about Dana." Dr. Randall had returned. "This is Vonda and Renee. Take all the time you need. The ladies are on their own time. I've got to catch up on some office work. Do let me know if you have any more questions, Agent Hunt."

"Thanks, Rand." Vonda was a heavier-set black woman with a friendly smile and impressive false eyelashes. Renee appeared to be the eldest, her short hair flecked with gray. She dabbed her nose with a tissue.

"Is Dana really dead?" Renee asked.

"I'm afraid so. Her son, too." Nikki sat down in the chair she'd hung her coat on, and the two women followed suit.

Vonda's eyes welled up. "She loved that little boy. He was all she talked about. Well, that and her selfish sister."

"Did either of the Andersons ever visit her?" Nikki asked.

"Not that I know of," Vonda replied.

"How well did you two know Dana?"

The women exchanged glances.

"We were friendly," Renee said. "She worked a lot. She was also studying to retake her teaching exam. I really thought she'd make it."

"She did," Vonda said definitively. "I don't believe for a minute she failed that court drug test."

"Why?" Nikki asked. "I know she passed one a couple of days before the trial."

"Yes, and other than work, she was here. No way she tried to smuggle drugs in here. The night before the custody hearing, she practiced what she was going to say with us. She wasn't tweaking then, and she hadn't been the entire time she lived here. Then the urine test at the courthouse comes back positive. I call bullshit."

"That's a big accusation," Nikki said.

"It's what Dana thought," Renee replied. "Ever since Dana realized that Maggie went to high school with that judge, she'd worried Maggie would pull something. We told her to put it out of her mind. She was clean and had nothing to worry about. Man, I never dreamed she was right."

Nikki leaned forward. "Really? Cam and Randall didn't mention that."

"She probably didn't want them to think she was paranoid," Renee said. "But she sat right in that chair the night before the hearing and said she'd talked to her sister a while back. Maggie told her she'd never get Kellan back and she'd do whatever it took to keep him. I guess Dana tried to tell the judge that, but he didn't believe her."

Maggie Anderson was starting to sound almost comically diabolical. How much of Dana's view of her sister had been impacted by their strained relationship, and how much had been Dana's own issues or paranoia caused by her addiction?

"We had a cake ready for her," Vonda said. "But someone called Randall and told him before Dana got back. He searched her room, and she let him have it."

"He was in a difficult position," Nikki replied.

Renee shifted in her seat. "She went straight to his office. We could hear her yelling from the common area. She kept telling him to have someone do a blood test right now. Next day, she's being escorted out. Randall said the board had made the decision."

"Did you hear from her after that?"

They shook their heads. "We tried to call her, but she never answered."

Nikki spoke with Vonda and Renee for a few more minutes and thanked them for their time. She made sure to give each one a card and asked them to call if they remembered anything else.

Dr. Randall's office door was partially closed, and he appeared to be on a call, so Nikki stopped by the front desk.

"Drew, could you thank Dr. Randall for his time? I've got to get going."

"No problem."

"By the way," Nikki said. "Do you happen to know if Dana kept receiving mail here or left a forwarding address?"

His smile faded. "I'm sorry, I don't. I have her office records, but she paid in cash. These records are mostly about court dates and visitors' logs, stuff like that. But I can't legally show them to you."

Nikki found the signed warrant in her bag again and handed it to Drew, along with a business card. "I'll need the records emailed ASAP."

He nodded. "You'll have them by the end of the day."

"Perfect. I'll keep an eye out for them."

Nikki slipped her coat on and headed outside. Bright morning sun glinted off the snow and ice, and she shaded her eyes to find her jeep. She tossed her bag in the passenger seat and checked her phone, hoping to see a call from Liam. He'd secured the warrant for the bank records this morning and planned to stop before he met Nikki in Stillwater. He hadn't called, but Rory had texted her about meeting for lunch. Her stomach knotted as she read the message.

Please meet. Need to talk asap.

Those words usually meant bad news was coming, but things had been good between them. What did he want to talk to her about?

CHAPTER ELEVEN

Patriots Tavern took up the ground floor of the colonial-style building that would have fit in nicely in New England despite its lack of history. Nikki's pulse increased when she saw the full dining room. The impressive wood-and-brick bar was full as well.

Nikki smiled at the hostess and asked for Rory's table. She directed her to a table in the back—Rory's usual preference. His head was down, and a single wavy curl dangled into his eyes.

"Hi." She sat down across from him. "Sorry I'm a little late."

"No biggie." He leaned across the table and grabbed her hand. "You could sit next to me, you know."

"Then I have to turn my head to talk to you. I'd much rather see your face. What's good here?"

He grinned, and the familiar look in his eyes made her pulse quicken. "Everything. But the burgers are my favorite."

"Sounds perfect." Nikki's stomach growled at the mention of food. She'd grabbed a protein bar on the way out of her house this morning and had gotten sidetracked before she even finished.

Rory flagged the server down, and they both ordered burgers and fries. Nikki ordered an iced tea, hoping the caffeine would give her an afternoon boost.

As soon as the server left the table, Nikki swallowed her nerves and leaned forward. "What's going on? 'We need to talk' is never a good thing to hear."

He looked sheepish. "Yeah, I thought about that after I sent it. It's nothing bad really. I have to tell you something that's probably going to royally piss you off." Rory looked at her nervously.

She relaxed a little. "Well, that sounds ominous. Is everything OK?"

"Caitlin Newport called me earlier." He worried his lower lip. "You can probably guess what she wanted."

"The interview she wants me to give." Nikki tried to keep her voice at a normal tone. "I told her I'd get back to her."

He ran his hands through his already tousled hair. "Actually, no. She found out that the house I'm building is for Sheriff Braintree's parents and wanted me to talk to you about a case she's following."

Nikki stared at him. "The boy from Chisago County who probably went through the ice on the St. Croix? Did she ask you to talk to Sheriff Braintree, too?"

"Zach Reeves is his name," Rory said. "And no, thankfully. I told her that you were really busy with this case, but you know how she is. She wouldn't quit until I promised that I'd say something. Apparently, you're not taking her seriously." The corner of his mouth twitched, but Nikki was in no mood for humor, even at Caitlin's expense.

"Damn her," Nikki said. "I told her that I'd spoken to Miller and he followed up. She knows I can't just waltz in and take over, and there's no real evidence anything else happened to Zach." Nikki tapped her nails on the table, trying to ignore the nagging voice in the back of her head. This wasn't the first time Caitlin had been fixated on a case—and she'd been right before. Nikki had to remind herself that she'd done her best getting Miller to ask questions; there was nothing so far that suggested Zach had been taken.

"She knows the kid and his family," Rory added.

"And I feel for her, really. But she's overstepping her boundaries. You talking to Braintree is going to do nothing but make him mad and that could jeopardize your livelihood. And if he's got the ego both she and Miller say he does, he's not going to be very empathetic to her trying to undermine him."

"I tried to tell her that," Rory said. "But she won't take no for an answer. I guess that's what makes her such a good reporter."

Nikki rubbed her temples.

"What if she's right?" Rory asked. "I mean, it is weird that both these boys disappeared on the same day. Zach was terrified of water. She says the only thing the sheriff has that indicates he might have driven across the ice is a hat that he never would have left behind. What if Braintree's got tunnel vision, just like Hardin did with my brother?"

Nikki sighed. "That was a different time, and an entirely different situation. Hardin had personal issues with Mark. What possible reason would a sheriff have to be so narrow-minded about a missing kid? Miller doesn't like the guy, but even he admitted there wasn't any evidence to follow. Nikki knew the hat had also bothered Miller, but Zach had been seen near the river. "And from my understanding, Braintree did have deputies check other possibilities. And Miller has one of his guys on it right now. Not everything is a conspiracy."

"I didn't say that it was. I guess it was just the way she sounded…" Rory sighed, fiddling with the salt and pepper shakers on the table, not quite meeting her gaze. Nikki could tell he was frustrated. "I know you don't like her," he finally said.

Nikki tried to keep her expression neutral. "My personal feelings have nothing to do with my professional opinion. You of all people should know that."

He held up his hands. "You're right, I'm sorry. I guess she just got to me. The kid's only twelve, for Christ's sake."

Nikki almost mentioned that Rory had been the same age when Mark was arrested and that connection could be driving his interest in the case, but she didn't want to get into that conversation. "I'll talk to Miller and make sure his deputy still agrees with Braintree."

She settled against the booth, too tired to argue anymore.

Concern shined in Rory's eyes. "Are you OK?"

She shrugged. "I'll perk up after I eat."

"This is the second case I've seen you work, and I've already figured out your M.O."

"Oh really?" she replied.

He smirked. "You keep going until you crash. That's why you barely take time for regular things like eating because once you sit, it hits you."

He wasn't wrong, but Nikki only shrugged. "It's next to impossible to rest when you're on a case, especially when one of the victims is a kid." Nikki pitched her voice low. "I shouldn't even be here. But something has been niggling at me, and I did want to ask you a little more about the family. When we volunteered for the search, you mentioned Joe had done some custom stuff for one of your houses?"

"He's incredibly talented," Rory said. "Pays serious attention to detail."

"We saw his workshop yesterday." Nikki told him about the custom log set he'd made for Kellan. "It's obvious both he and Maggie deeply cared for Kellan."

"Mom and Dad bought a couple of cows from Joe's family farm when I was a kid," Rory said. "Betsy and... God, what was the other one's name?"

"Bonnie." Nikki grinned. "I remember Mark trying to learn how to milk her. She kicked the pail, and it hit him in the chin." Nikki had spent so many years working hard to forget about Stillwater that the good memories were hard to recall. Before her parents' murders, Nikki and Mark had been friends. The Todds lived less than a mile from Nikki's house, and she was always welcome in their home. Rory was a few years younger than Mark and his friends, but he often tagged along with them. Back then, Nikki had been too cool to hang out with a younger guy, so she'd barely given Rory a second thought.

He grinned. "That's right. He still has that scar. She was a good cow."

Nikki laughed. "I was always grateful my parents just farmed. I loved the animals, but I didn't envy Mark having to help take care of them."

"Me either," Rory said. "After he went to prison, I did most of his chores." He looked down at his plate, and Nikki wondered if the awkwardness that inevitably came from talking about Mark would ever go away.

"I'm sorry."

"We've had this conversation already. You don't have to apologize every time."

"I know. But it feels wrong to ignore the elephant in the room."

Rory shrugged. "Doesn't mean you have to keep apologizing."

She hated hearing the edge in his voice. "I'll try to remember that."

"Thank you." Rory's shoulders relaxed.

Nikki decided to change the subject. "Do you remember when Joe sold the dairy farm?"

"Oh yeah," he replied. "Dad always said that some farmers were upset with him because he allowed the big corporations to come in and raise prices. Personally, I think Joe saw the writing on the wall. Good for him for making money when the dairy business was still profitable."

"He doesn't seem like the farming type," Nikki said. "He's certainly found his calling now."

Rory nodded. "He's in high demand. The owner of the house we're working on wants him to do a custom dining hutch."

"I'm sure it will be incredible," Nikki said. "The house, too. It's a beautiful design."

Red dotted Rory's cheeks. "Thanks. You'll have to come over when it's finished."

"I'd like that."

"I'm going to use the restroom." Rory squeezed Nikki's shoulder as he headed across the room.

Nikki stared out of the window, thinking about what she'd learned at the sober living house. How could Maggie—or anyone—have falsified Dana's drug test? Nikki had left a message for the family court judge who'd handled Kellan's case. She knew meth could stay in a person's system for up to a week after using it. Dana had passed Gateway's bimonthly test, so she had to have used in the few days between that test and the courts. Nikki had checked with Courtney, and she'd confirmed that errors were extremely rare but could happen. Falsifying tests was certainly difficult, but not out of the realm of possibility. Nikki knew of at least two private labs in the country where upper-level administration had been caught making big money from doing just that. Maggie Anderson had the funds, but Nikki couldn't figure out how Maggie would have found someone at the lab willing to take such a big risk. And would she go that far to keep Kellan?

"Dang, I was hoping our food would be here." Rory slid back into the booth. "I forgot to ask—how's Lacey?"

Nikki warmed at the mention of her daughter's name. She told Rory about the butterfly garden plans. "I have a feeling we're going to have them everywhere if she gets her way."

He laughed. "That's cool, though. She's interested in science."

"Oh yes, and everything else. She's one of those that has to know the why and how of everything. And she'll keep asking questions until she fully understands."

Rory leaned back as the server arrived with their food. "I wonder who she gets that from."

Nikki rolled her eyes. "That's why I'm good at my job."

After the server left, they spent a few minutes making small talk, although Rory did most of the talking, while Nikki demolished her burger. She hadn't realized just how hungry she'd been until the plate was set down in front of her.

"I have a question for you," Rory said.

Nikki smeared a fry in ranch dressing. "Go for it."

"If I could talk my parents into meeting us and Mark for coffee, would you do it?"

Nikki balked. She finished chewing and then took a long drink of iced tea. "That really came from nowhere," she said, straightening up. How long had he been trying to get the courage to ask her? And did he really think she would agree while in the middle of a murder investigation?

"Not for me," Rory replied. "I've been trying to find the right time, and then I figured there never will be a good time, so I just took the shot."

"Why would your parents ever agree to that?"

"Mark has been working on them. If he asks, I think they'll do it."

"Because they want him to be happy," Nikki said. "That's a little unfair to take advantage of them like that."

He stared at her for a few seconds as though she'd spoken in a different language. "Wait. You're defending my parents?"

"It's not a matter of defending them. They shouldn't have to be convinced to spend time with me."

"They're not going to come around without a lot of convincing."

"That's not how I want it to be," Nikki said. "And you need to let them enjoy Mark." Growing up, their mother had doted on Mark and Rory. She and their father had been kind to all of their friends and had had an open-door policy. Nikki had even gone to their mother about her first real crush in high school instead of her own. And then Nikki had helped to turn their world upside down; they deserved a normal life with Mark now.

Rory picked up his cheeseburger and resumed eating. He glared out the window, shaking his head. "I don't think that's it at all."

"Really?" Nikki crossed her arms over her chest. "I'm all ears."

"I think you're afraid to spend time with my family because then all of this is real."

She looked around. "Are we living in a fantasy world, then?"

"That's real mature."

Nikki took a deep breath. "What are you getting at?"

"You don't think we're going to last because of my parents and the past, so you don't want to take that step."

Nikki pushed her plate out of the way, her appetite gone. "That's not true," she said, but Rory had hit a nerve. Is that why she was so worried?

But she didn't have time to wonder for too long. Her phone vibrated with a text from Liam. He had found Dana Rhodes' current address.

"I have to go. I'll see you later," she said.

Rory stared at her for a moment before going back to his meal, the tension between them creating a chill in the air.

CHAPTER TWELVE

Nikki tried not to break too many traffic laws as she rushed across town to the address Liam had texted. She couldn't stop thinking about the hurt in Rory's eyes when she'd abruptly left. He probably thought she was running from the argument, and if she were being really honest with herself, she'd been happy to have an excuse to leave.

Why was he so intent on pushing her onto his parents? The entire family had spent the last twenty years in turmoil, and Nikki was partially responsible for that. If Nikki were in his parents' shoes, she'd have the same angry reaction to her and Rory's relationship. It had to feel like a slap in the face. Rory and Mark both had a capacity for forgiveness that many people just didn't possess. The idea of forcing her presence on the Todds as though she had every right to be in their lives made her feel ill. And maybe that meant Rory was right and Nikki didn't see a way for the relationship to last, no matter how much she wanted it to.

She ignored the sadness washing over her and followed the GPS's instructions. Liam had found out that Dana had rented a studio apartment not far from Lily Lake Park. The affordable area was relatively quiet and tucked away from traffic. Nikki didn't see any sign of Dana's car in the parking lot as she pulled up.

Liam was standing with a short woman in front of the manager's office. He leaned down and said something to the woman, and Nikki swallowed a laugh. Between his height and her lack of it, they reminded her of the old comic strip Mutt and Jeff. Her father had read it every morning over breakfast.

Liam met her on the sidewalk. "Fair warning, the project manager's a fan."

"Of who?"

He rolled his eyes. "You. Big crime television watcher."

Nikki smiled tightly. She'd managed to shake off the media interest after her parents' murders and fade into the background during college, but her career as a profiler had put her in the national headlines more than once. "Fantastic. I assume the bank gave you this address?"

"Yep. And I found out something else. You know how Maggie's the executor of her mother's estate, which includes the trust set up for Kellan? She did agree that the monthly interest could go to help with Dana's rehab and stay at Gateway, as long as she stayed clean, but she also called the bank the morning of the test and told them to stop funding because Dana was using again. They don't remember what time she called, but the switch was made effective the next day. They'd already sent out that month's check. Dana came in two weeks ago to change her address and have them reissue February's check because she hadn't received it and assumed it had been sent back since she wasn't at Gateway. According to the clerk on duty, she was floored. It sounded like Maggie hadn't told her anything about making the change. Dana told them that she was going to talk with her sister and get it fixed—she spoke with an investment assistant about resolving the issue and gave him her new address. He never heard from her after that."

"Interesting. I've also been told by more sources that Dana thought Maggie somehow changed the test. Initially I thought Dana said it because she couldn't handle facing the truth and that she'd screwed up. But her friends at Gateway and the staff say she never exhibited signs of using again. They didn't kick her out because they didn't believe her; the director's hands were tied by the board."

"I double-checked, and the trial started at 10 a.m. that day," Liam said. "So it's feasible Maggie called the bank right after the hearing."

"So one of the first things on her mind when she had been awarded custody of Kellan was making sure her sister was cut off. I just find it strange her initial reaction was about money. Not her elation at finally winning custody, not her sister's emotional well-being…" Nikki glanced at the two-story building. "Have you gone inside?"

Liam shook his head. "Waited for you. Ready to meet your fan?"

"Shut it." Nikki couldn't help but smile.

The short, portly woman's eyes widened as Nikki approached and extended her hand.

"Special Agent Nikki Hunt."

The woman grabbed her hand and began shaking it. "I know who you are," she said. "You're a hero."

"I'm sorry?" Nikki replied, taken aback. She'd met people who were particularly interested in her job before, fascinated by crime scenes and big cases and killers like Frost, but after everything that happened last year with Mark Todd's release, she was surprised to still be someone's hero.

"You helped get that man out of prison without worrying about your reputation," the woman replied. "That's a hero in my book. And you hunt serial killers. I'm Sandy by the way. I've been the property manager here for almost ten years. Is Dana really dead?"

Nikki caught the irritated look on Liam's face. She knew he'd likely answered these questions already, but Sandy clearly liked having the attention on her. Nikki decided to press on quickly to keep her from asking questions Nikki couldn't answer. "I'm afraid so. How long did she live here?"

"Just a couple of weeks. She paid her first and last month's rent in cash."

"She rented a garage space too," Liam added. "I haven't had a chance to see if her car's—"

"Oh, it is," Sandy said. "I checked before I came over. Would you like to see it?"

"Please," Nikki replied. "Which units have garages?"

"They're a separate building," Sandy explained. "With the units built directly on top. Only twenty-five dollars a month for the garage. It's very reasonable."

They followed Sandy across the large parking lot to a building partially hidden by trees. It looked newer than the main building, with small balconies above the garages.

"Dana's in number three, apartment 3B." Sandy punched in a code on the keypad next to the garage.

Nikki's heart hammered as it slowly opened. Was this where Kellan's body had been kept? If so, they might be about to be faced with a grisly scene.

Dana's sky-blue VW Bug sat in the small space. Sandy started to go into the garage, but Nikki blocked her path. "We're not sure what we're walking into, and we need to preserve the scene as much as possible."

Sandy looked as though she'd won the lottery. "A real investigation? Is this where Dana was killed?"

"We don't know," Liam said. "Please stay back."

He and Nikki entered the garage, with Liam on the passenger side of the car.

Nikki peered into the driver's window and slipped her gloves on. The car appeared relatively clean, with a sweatshirt in the backseat. She tried the door handle.

"It's unlocked." Nikki carefully opened the door, half-expecting to smell cleaner. But she only smelled the pink air freshener. A Styrofoam cup from a chain gas station sat in the single cup holder.

"Look how far the seat is pushed back." Liam opened the passenger door. "Dana was too short to drive it like that." He opened the glove compartment. "Owner's manual. Registration and insurance information."

Nikki tipped the driver's side visor down, and a set of keys attached to a large, bejeweled 'D' fell onto the seat. She and Liam looked at each other. Dana likely hadn't driven this car into the garage.

"I'll call Courtney," Liam said.

Nikki rejoined an impatient Sandy. "Do you have security cameras?"

"No. I've been begging the management company to install, but they won't listen. We do have controlled entry."

"Meaning someone would need Dana's code to enter the garage or her unit?"

"Exactly. Would you like to see the apartment?"

Nikki motioned for Liam to stay with the car as Sandy unlocked the front door. Concrete stairs led up to her unit on the second floor.

Sandy entered another code and opened the door. "I guess you'd like me to stay in the hall."

"Yes, please."

Dana's apartment appeared neat. Her furniture was clearly secondhand, and she had only a love seat, coffee table, and a double bed in the tiny bedroom. A large, faded flannel shirt was on the floor next to the bed. Nikki opened the closet. It was small, with two shelves that Dana had used to store socks and underwear. A couple of pairs of boxer shorts were tucked in with Dana's items. Nikki checked the other obvious places but saw no sign of drugs. If Dana were using meth, she'd expect to see a pipe or residue, but she'd have Courtney do a full sweep.

A couple of plastic bins sat at the end of the bed. Nikki's throat tightened when she opened the first one. The clothes were clearly Kellan's, along with several books and a few toys. A business card was tucked into the corner. Kim Kroll, Private Investigator.

Cam had been right about Dana's determination to clear her name. Had she been disappointed in the investigator's advice and decided to take matters into her own hands, or had something else prompted her to kidnap Kellan?

Nikki made a mental note to have Liam track the PI down and see if she'd spoken to Dana.

"Courtney's on her way." Liam had joined Nikki in the apartment.

She walked him through the small space. They sifted through her clothes in the closet and bins, finding a few more men's items mixed in.

"This is weird." Liam pointed to one of the lids. "These are marked 'property of Dana Rhodes.'"

"So? They're pretty beat up. She's probably carried them around for a while."

"Exactly. Her clothes aren't new. Yet these"—he held up a pair of men's boxers—"look and feel like they just came out of the package."

"How can you tell?"

Liam showed her the label. "These are cheap, which means scratchy and not soft. They get better after they're washed, but I'm telling you, these are right out of the package."

"And stuck in the middle of her clothes. There are some male residents at Gateway, and they all share a laundry room. Maybe she accidentally wound up with some guy's underwear and never got around to giving it back to him."

"Maybe." Liam walked over to the closet and pulled out the men's clothes. "Extra larges. These underwear are mediums."

"So the shirts belong to someone else."

"The shorts are new, I'm telling you."

"We'll have everything fingerprinted. Courtney might be able to get something off the shirt and underwear."

Nikki put the lid back on the top bin and opened the second. A few more clothes sat on top, but books and other odds and ends took up most of the bin.

"Self-help books, a couple of teaching textbooks. Oh, I know what this is." Several photocopied papers had been stapled together like a book, with the title page reading "Freshman year at Frontier, '06–'07. Second Floor Girls Rule." A wave of nostalgia washed over her. "Frontier Hall is one of the freshman dorms at the University of Minnesota. I lived on the second floor as a freshman and sophomore. Our resident advisor made something similar." Nikki leafed through the booklet. "Everyone shared their favorite pictures and moments." All of the pictures had handwritten captions. She stopped at a picture with three girls. They'd posed with their arms around each other, wide smiles on their faces. Sylvia, Dana and Shelly, the three amigas. "It will take some work, but I should be able to track Sylvia and Shelly down," Nikki said, feeling pleased. She felt sure there was something hidden in Dana and Maggie's past, something about their relationship that she just wasn't understanding, and these women could help her get a clearer picture of things back then.

"It's unlikely she's had contact with them recently. How does that help us?" Liam looked confused.

"I'm not sure yet. Just a gut feeling." Nikki replied. She didn't want to share her thoughts in case they clouded Liam's judgment. It was important her team investigated all angles.

They went into the tiny kitchen, and Nikki checked the three drawers next to the stove while Liam searched the few cabinets. "A few basic items, plastic silverware," Nikki said. "Makes sense. She just moved in."

"There are a few small, suspicious spots in her car," Liam noted. "May or may not be blood."

"Courtney'll figure it out." Nikki held up the private investigator's card. "See if you can track this woman down. Dana might have spoken with her before she died."

Nikki left Liam to photograph the apartment and went in search of Sandy. She found her hovering in the stairwell, phone to her ear.

"It's true," Sandy whispered. "She's dead and the FBI are here." Nikki cleared her throat. Sandy turned around and flushed red. "I'm sorry. I'm just talking to my husband," she said, clearly embarrassed at being caught out.

"Please ask him to refrain from telling anyone else. We'd like to keep the media away from the area as long as possible. May I ask you a few more questions?"

"Of course." Sandy hung up on her husband without saying goodbye and looked at Nikki eagerly. "I'll help in any way I can."

Nikki smiled tightly. "Great. Did you ever see Dana with anyone while she was living here?"

"No," Sandy said. "But she's only been here a couple of weeks."

"She didn't bring anyone with her when she signed the lease or to help move in?"

"I didn't notice, but my office is on the other side of the complex. I wouldn't have seen her moving in unless I happened to be at these units." Sandy sounded disappointed she couldn't come up with any useful information.

"What about her neighbor?" Dana's end unit gave her a bit of privacy, but she still shared a wall with another renter.

Sandy nodded excitedly. "Joanne. She's on disability and is home almost all the time. She might have heard something. Would you like me to introduce you?"

"That would be great, thank you."

Sandy hurried up the stairs. "She's just right across the hall."

"So there is a shared entrance?" Nikki asked.

"One for every two units, yes. The garages have separate entrances, as you know. Joanne doesn't have a car, but she keeps a lot of things in her garage."

Sandy knocked on the door, bouncing on her heels. Nikki wondered how many crime shows she'd watched.

A heavy woman with square glasses opened the door. "Sandy, what's going on? I've been watching—"

"Dana's dead." Sandy spoke before Nikki could even open her mouth. "This is Agent Nikki Hunt with the FBI. You know the one. She wanted to talk to you."

Joanne looked Nikki up and down. "You look taller on television. Come in, I can't stand long."

Leaning heavily on her cane, Joanne led them into the small apartment. It was laid out exactly like Dana's, but considerably more lived in. Stuffed to the gills, as Nikki's father would have said. No wonder Joanne needed the garage for storage.

She sat down in her recliner with a huff and propped her cane against her knee. "What do you want to know?"

"I know Dana only lived here a couple of weeks, but did you have any interaction with her?"

"Just pleasantries when she moved in. She seemed nice. I don't get out of the apartment much. Thank goodness for delivery service."

Nikki glanced onto the tiny patio, where a plastic chair and table had been wedged in. A full ashtray sat on the table, along with a pack of cigarettes.

Joanne followed her gaze. "Yes, I smoke. I know I shouldn't. I don't need a lecture."

"No judgment," Nikki said. "I was just thinking that you must spend some time outside every day. Did you ever see Dana with anyone?"

"No, but I heard her arguing with some man not long after she moved in. It was Thursday night, and *Supernatural* was on. I remember being ticked off that it was a repeat and that stupid Chuck was screwing over the boys again."

Nikki nodded as though she understood Joanne's reference. "Did you hear what they were arguing about?"

"Another man, I assume. She wanted to get him back, and the guy kept telling her she was crazy. I heard a couple of thumps, too. If I was more mobile, I would have gone over there and made sure she was OK."

"If you thought she was in danger, why didn't you call the police?"

Joanne shifted in the chair. "I would have, but the fighting stopped. He left a few minutes after."

"Did you check to see if she was OK?"

"I heard her crying when he left," Joanne said. "My window has a view of the parking lot, and I wanted to make sure he left. He was kind of thick and average height. I couldn't tell what color his coat was, but he had a hood covering his face."

"What about his vehicle?"

"I think a dark, four-door car. Nothing special," Joanne replied. "Like I said, it was dark, and I need new glasses."

Sandy patted her knee. "You've been so helpful. Can you think of anything else?"

Nikki gritted her teeth. She could tell Joanne liked having Sandy's attention, so she let her interference slide, but that didn't make it any less grating.

"Yes, I can." Joanne leaned forward, looking at Sandy intently. "I told you to get some damned security cameras."

Nikki thanked the women for their time and then headed back to the garage. Nikki was relieved to see that Courtney had arrived, along with two of her crime scene techs. Liam had also joined them.

"That's record time from the lab," Liam said to Courtney. "How fast did you drive?"

"Fast enough." She zipped up her clean suit. "Which apartment is Dana's?"

Nikki pointed to the interior garage door. "3B. It's the one on the left. The apartment manager's still upstairs with the neighbor. She's a crime enthusiast, so make sure she doesn't try to follow you guys into the apartment."

"Good to know." Courtney turned to the two crime scene techs, who were also in clean suits. "You guys handle the apartment. Make sure you print everything. I'll be working on the car if you need me."

Liam held up the two evidence bags. "Men's underwear and flannel shirts."

"Nice. I'll look for any biological evidence."

"And fingerprints."

Courtney made a face. "That's not as easy as television makes it sound, but I'll try."

"Have you had any luck with Kellan's and Dana's personal effects?" Nikki asked.

"Some tiny black fibers under Dana's fingernails," Courtney said. "They're so minuscule they might have come from anywhere. No viable prints."

"Meaning whoever brought them down there wore gloves," Liam said. "No big surprise."

"This is her car?" Courtney asked. "What a cute Beetle. I've always wanted one."

"Tyler drove one when we first got together. It was the same drab color as Ted Bundy's. The first time I rode in it, I asked him if he was going to remove the passenger seat, and he looked at me like I was crazy." Nikki smiled ruefully. "I should have known then that we wouldn't last."

"It looks pretty clean." Liam walked around and opened the hatchback. "Basic winter safety stuff in here. But do your thing. Maybe we'll get lucky and our suspect looked in the back for some reason."

"Cam Fletcher probably has prints in the system," Nikki said. "It's pretty standard for drug counselors. We know a man was here a few days ago, and he's the most likely candidate."

"I'll compare them as soon as I can."

Nikki tucked the evidence bag with the private investigator's card in Courtney's pocket. "See if you can get any prints from this. Whoever gave it to her was probably in her apartment at some point."

Courtney nodded, shooing Liam out of the way so she could take photos. "Hopefully they're in the system."

"My bet's on Cam Fletcher," Liam said. "Whether or not they acted on their feelings, they were closer than he wanted to admit."

Nikki agreed, and Cam was the logical choice to give her the card. If he hadn't, she could have gotten it from one of the residents at Gateway. "And if he did give her the card, I want to know why he never mentioned it to us."

"And who else he might have put her in contact with," Liam said. "Including the muscle needed to help her kidnap Kellan."

Nikki's gut told her that Cam hadn't been directly involved, but if he'd put Dana in contact with the person who killed Dana, he needed to come clean. She retrieved her phone from her bag and called Gateway to see if Cam was working in the office today, but the front desk said he was in family court testifying for another client. He wasn't expected back today. Nikki debated texting him, but she preferred to catch him off guard. She thought she recognized the peppy male voice. "Is this Drew?"

"Sure is," he replied. "Do you want me to see if I can reach Cam by phone?"

"No, not if he's in court. I don't want to distract him. Would you be able to tell me which district? I'll try to catch him after the session's over."

"Let me see if I have the information," Drew said. "We should, since the client is also living here. OK, here it is. The case is at the Chisago County Government Center. I can't give you the client's name, but I can tell you that Judge Marnie Loeffler is assigned to her case."

"Thanks, so much, Drew." Nikki ended the call and motioned Liam over. "Can you stay here and help process the scene? Cam Fletcher's in court this afternoon, and if I hurry, I think I can catch him after he's done. I want to speak with him in person. If Cam did facilitate a meeting with someone and that person wound up killing Dana, he could be in danger. And tell the office to rush that background check."

Nikki scanned the posted court assignments for the day. Judge Loeffler's cases were being heard in a second-floor courtroom, and

Nikki crossed her fingers that Cam hadn't finished. She found the court room and sat down in one of the hard, wooden chairs in the large hall, and then checked her phone to see if Liam had texted any new information. Nothing so far, but Rory had responded to the text she'd sent after leaving Dana's apartment, telling him that she'd probably be working late and not to wait for her to eat. He replied abruptly.

K. Working late too.

Nikki felt cold with disappointment at the short text. She told herself that he was just busy, but that didn't stop the nagging fear that they might have reached a serious impasse in their relationship that she didn't have time to deal with.

The courtroom door opened, and a handful of people filed out. Cam finally emerged, looking tired and a little less dapper than yesterday.

"Agent Hunt." He looked up from his phone in surprise. "What are you doing here?"

"Waiting for you, actually," Nikki said. "Can we talk privately?"

He hesitated and then nodded. "Of course."

Nikki gathered her things and walked toward an open, empty courtroom across the hall. "This will only take a few moments."

Apprehension resonated from Cam, and she could feel him tense as soon as she closed the courtroom door. The room was small, stuffy and uncomfortable, which made it perfect for interviewing a nervous person of interest.

Nikki got right to the point. "We did find Dana's apartment, along with her car. She was living in Stillwater to be close to Kellan. I don't think the Andersons knew. Someone likely parked the car in the garage in an effort to hide their involvement in her death."

Cam sat down on the nearest bench. His eyes filled with tears. "She really was murdered?"

"Yes," Nikki said. "We found a card for a private investigator. Did she ever mention talking to one?"

Cam shook his head. "No, but we hadn't talked in a little while."

Nikki shifted so that she could look him directly in the eyes. "I need you to be honest with me. Do you know of anyone Dana would have asked to help her kidnap her son?"

"No," Cam said. "I still can't believe she even tried. The last time we spoke, she was so adamant that she would stick to the legal route and try to get Kellan back. If she talked to a private investigator, why didn't she let them do their job?"

Nikki found a tissue in her bag and handed it to him. His grief was so palpable she didn't think he had anything to do with the kidnapping or murder. "Something must have changed her mind," Nikki said. "You're certain that's all she told you?"

He looked up at her with wide eyes. "I don't understand why you're asking me this."

"You were close to her," Nikki replied. "If she let anyone in on her plans or went to someone for help, you're the obvious choice. So, if there's anything else you need to tell me, now is the time. If you're afraid of losing your job, I'll do what I can to make sure that doesn't happen."

Cam sighed. "If I thought I knew anything that would help you find out who did this, I would tell you."

"We have a warrant for your phone records," Nikki said. "We'll have them later today."

"That's fine. I have nothing to hide."

She searched his face, looking for any sign of dishonesty but saw none. "Whoever put Dana in contact with her killer is in danger."

"I see where you're going with this," he interrupted. "You assume I probably know of people who live on the outskirts of the law and might be willing to help. I'm not sure that I do, and if I had given Dana any names, I would tell you." His jaw quivered. "I want the person who did this to be held responsible."

Nikki sighed. She believed Cam was telling the truth, meaning she'd hit yet another dead end. "Her neighbor overheard an argument with someone the day before Dana and Kellan disappeared. The neighbor didn't get a good look at the person, but described them as a short, stocky male wearing a hoodie. Does that ring any bells? Someone she might have met at Gateway or in rehab?"

Cam shook his head. "Not that I know about, anyway. We only have two male residents, and neither is short and stocky. They both arrived a month or so after Dana."

"Well, it was a long shot," Nikki said, defeated. "Thanks for your time."

Cam grabbed Nikki's arm, stopping her from leaving. "Look, I know you still think Dana was involved in taking Kellan, you probably still think she might have been using. But I knew her. I saw her daily in the weeks leading up to the hearing. She was sober. She always seemed scared of Maggie," he said shortly. "Not physically, but she lived in fear that Maggie would find a way to keep Kellan. Turned out she was right."

Nikki shuddered against the biting wind as she walked to the jeep. The gray afternoon had turned to a cold early evening. Nikki usually took the miserable Minnesota winters in her stride, but she longed for spring more than ever this year. She was sick of looking at the same dreary skies and dirty, slushy streets.

She spotted a Chisago County Sheriff's cruiser and remembered her conversation with Rory earlier. Maybe her arriving at his place with information from a Chisago deputy about Zach would ease the tension between them. But what would she say to the deputy that wouldn't get back to the sheriff and set off unnecessary friction in an already tense case?

Nikki sighed and continued walking to her jeep.

CHAPTER THIRTEEN

Nikki keyed in the code for Rory's garage door. She knew he wasn't home yet, because his work truck was always parked outside, and he saved the garage space for the snowmobile, lawnmowers and the motorcycle Nikki had yet to ride on. Rory lived in his parents' old split-level home, not far from Nikki's childhood home. His parents had taken good care of the place, and Rory had been slowly putting in updates like the bathrooms and flooring. She walked into the lower level and slipped her boots off.

Growing up, Mark and Rory's rooms had been downstairs, along with the laundry room and a small living room area. Rory lived mostly upstairs, and the lower level still had the same old furniture it had when Nikki and Mark were in high school. His parents didn't like Mark's friends congregating downstairs because "that's how trouble starts," as Mark's father had put it.

She was sifting through the things she kept at Rory's place looking for a change of clothes when her phone chimed with a video call from Tyler. She debated not answering, but Lacey was probably calling to talk.

"Mommy!" Lacey's sweet, singsong voice and happy face immediately lifted Nikki's spirits. "Guess what I learned today?"

"Hi, baby. What did you learn?"

Lacey chattered excitedly about an experiment her teacher had done that turned pop into a fizzing volcano.

"That's very cool," Nikki said. "We'll have to try that at home."

"Me and Daddy are going to do it tonight."

"Oh, right." Nikki reminded herself she was lucky that Tyler was able to be so flexible with Lacey. Still, she hated missing out on things. "Make sure Daddy records it for me."

Nikki listened to Lacey's chatter for the next twenty minutes. Her enthusiasm and silliness always took some of the edge off Nikki's day. She was so engrossed in the story that she didn't realize Rory was home until he came into the bedroom.

"Hey, baby, can we—"

Startled, Nikki dropped the phone. "Shit." She put her finger on her lips, motioning for him not to say anything.

He looked a little annoyed but nodded. He pulled his sweatshirt over his head and tossed it onto the dresser.

Nikki held the phone up again. "Sorry, Lace. You made me laugh so hard I dropped my phone."

"Who came to see you?" Lacey asked. "Is there a baby with you? That's not fair. I love babies. Me and Jules both want two babies, and they both have to have blond hair. And not be ugly. I can't be seen with an ugly kid, Mommy."

Rory choked back a laugh on his way to the shower.

"That's just the television, honey."

Lacey launched into another story, but Nikki couldn't concentrate. Lacey wouldn't forget about hearing the voice, and then she'd probably say something to her father. He'd probably been within earshot, anyway. Nikki wasn't sure she'd be able to lie to him if he asked her outright. Their relationship had never been perfect, but they'd always been honest with each other.

"Daddy says you probably have to work and it's time for my supper." Lacey sighed dramatically. "I have to go, Mommy."

Nikki blew her a kiss and promised to call tomorrow. She ended the video chat before Tyler returned and asked questions.

Rory emerged from the bathroom with a towel around his waist. "No uggos for Lacey, then."

Nikki laughed. "Be glad you didn't see her expression. That's what makes it so priceless."

"I'd like to see it sometime," he said softly.

Nikki pretended she hadn't heard and grabbed her overnight bag.

"What are you doing?" Rory asked.

"I'm heading to the sheriff's station. There's been new developments in the case, and I want to be able to concentrate on them."

"Meaning you don't want to talk about earlier?"

"I just can't right now."

Rory sighed. "Mark worked overtime today helping me to fix the issue with the cabinets. He told me what our cousin said. Why didn't you say anything to me about it?"

"Because it's not important." Nikki touched his arm. "You can't expect everyone to be as forgiving as you are. I still can't believe Mark is."

"Because we know you were a victim, too," Rory said. "Anyone else in your place would have done the same thing. What matters is that you were willing to listen and open up a lot of old wounds to get to the truth. I know it hasn't been easy finding out that John—" He stopped and exhaled. "I'm sorry. I shouldn't have brought that up."

Nikki tried to ignore the rock in her stomach. "It's fine. Yes, it's hard. I'm angry as hell, and I don't feel bad about that. He doesn't deserve my forgiveness, and I'm not that good of a person, anyway. I think your family probably feels the same about me, and who am I to blame them?"

Rory shook his head. "They'll come around. Without your help, even with the DNA evidence, Mark would still have that hanging over his head. People would still whisper behind his back because he was the most obvious suspect."

Nikki knew they would just continue to go in circles, and she didn't want to get back into the conversation about his family. "Don't be mad at your cousin, please. Mark shouldn't be, either."

"Is she the reason you got upset at lunch? I didn't mean what I said. It all came out wrong."

The ding of a notification on her phone saved Nikki from further debate. "The Department of Transportation just sent me traffic cam footage. I have to deal with it."

"Don't go to the station unless you absolutely have to," Rory said.

"I can't do this with you right now." Nikki stood, balancing her laptop in one hand.

"I'm not asking you to do anything with me," Rory said tightly. "I'm saying do your work here. I'll leave you alone." He yanked on a T-shirt and walked out.

Nikki ignored the guilt washing over her and opened her laptop, quickly logging into her email. There were four attachments taken around 4:55 p.m. Friday, capturing Dana's car going through the intersection and then turning right into the complex. According to the email from DOT, one of the streetlights at the intersection was burnt out when the photos were snapped, making already subpar pictures even harder to make out.

Nikki enlarged all of the pictures but still couldn't tell who was driving. The person behind the wheel had the seat reclined, making sure their face was out of view of the cameras. She'd assumed the seat had been pushed back to accommodate height, which meant they were dealing with a taller individual. But if the driver purposely moved the seat back to avoid the camera, then they were back to square one. It was impossible to tell if the driver was a man or woman, let alone height. Had Dana been driving after all?

The car hadn't been photographed since Friday night, but Nikki doubted that Dana would have taken Kellan back to her apartment, even if few people knew where she lived. Had someone else been driving while she and Kellan kept their heads down? Blanchard believed Kellan had died within a few hours of his disappearance, but Courtney hadn't found any blood in the car. Perhaps whatever happened to Kellan occurred after Dana and her possible accomplice stashed the car. They could have left in another vehicle with no one noticing. Dana had to have known she wouldn't get very far in her own vehicle.

A text from Courtney flashed on her screen.

Still at scene. Guys found almost $100 in cash hidden underneath mattress.

Nikki's stomach somersaulted. Dana not taking her things with her was one thing, but leaving cash when she intended to disappear with—or without—her son made no sense.

"Oh my God," Nikki said to the empty room. Until now, she'd assumed that Dana and her killer had laid low over the weekend, trying to figure out what to do, and her accomplice had likely talked her into leaving Kellan's body in the gulley so that he could stage her suicide.

Nikki found the preliminary autopsy results from Dr. Blanchard. She was positive Kellan had died within hours of eating his school lunch, and the bleeding in the brain suggested he might have lived for a while after being hit—or falling. Dana had wrapped the scarf around his head wound to try to stop the bleeding, and Blanchard believed enough blood had stained the scarf to indicate Kellan had been alive for a little while after his mother tried to help him.

Nikki immediately called Liam and explained her theory. "Dana wasn't lying low. I think she was being detained with her dead son's body."

"Christ," Liam said. "Who would do that to her?"

"Someone who truly despised her," Nikki replied. "Which brings us back to Maggie. Dana tried to take Kellan and either Joe or Maggie caught her. Kellan's death was an accident, and Maggie could have snapped. So she punished her sister by making her stay with him."

"I don't know." Liam still sounded unconvinced. "Miller's guys searched thoroughly, and so did we. Where would Maggie have hidden them?"

"I don't know," Nikki replied. "See if the Andersons own other property nearby, like a lake cabin or a hunting cabin."

"That shouldn't be too hard to find out as long as it's in one of their names."

"Check for the family name as well," Nikki said. "If they inherited a place, there's a chance the title isn't in their names."

"Good idea," Liam replied. "But maybe Dana didn't have anyone helping her at first. What if Kellan got hurt and she panicked and wound up calling the wrong person for help?"

Nikki had been considering the idea since she'd spoken with Cam Fletcher. Dana likely would have called him for help, but Nikki was certain he hadn't been involved in her death. "We need to find out what Dana told the private investigator."

"I left a message," Liam said. "If I don't hear from her tonight, I'll track her down in the morning."

Nikki forwarded the DOT's email and attachments to Courtney. Photographs weren't usually part of Courtney's job, but she had a keen eye for detail and had spotted things Nikki had missed more than once.

Shifting on the bed, Nikki logged onto University of Minnesota's alumni website. Hopefully at least one of Dana's old roommates had provided current information for the alumni events.

Nikki started with "Sylvia" for the class of 2006, hoping the old-fashioned name made the search easier. Thankfully, only two results popped up. Nikki quickly read through the personal information. Neither had provided a photo for the alumni association, but Nikki searched through the various alumni events featured on the website and finally found a picture of Sylvia Smith. She was African American, and the girl in Dana's picture had been white with lighter hair.

Nikki searched for the second result, Sylvia Kline, finally finding her in reunion photos from a recent reunion. Sylvia was one of at least a hundred people in the picture, but Nikki still recognized the girl from Dana's picture. She went into Sylvia's personal information. She didn't have an address, but she did have an email. Had Sylvia even heard of Dana's death? Nikki hated to be the one to tell her, especially in an email. She decided on a simple message stating that she was working on a case involving Dana and asked Sylvia to call her as soon as possible.

She could hear the hockey game on the television downstairs. She should go talk to Rory, but Kellan and Dana needed her more right now.

CHAPTER FOURTEEN

The next morning, Nikki was showered and gone before dawn. Rory had fallen asleep on the couch, and she managed to slip out without waking him. She knew avoiding Rory wasn't the right way to handle their issues, but she had to focus on the case. She needed to brief Miller on new developments and Dana's college roommate had replied asking to meet later this afternoon. Nikki emailed her back to confirm the time and place before meeting Miller at the sheriff's office.

On the way to the station, Cam Fletcher's phone records finally arrived in her email. Nikki went straight to the conference room and opened the file. She scanned through the numbers, her excitement waning quickly. He'd been honest about the last time he spoke to Dana—at least on her cell phone. A handful of numbers had unknown names, but none occurred during last weekend. Unknown numbers on a drug counselor's phone records weren't all that unusual.

"Not sure I like being acting chief." Miller entered the conference room, carrying coffee and a notepad. "So much red tape and paperwork."

"Better pay, less risk than being in the field."

"I think I'd rather face a bullet than keep dealing with the mayor and city council." He sat down across from Nikki. "Give me good news, please."

"Cam Fletcher's phone records are a bust," Nikki said. "Unless we get a print match, I think he's officially off our suspect list."

Miller cocked his head. "Nikki, do we need to discuss the definition of good news?"

She smiled. "I like Cam. I'm glad he's probably innocent."

"I suppose. But we don't have any solid suspects. Where's your team?"

"Liam's in Minneapolis to track down the private investigator we think Dana might have contacted, and then he's going to the lab that handled Dana's testing. Courtney's supposed to call—" Nikki's phone rang, and Courtney's face popped on the screen. "Right now," she finished. "Hey, Court. Miller's here. Liam's running down leads. You're on speaker."

"Well, good morning to you, too."

Nikki could hear Courtney shuffling papers. Her office was such a disaster, Nikki had no idea how she excelled at her job.

"OK," Courtney said. "The fingerprints in Dana's apartment belonged to someone named Drew Barnes."

"Drew Barnes?" Nikki echoed. "That's the office manager at Gateway. He acted like he barely knew Dana."

"Well, he's the only other person who's been in her apartment, as far as I can tell. His prints are in the system because of a DUI last year. His address is in downtown Minneapolis, within walking distance of several nightclubs and bars, but I guess you don't need that if you know where he works."

Nikki drummed her fingers on the table. Drew was young and seemed helpful, and it was easy to imagine the residents chatting him up and maybe even confiding in him. She would get his phone records, but Drew struck her as an easy egg to crack with a little pressure. She debated texting Liam and asking him to stop by the sober living house, but Nikki wanted to talk to Drew in person. "What about Cam Fletcher? His prints should be on file. He was arrested several years ago before he got clean."

"They are," Courtney said. "But they don't match any of the ones we lifted. And before you ask, I'm still working on the clothes. I think there's a partial print on the underwear tag I can lift, but it's a delicate process."

"What about the prints from the car?" Miller asked.

"All Dana's. I didn't even find Kellan's. The spots Liam thought might be blood turned out to be hot sauce. I did take the driver's-side floor mat because it's got some stains. It will be a few days before I have any results."

"And no prints on the utility knife used to slice Dana's wrists?" Nikki said.

"No, but it's brand spanking new, save for the whole murder thing."

"How can you tell?" Miller asked.

"Because everything leaves trace. If it had been used to cut anything before, I would have seen markings under the microscope and possibly found particulates. By the way, thanks for sending your deputies over yesterday. I needed the extra hands and the property manager needed a babysitter."

Miller looked at Nikki for an explanation.

"The property manager's a crime buff."

"And a fan of Nikki's," Courtney chimed in.

"What about Dana's and Kellan's personal effects?" Nikki asked.

"Nothing useful, I'm afraid."

Nikki sighed. "OK, thanks for the hard work. Let us know if you get anything from the clothes at Dana's or the floor mats."

"Will do," Courtney said.

Nikki ended the call. "Let's hope she gets something we can use." She opened her notes and spent the next ten minutes filling Miller in on everything she and Liam had found out since having coffee with Cam. "Drew lied about how well he knew Dana, and I want to find out why. We also need to compare his boot prints to the ones at the scene. And there's another option we need to discuss." Nikki showed him the photos from the traffic cameras near Dana's apartment and explained her theory. "Leaving her clothes is one thing, but the cash? It doesn't make sense."

Miller dragged his hands across his face. "You think Maggie was somehow involved."

"I think we have to seriously explore that possibility. Who else would want to punish Dana so badly they would hold her hostage with Kellan's body before killing her? We have several accounts—including Maggie's own words—that make it clear the sisters didn't get along. Maggie bore a lot of resentment, and Dana believed Maggie had something to do with her failed drug test. Dana could have found out about Kellan's early out and showed up to take him. Maybe he refused and then Maggie and Joe somehow got involved. I know she was still working when Joe realized Kellan was gone, but what if she rushed home to find Kellan gravely injured and snapped?"

"Maybe," Miller said. "But she loved that kid. If he was alive, she would have called the ambulance."

"Probably," Nikki replied. "We don't know the exact timeline, but Maggie could have tracked them down and Kellan was already dead."

"Joe would lie to protect her," Miller said.

Nikki agreed. "It makes more sense than any other scenario we've come up with."

Miller looked resigned to the theory. "Joe said he got home roughly ten minutes before he expected Kellan to, and he's got a gas receipt that backs his alibi about delivering to a customer. He called Maggie at work shortly after arriving home."

Nikki shuffled through her notes even though she had all the details memorized. "Let's go over the timeline. Joe said he first thought the bus was late but then found Kellan's backpack, so he called Maggie around 4:45 p.m. He didn't realize Kellan had an early out until then. Yet they didn't call the police until after Maggie got home—" Nikki double-checked her scribbled notes. "At 5:35 p.m. The delay in calling doesn't make sense to me since at that point they knew he could have been missing for at least three hours."

"We should have looked closer at their story," Miller said. "It would have been tight, but they had the time to drive her car back to her apartment and drive home before calling us."

"You didn't have the traffic camera footage or know where her apartment and car were," Nikki said. "I didn't put it together until we had those. I'll have the DOT search for both of their vehicles in the same area, but remember, this is just a theory. Someone else could have held Dana captive with Kellan because they were trying to figure out how to save their own ass."

"Like Drew Barnes?"

Nikki's phone vibrated. She checked the caller ID and rolled her eyes. Caitlin Newport. Again. "Given his lie, definitely. I'm headed there this morning before I meet with Dana's college roommate. But you and I both know that Dana's accusation about the test deserves a closer look. Maggie is dominant over her sister. She's been in control since Kellan was removed from the home. By her own words, she spent a lifetime building resentment toward Dana. I don't doubt that Kellan should have been removed, but put yourself in Maggie's shoes. She's bitter and angry and probably still grieving their mother's death. I've no doubt she wanted to help Kellan, but I find it hard to believe that, deep down, she didn't relish having the control over her sister. She would have seen it as some kind of well-deserved punishment."

"Then Dana accuses her of interfering with the drug test somehow?" Miller said.

"We found the private investigator's card in her apartment. We're looking into whether or not Dana actually contacted her and why she wanted to in the first place," Nikki said. "She could have threatened Maggie with proving what she'd done to Dana. Maggie wouldn't have responded well to that." Nikki's phone vibrated. She glanced at the screen. "B. Reeves. Why does that last name sound familiar?"

"Ben Reeves is Zach's grandfather. That's the boy who went into the St. Croix, according to the Chisago guys."

Nikki sighed. "Caitlin must have given Ben my number. I have to give her credit for her determination." Nikki answered the call before Miller had a chance to respond and put it on speaker. "This is Agent Hunt."

"Hello, ma'am. My name is Ben Reeves. I'm sorry to bother you, but my grandson is missing. Caitlin Newport gave me your contact details. I believe she's spoke with you already?"

"Yes, she has," Nikki said. "I'm very sorry for everything your family is going through. Sheriff Miller is here with me, on speaker. He followed up with the team in Chisago County about the search for Zach. I know this is hard to hear, but it really does appear that Zach took the snowmobile out on the ice and went through."

"They're wrong," Ben said gruffly. "He's hotheaded enough to take the snowmobile out, but he's scared to death of water. Can't swim. There's no way he would take that risk."

"Does Sheriff Braintree know this?" Miller asked.

"That man don't know his ass from a hole in the ground," Ben replied. "He's putting on a show with divers and not looking anywhere else."

"Mr. Reeves," Nikki said, "it's my understanding that Zach's stocking hat was found on the banks of the river."

"It was bone-dry, never been in the water," Ben said. "That hat belonged to my son. Zach would never leave it. Something else is going on."

Nikki remembered Caitlin's theory about both Zach and Kellan being targeted because of custody disputes. "Is your son around? Or Zach's mother?" Nikki asked. "I'd be happy to—"

"My boy was killed in Afghanistan when Zach was just a baby. My wife and I are raising him."

"I'm so sorry." Nikki could tell by his tone that Ben wasn't going to talk about Zach's mother.

"Mr. Reeves, I understand your frustration and I can't imagine what you're going through," Miller said. "I'm no fan of Braintree's either, but my deputies are searching on our side of the county line. I hate to say it, but it looks like Braintree is right about what happened to Zach."

"No, he isn't. Please, Agent Hunt. Would you mind talking to Braintree? You're an FBI Agent, and this is a missing child case. I thought the FBI was automatically involved and took charge."

"That's not how it works, I'm afraid." Nikki was beginning to feel like a broken record. "Unless we know a kidnapping has crossed state lines, we don't have jurisdiction. If Braintree requests help, that's different. But, to my knowledge, he hasn't."

"And he won't. Idiot's out there dragging the river when someone has my grandson. I heard about the boy and his mom being murdered. Zach isn't much older and looks the same age. Caitlin thinks that maybe the same person took them both."

"We considered that," Miller said. "But there's just no evidence to support that theory."

"Please," Ben's voice cracked. "Please, Agent Hunt, can you just speak to Braintree? Someone has to make him listen."

His distraught tone made Nikki's throat ache with emotion. She would probably catch hell from Braintree and her own boss, but she couldn't sit around doing nothing.

"All right, Mr. Reeves. I'll talk to Braintree."

CHAPTER FIFTEEN

Nikki followed Miller's SUV down the narrow park road. According to the deputy Miller had sent to keep tabs on things, the ice divers were searching near Riverway campground, which was located on a peninsula nestled between Lake Alice and the St. Croix River. The tight road widened to the main parking area of the campground. The campground was closed for the season, but several Chisago County Sheriff's vehicles were parked in the lot, including the Boat and Water Patrol unit and a K-9 unit.

Miller was already out of his SUV by the time Nikki parked and joined him, trying not to show her impatience. She needed to speak with Drew Barnes, and she hoped the conversation with Braintree wouldn't take long.

"Isn't this Washington County?" she asked.

"Yes." Miller's upper lip curled. "And if Zach went into the water on Friday, his body is likely to be a lot farther south by now."

"What are the ice reports?" Nikki asked.

"It's typical March. Patchy." His gaze focused on a figure in the distance. "There's Braintree, walking around like a dumb ostrich."

Nikki suppressed a laugh. Braintree was tall and gangly, with a longer than usual neck. Hands on his hips, he strutted toward them.

"Miller, I didn't expect to see you here," Braintree said. "Your deputy's doing great directing traffic." Braintree fastened his eyes on Nikki. "Why are you here, Agent Hunt?"

"Ben Reeves asked me to come. Have we met before?"

"You're famous," Braintree said shortly. "We all know who you are. As for Ben Reeves' concern, I can assure you, Zach Reeves drowned. Your services aren't needed here."

Nikki plastered a smile on her face. "I understand you have things under control, but I keep being contacted. Appeasing Ben might help him start to accept the truth, so I'm just here to give him the reassurance he needs. Would you catch us up?"

Braintree grunted. "As I told Miller here, the K-9 tracked the snowmobile about five miles away from his house, near the Falls Creek area. His hat was stuck in some frozen weeds, and the ice around that area is real patchy. We're on a recovery mission now. That's it."

"Why aren't you searching farther south?" Miller asked.

"Because there's a ton of debris in this area of the river for the kid to get caught up on. Believe it or not, Miller, I've got the situation under control."

Depending on the current and amount of debris in the river, it could be weeks, if not months, before they found Zach's body. The St. Croix eventually ran into the Mississippi River, but the chances of a body getting that far south were pretty slim. Nikki couldn't see the fault in Braintree's logic, but if he spoke to the Reeves this way, no wonder they didn't think he knew what he was doing.

Nikki must have done a lousy job keeping her expression neutral. Braintree's angry gaze landed on her. "You can tell Ben Reeves we've got the situation handled. But thanks for checking on us."

"Fine." Nikki turned on her heel and headed back to her vehicle. She debated texting Rory to tell him that she'd spoken to Braintree personally and believed he had things under control, but she didn't. Instead, she texted Caitlin and reiterated the unfortunate truth that Zach had likely drowned.

It was nearly lunchtime when Nikki finally arrived at Gateway. She squeezed her jeep into the first available space and killed the engine. She was halfway to the front door when Drew Barnes walked outside, looking at his phone.

"Just the person I came to see," Nikki said.

Drew looked up in surprise, and fear flickered in his eyes. "Agent Hunt. I didn't expect to see you again."

"Really?" Nikki asked. "Because you look scared."

"I don't know what you mean."

"Listen," Nikki said. "I've had a long day, and it's barely noon. Let's cut to the chase. We found your fingerprints in Dana Rhodes' apartment. I need to know when you were there and why."

Drew looked deflated. "I knew this would happen. My prints are in the system from the stupid DUI, right?"

Nikki nodded. "Let's go inside and talk."

"Can we talk out here? I don't want Randall finding out. I could lose my job."

Wet snow had started to fall, and Nikki hadn't bothered to put her coat on. "Come sit in my jeep. It's cold and wet."

Drew nodded, and Nikki unlocked the doors. He sat down in the passenger seat with a nervous look on his face. "My fingerprints are in her apartment, so I'm a suspect," he said flatly.

"Yep," she replied. "You said you didn't have a relationship with her, but you were in her apartment, and you didn't tell police where she lived. That doesn't exactly make you look innocent."

"We didn't have a relationship," Drew said. "I mean, we were friendly but not close."

"You weren't having some kind of sexual relationship?" Nikki asked.

"I'm gay," he said flatly, relaxing a little. "I need this job. Randall was livid when I got the DUI. It's not exactly great PR for a sober living house. I convinced him to give me another chance. I don't drink much, and my boyfriend at the time was supposed to be the designated driver. But he was so drunk, I was afraid to get in the car. I barely blew over the legal limit."

"Everyone makes dumb decisions," Nikki said. "I just need you to be honest about Dana."

He shrugged. "She didn't tell me her deep dark secrets if that's what you're thinking, but I knew she was working her ass off to get Kellan back. Sorry for my language."

He was so sincere, Nikki had to fight back a smile. "Were you here when Randall had to ask her to leave?"

"It was awful. She was just unhinged. Normally she was an even keel kind of person. She put a lot of work into trying to handle her emotions and not get back into bad habits. But she snapped. She threw a stapler at Randall."

"How did he handle that?"

"Gracefully," Drew said. "Randall is a good guy. He's very compassionate. He told Dana that if she got sober again and went into rehab, he would make sure she had a place. But it didn't matter. She packed her things and left. Cam went after her, and he told us the next day he knew where she was and that she was safe."

Nikki didn't mention that Dana had spent the first few weeks staying with Cam. "Did Cam say anything about the test being wrong?"

"Not to me. He was just shell-shocked. But I heard him telling Randall later that there was just no way she was using again."

"So where do you come in?"

Drew sighed. "Cam had been taking her mail, but then he said he didn't know where she was, and she had a check. She called me and asked me to bring her the mail and not to tell anyone where she lived. I felt bad for her, so I agreed."

"When was this?"

"A few days before she and Kellan went missing." Drew looked down at his hands. "I knew something was going on with her. I should have told Cam, but she made me promise not to."

"What made you think that?"

"She had bruises around her neck and a black eye," Drew said. "She wouldn't tell me who did it at first, and then she kind of broke down crying. She was supposed to have a job interview and couldn't go because of the bruises. I told her I'd loan her some money, but she wouldn't take it. I managed to get her calmed down, and she told me that the day before, a man had shown up at her place. She thought he looked familiar but couldn't place him. He pushed his way in and told her to drop the questions about the test and move on with her life. When she said that she wasn't going to stop until she had her son back, he hit her and then started to strangle her. She managed to knee him and get to her phone. He took off."

"Did she make a police report?"

"I don't think so," Drew said. "I told her she had to, but she'd lost faith in the system. No one believed her, and she knew she sounded paranoid."

"About her sister?"

He nodded. "She said that her sister was out to get her and make sure she kept her mouth shut. That's why she sent that pock-faced goon to threaten her."

"Pock-faced?" Nikki asked. "Those were her words?"

"Yes. I guess she meant acne scars."

"I have to ask you where you were Friday night and on the weekend," Nikki said.

Drew flushed. "With my new boyfriend. I have a roommate and we wanted privacy, so we got a room at the Doubletree downtown. I swear I'm telling the truth."

Confirming his story with the hotel would be easy. "I believe you," Nikki said. "But you should have told us earlier. It would have saved a lot of time and energy."

He looked at her with misty eyes. "If I'd told someone, would she and Kellan still be alive?"

Nikki didn't have the heart to say yes, so she shook her head. "Probably not, but now we have to find the man who attacked her. That's our best lead."

And thanks to Drew's silence, the guy could have easily left town and gone off the grid by now.

Dana's college roommate had asked to meet at a Starbucks on the east side of Saint Paul, and the place was busy. Nikki searched the small crowd, and a slim, blond woman sitting at a high-topped table waved shyly. Sylvia's hair was several inches shorter than in the college photo and Nikki could see that she'd traded the miniskirts she wore as a girl for business casual. Behind her trendy black glasses, her eyes were red and swollen.

"Sylvia?"

"Agent Hunt. Thank you for meeting me. I just didn't want to discuss Dana over the phone."

"No problem." Nikki shrugged out of her winter coat and put it and her purse on the chair next to her. "Thanks for talking with me. I know this can't be easy." A server stopped by, and Nikki ordered a coffee and warmed cinnamon roll. "When was the last time you spoke with Dana?"

"I'm ashamed to say years ago," Sylvia said. "When Dana lost her way, I tried to be there when I could. But she drifted away, and I was too consumed with grad school to chase her."

"From what I've heard, I'm not sure it would have made any difference. Dana was in bad shape for a long time, and her mom did everything she could to help her. Dana and Kellan lived there until her mother died. She eventually lost custody of her son."

"To who?"

"Her older sister, Maggie."

"You've got to be kidding me." Sylvia sat her coffee cup down. "Dana had to have been beside herself."

"Was it that bad between them?"

"When I knew Dana, yes. I know the age gap didn't help, but it was more than that. They didn't like each other at all. Dana said it was because Maggie resented her so much."

"Did she ever talk about why?"

Sylvia's account of the family's financial situation backed up what Nikki had been told before. "Maggie told Dana that she didn't get to go to college because her parents put Dana first. She was so bitter. I can't imagine Dana was happy with her being named Kellan's guardian."

Nikki sighed. "Well, the state always prefers to place a child with blood relatives, and Maggie was Kellan's only other blood relative."

"I hope Maggie didn't mistreat the little boy because of how she felt about Dana," Sylvia said.

"No, she and her husband loved him deeply. By all accounts, he was a happy kid," Nikki said. "Do you think Maggie's capable of that?" Nikki asked.

"I don't know," Sylvia replied. "I will say that I remember Maggie visiting with their mother, and I could tell there was jealousy long before Dana told me the whole story. It just resonated from her, like she was just waiting for something she could nitpick and use to start an argument."

"She was manipulative, then?" Everyone in Dana's life—both past and present—had described Maggie as jealous and resentful. Had she snapped when Dana tried to take Kellan and decided to get rid of her for good? Maggie had a distinct height and weight advantage over Dana. She could have overpowered her, especially if Dana was busy trying to help Kellan.

Sylvia played with an empty sugar packet. "When did she lose custody?"

"Three years ago. She went on a bender and left Kellan alone in their apartment for three days. He called Maggie when he couldn't find anything else to eat."

"Jesus. But she got sober, didn't she?"

"For more than a year. She was staying at a sober living place that tested bimonthly. She was clean until the final court date." Nikki made a mental note to ask Drew Barnes about that, too. Did he have access to the center's drug test results? Could he have covered something up for Dana?

"Why would she do that?"

"Some people don't think she did." Nikki explained what she'd learned from Cam and the others in Dana's life. "Dana believed Maggie would take Kellan from her eventually."

"I wouldn't put it past her," Sylvia said. "I only met her a couple of times, but the way she looked at Dana made it obvious she only tolerated her because her parents were around."

"Her drug counselor said that Dana was on a mission. She was determined to get her son back and believed she would until the judge read the test results. I have to admit, her reaction doesn't sound like someone who'd been using."

"I can't believe Dana's gone." Sylvia shook her head. "And her son. Do you have any idea who did this?"

"I can't really talk specifics, but we're investigating several leads. I was hoping you could tell me more about the Dana you knew and if you had any idea why she started using?"

Sylvia dabbed at her eyes with a wadded-up napkin. "The Dana I knew was smart, funny, shy. Wicked sense of humor. She loved kids and couldn't wait to be a teacher. But then everything fell apart."

"When did you notice her changing?"

"Senior year, right after Christmas break. Dana, Shelly and I had an apartment off campus. She came home kind of... subdued, I guess. We asked her about her vacation, and she said it was fine. Shelly and I both thought something had been bothering her, but Dana insisted she was just tired and nervous about student teaching. Then the nightmares started. At least twice a week, she'd wake up screaming at someone to 'stop it.' She always said she didn't know what she was dreaming about, but we knew she was lying."

"Did she ever tell you anything more?"

"We tried to ask her, but she'd just get angry. And then she started staying over at other people's places—people we hadn't met. We found out she was using and begged her to stop. She broke down and was ashamed. She'd tried meth because she wanted to forget. That's all it took."

"Forget what?" Nikki asked.

"She refused to say. Shelly thought she might have been assaulted over break, but we never outright asked her."

Nikki drummed her fingers on the table. "Do you remember if she went to any counseling or the university clinic when she came back? Maybe made a report?"

"Not that I know of."

Nikki might be able to get a subpoena for the university clinic's medical records, but proving that whatever happened to Dana during college was pertinent to her death investigation would be a hard sell. "Did she stop using after you confronted her?"

"For a while. We graduated, and she was getting ready to take her teacher's exam. Then her father died, and she started having panic attacks. I told her to go to the doctor, and she started taking Xanax. She said it made her feel like a zombie, and she was really tired at first, but she seemed to adjust. Then Shelly caught her doing meth in the morning. Dana said it was just one hit—she called it a bump—to help wake up from the Xanax."

"And then she failed the teacher's exam, right?" Nikki asked.

Sylvia nodded. "I knew in my gut things were going to get bad. Soon, Dana moved out and that's when we really started growing apart. She didn't want to be helped, and back then I told myself that I'd done enough, and I had to take care of myself."

"You were right," Nikki said. "Addicts don't stop until they're truly ready. And some never are."

She thanked Sylvia for her time and promised to contact her with any new information about Dana's killer.

Nikki's jeep was parked a few blocks from the coffee shop, and she walked slowly, lost in her thoughts. It had become clear that something had happened during college that shattered Dana's life, and she was never the same. Nikki's tragedy had already happened by the time she started at the University of Minnesota, but it would have been so easy to go down the same path as Dana and try to numb the pain.

Her freshman year, she'd gone to one of the frat houses with her roommate, who was dating one of the pledges. She was actually having a decent time until someone brought out the cocaine. Nikki's roommate had immediately taken a hit and encouraged her to do the same, saying that normal people without a bunch of baggage could use cocaine recreationally without becoming addicted.

"If you're just doing it to party, it's fine," her roommate had said. "We're too young to be that screwed up, anyway."

Nikki had almost laughed out loud. At that time, no one knew about her past or the notoriety her parents' murders had created. She remembered thinking about how wonderful it would be to feel numb, but she knew in her gut that just one hit would probably lead her down a disastrous road.

Had Dana had one of those moments?

CHAPTER SIXTEEN

Nikki called Miller from the jeep and told him about Drew's visit to Dana. "Drew's alibi checks out. The Doubletree confirmed his check-in and out times. He also paid with a credit card. Dana's neighbor mentioned a stocky guy in a hoodie. And now we know he had acne scars."

"Damnit," Miller said. "Why didn't Barnes say anything earlier?"

"He was afraid of losing his job," Nikki replied. "Dana's college roommate had some really interesting things to say." Nikki explained Dana's changing after break and eventual medicating with drugs. "I honestly think something happened to her that last winter break. I'd like to get a peek into the university records and see if she went to the clinic, but I'll never get the warrant without proving a direct connection to her murder."

"When do you want to sit down with Maggie Anderson again?"

"I need to see my daughter tonight." Lacey was the only person in the world Nikki would drop everything for, and she longed to see her.

"We can swing by in the morning," Miller said.

"Did you talk to Ben Reeves?" Nikki asked.

"I tried. But he's a wreck and doesn't want to hear that someone else is giving up on his theories. I'm going to stop by their place tomorrow if I can."

"Try to get some rest," she said. "Go home and hug your daughters. That's what I'm going to do."

Lacey had gymnastics practice after school, but she would be finished by dinner time. Tyler would be watching practice and his phone on silent, but he usually kept it in sight in case an important call came in.

"Hey." He sounded out of breath when he answered. "I had to run out of the gym and into the hall at Lacey's practice. What's up?"

"Several things," Nikki said. "I'm close to Saint Paul and thought I'd see Lacey. What are you guys doing for dinner?"

"Going over to my parents. You're welcome to join us."

Nikki's heart sank. His parents probably wouldn't be so welcoming. They appreciated that Nikki and Tyler were on good terms, but they resented her divorcing him. Nikki wasn't in the mood for his mother's chilly reception and barely veiled digs. "Thanks, but I know they don't see Lacey as much as they'd like. I don't want to take her attention off them."

"Right."

Nikki didn't miss the edge in his voice. "Everything OK?"

Tyler said nothing.

"You know you're every bit as bad as a woman who says she's fine when she's really ready to explode." She tried to tease him. "What's going on?"

"I just thought you wanted to see Lacey."

"I do," Nikki said. "But your parents aren't big fans of mine. I want Lacey to enjoy her night, and, frankly, I'm not in the mood for your mother's digs about my breaking your heart."

"Is that the only reason?"

"What other reason would there be?"

"Nik, I know you weren't at a hotel last night. I called the Comfort Inn and all the hotels in the area. You're not registered."

"Jesus, Tyler."

"What if something happened to you and we didn't know where you were staying?"

"I don't know," Nikki said. "Maybe try the GPS on my phone or in the jeep. Checking at the hotel is way over the line."

"Then where were you?"

"None of your business."

He snorted. "I'm your husband—"

"Ex," she snapped. "You have every right to keep tabs on Lacey. But not me."

"Who is he?" Tyler asked quietly.

"I don't know what you're talking about."

"Yes, you do. I know you're not home a lot when I have Lacey."

"How?"

"It doesn't take an FBI agent to notice the overnight bag in your backseat, Nikki."

"And that means I must be seeing some guy?"

"I know you," he said. "You're acting different. And Lacey heard you talking on the phone about staying over."

"You're having our daughter spy on me?"

"Don't be ridiculous. She mentioned it. That's when I got suspicious. I know you're hiding something from me."

Nikki took a deep breath and slowly released it. "I'm only going to say this once. My personal life is none of your business unless Lacey is affected. And she's not."

"Yet," Tyler said. "But you'll introduce her sometime."

"If things get to that point, we'll have this conversation. Until then, mind your own business. And don't tell Lacey I asked about coming home tonight." She ended the call before he could respond.

Rush-hour traffic was in full swing now, and Nikki really didn't have the patience to deal with angry commuters. She thought about going to the office, but the drive would be just as bad. What the hell was Tyler thinking? Calling the hotel went too far. She knew there were still feelings there, and it seemed to Nikki like Tyler was holding onto them. She wanted him to be happy. He had to let go.

Had she brought this on herself? She had tried so hard to make sure that she and Tyler stayed friends after the divorce because it made things easier for their daughter, but she'd also selfishly wanted him in her life. She'd thought he would move on in time, but maybe

Nikki's dependency on their friendship had been unfair. Maybe Tyler saw it as the door being left open and wasn't able to move on. After this case was over and things were at some level of normal, she and Tyler would sit down and hash everything out. Right now, her mind was too clouded and too damned tired.

Traffic barely moved, which usually meant a wreck somewhere ahead on the interstate. Nikki checked her messages, hoping to hear from Liam. Instead, she had a missed call from Stillwater Public Schools.

Kellan's teacher had left her a message about Lindsey, the friend she'd suggested Nikki talk to. According to Kellan's teacher, Lindsey had gone home upset yesterday, and her mother had called her out sick for the rest of the week. Apparently, during Lindsey's breakdown yesterday, she had said several times that Kellan's death was her fault and she could have done something about it. Nikki wasn't sure how the little girl would have saved him, but she wanted to talk to her as soon as possible. Kellan might have told her something that would lead them to their suspect. The teacher wasn't able to give out personal information other than Lindsey's mother's phone number.

Traffic was still pretty thick, so Nikki went ahead and called.

"Hello?"

"Hi, may I speak to Kim Chalmers?"

"This is she." The woman's pleasant tone became guarded. "Who's calling?"

"Special Agent Nikki Hunt with the FBI. I know your daughter Lindsey was a friend of Kellan Rhodes. Her teacher called and mentioned that she had a bad time yesterday and went home. Would it be all right if I stopped by and spoke to her for a few minutes?"

"Absolutely not. She's been through enough and doesn't need to be bothered. She doesn't know anything, anyway." Kim ended the call abruptly.

Nikki understood the woman's protectiveness. She would have fought to shelter Lacey just as much. Still, Nikki felt it was important that she talk to the little girl in person. She'd get her address in the morning and stop by. Nikki hoped she could persuade the mother to give her just a few minutes.

Nikki was debating getting off the interstate and taking the longer route through the suburbs when a text from Courtney flashed on the screen.

Still in town? Shall we swap notes over some dinner?

Nikki quickly replied: *God, yes. Just tell me where.*

Degidio's was one of Saint Paul's Italian staples and almost always busy. Courtney must have come at just the right time because she and Liam already had a table when Nikki arrived. She ordered a glass of red and her favorite dish, baked mostaccioli and meatballs.

"What a day." Nikki sipped her glass of wine. Between Ben Reeves' grief and her argument with Tyler, Nikki was completely drained. She'd done nothing wrong, yet Tyler somehow managed to make her feel as though she had. "Does anyone have good news to share?"

"Cam Fletcher's background check came back clean," Liam said. "The private investigator was a dead end. Dana had an appointment but never showed up."

"Fantastic," Nikki replied. "How'd it go at the lab?"

Washington County had contracted Hennepin Partners for Healthcare for most of their court-ordered drug testing. Nikki had never encountered HPH, but they had a solid reputation.

"I met with the associate director," Liam said. "Dana physically came to the lab and provided the urine. The associate director walked me through the process, but it's pretty straightforward. The individual comes in and submits the test. One of five technicians is randomly assigned to perform the test. Negative tests come back faster, but a positive can take up to seventy-two hours to fully process."

"Do they keep a record of findings?"

Liam nodded. "Yes, but she couldn't give me the details without a warrant. I asked her how a test could be falsified, and she said it's extremely unlikely. They're very strict about the chain of custody with the samples, so switching them out would be nearly impossible."

"But it's up to the technician who ran the test to then translate that to a report, right?"

Liam nodded. "Why?"

"I don't know," Nikki replied. "As unlikely as it seems, it's happened before in other states. Not a single person in Dana's daily life believes she was using again."

"Meth is a really tough one to beat," Courtney said. "Maybe she freaked out about having to be on her own again with Kellan."

"And sabotaged herself?" Nikki asked. "That doesn't match with the reaction she had in court. Cam said it was visceral and she had to be restrained."

"Maybe that was the meth talking," Liam suggested.

Nikki shrugged. "I guess. Miller and I are going to talk to the Andersons tomorrow. I plan on asking Maggie point blank and hopefully knocking her off her game. Assuming she's involved at all."

"I should be able to pull their financials and see if they had any large withdrawals," Liam said. "But even if Maggie did pay the tech off, how does it help us find out if someone helped Dana take Kellan?"

"I don't know that it does," Nikki replied. "But we might be able to shake more information out of Maggie if we have that as leverage."

"You really think she'd hurt Kellan? Or that Joe would?"

"No," Nikki said. "If one or both of the Andersons are involved, Kellan's death was probably an accident. Dana's a different story."

"Even if she hated her sister, cutting Dana's wrists is as cold as it gets," Liam said. "I can't see her doing that. She has to care for her sister on some level."

"I don't disagree," Nikki replied. "But I still think she hasn't been honest. If she's holding back that information, she might have more that could help us figure out who else is involved."

Courtney slathered butter on the complimentary bread. "I could eat a pound of this stuff and still be hungry."

"And stick-thin," Nikki said. "Two pieces and I have two extra pounds on my rear."

"Rory doesn't seem to mind." Courtney smirked.

Nikki jokingly moved Courtney's glass. "You're cut off. Besides, how would you know that?"

"Given your upbeat and glowing attitude the last few weeks, I'm taking an educated guess. You have been spending a few nights a week at his place, right?"

"I'm not discussing this right now," Nikki said. "Interrogate Liam on his mystery girl."

"There's no girl," he said. "I had a date. That's it."

"A sleepover date," Courtney teased.

"What about you, Court?" Liam turned the tables on her. "How's your personal life these days?"

"More than you can handle."

The arrival of three plates of steaming pasta saved Nikki from listening to any more arguing. Liam and Courtney ate quickly, but Nikki picked at her food. She kept hearing Ben Reeves' voice begging her to find his grandson. She should make the time tomorrow and go to the Reeves' home instead of Miller dealing with it. The stocking hat did bug her a little bit, but it wasn't enough to make her think Braintree was wrong. And after spending a few minutes with him this morning, she'd love to have a reason to say he was wrong.

Liam ate his entire plate of pasta and part of Nikki's. He leaned back in the chair. "I might have to open my top button on the drive home."

"Please," Nikki said. "You have a hollow leg. Let's talk about tomorrow before I forget." She told Liam about the call from Kellan's teacher. "I want to talk to her as soon as possible. Dana's cousin agreed to have a video chat, so I'll do that first thing in the morning, and then we can head to Lindsey's before we sit down with the Andersons."

Liam snatched a pasta noodle off Courtney's plate before she could slap his hand away. "Did you pull a print off that underwear?"

She made a face. "I told you it's a delicate process. I've got a partial and not much else. And before you ask, there wasn't much in her car. If anything, it was too clean. Including the hatchback."

Their server brought the dessert menu. Liam surprisingly declined, but Nikki and Courtney split a piece of chocolate cake.

"I feel like I'm five months pregnant again." Nikki rubbed her stuffed belly.

"Yeah, I might explode," Courtney said. "But it was worth it. Are you heading back to Stillwater tonight?"

Nikki checked the time. It was nearly 7:30 p.m. She should just go back to her own house and try to get through some of her notes. But she would end up dwelling on Rory and trying to decide whether or not to call him. "Yeah. Hopefully the traffic isn't too bad by now."

"I'm going home and passing out in a food coma," Courtney said. "Drive safe."

Nikki waved goodbye and reminded Liam to meet her in the morning. Traffic wasn't as bad as she'd feared, and she got to Rory's in less than an hour. He was asleep on the couch again, with the hockey game muted on the television. Nikki debated waking him up and telling him to go to bed, but she was too afraid that he would reject her. She kissed his forehead before going into his bedroom to brush her teeth and change. Sleep probably wouldn't come easy tonight because she'd be on alert for Rory, hoping that he would at least sleep next to her.

After tossing and turning for an hour, Nikki had just started to nod off when she felt the bed shift and Rory lay down beside her. Neither one of them spoke, and they didn't reach for one another. But he was there, and that was enough for now.

CHAPTER SEVENTEEN

Nikki felt a heaviness on her shoulders on the drive to work the next morning. Rory had left the house early, but he did tell her goodbye. But something more than Rory was weighing on her mind. She felt no closer to finding out what happened to Dana and Kellan, and she was getting frustrated.

Alone in the car, looking out at the morning, her thoughts were interrupted by her cell phone.

"How could you side with Braintree?" Caitlin's shrill voice hurt Nikki's ears as she answered the call. "Can't you see that he's taking the easy route? Why haven't they found the snowmobile if Zach drowned? They've been diving for days now. The snowmobile's almost five hundred pounds. It's got plenty of edges for something to catch on. They should have seen it."

Nikki's frustration started to boil over as she listened to Caitlin go on. "Why are you so hellbent on this?" she interrupted her. "I spoke to Ben Reeves and Sheriff Braintree. There's no link between these cases. Why are you prying?"

"I'm not," Caitlin said. "I just want the truth."

Nikki snickered. "Right, because your intentions are always altruistic."

"You know nothing about me," Caitlin snapped. "I'm trying—"

"Just stop." Nikki tried to keep her voice steady. "I know you believed in Mark's innocence, but you also saw the opportunity for a career-breaking story. Is that what's happening here?"

Caitlin didn't answer right away, but Nikki could hear her breathing.

"Caitlin, I'll make sure you don't exploit this family's loss."

Caitlin's shuddering sob tore through the jeep's speakers, piercing Nikki's ears. "Just forget I asked for your help. I'll find him myself."

Nikki had seen countless people with the same inability to look at a case objectively because they were so deeply involved. But the raw pain in Caitlin's voice, the guttural cry and profound shock, were things only certain kinds of people displayed when a child had been lost. "Caitlin, you're Zach's mother, aren't you?"

Another keening sob filled the vehicle, followed by Caitlin's exhausted voice. "Please don't tell Braintree or Liam. Braintree hates me, and I don't want Liam to know yet. I've been avoiding him since Monday."

"Why are you avoiding Liam?"

"You don't know?"

Nikki wanted to bang her head on the steering wheel. So much for her keen observance of human behavior. Between the phone calls and furious texting, how could she have missed it? Nikki almost started demanding answers about their relationship but reined in her curiosity. Caitlin was going through enough right now.

"No, I didn't, and I won't say anything to either of them," Nikki replied. "I'm sorry about Zach, really. It's awful, and I swear if there were any reason to think he didn't drown, I would get involved."

"There is reason to think he didn't drown," Caitlin said. "But I have to show you in person. I don't trust Braintree. The cases are connected, and I have proof."

"I don't know when I can meet. You know how unpredictable a murder investigation is." She and Miller planned to speak with the Andersons, and Nikki had a feeling the conversation wasn't going to go very well.

"I know the first forty-eight hours after a child disappears are the most crucial," Caitlin said. "Those have already passed."

"All right." If Caitlin really had proof, Nikki wanted to see it. And if she didn't, then maybe sitting down with her, mother-to-mother, would help Caitlin start to accept the likely truth that Zach had drowned. "I have a full day, but can you swing by Rory's later this evening?"

Still reeling from her conversation with Caitlin, Nikki headed into the command center at the Washington County Sheriff's office. She had a video chat scheduled with Dana and Maggie's cousin in Iowa and didn't want to rely on her cell signal. She hoped to talk to Miller before they went to the Andersons, but his SUV wasn't in the parking lot.

Nikki stopped by the desk sergeant first. "Where's Miller?"

"One of his daughters fell on the ice this morning and fractured her arm, poor kid. They're going to have to put her under to set the bones. He may not be in at all today."

"Thanks." Nikki shuddered. She'd broken her arm as a kid and could still remember how it looked like a swan's neck. "Mind if I use the command room for a quick call?"

"Help yourself."

"Thanks." Nikki set her computer up in the small room and made a cup of coffee before opening the video chat and starting the call.

It took three tries for Dana and Maggie's cousin to get her video chat to actually have video. "I'm sorry. I'm just so technologically impaired."

Carrie Johnson looked a few years older than her cousin Maggie, with wispy gray hair and laugh wrinkles around her eyes.

Nikki adjusted her laptop. "You're fine. Thanks for talking over the computer. I'm a big believer in face-to-face communication if at all possible."

"Of course," Carrie said. "Although I'm not sure how much help I can be. I haven't spoken to Dana in years. I can't believe she's gone, though. And her child…" Carrie put her hand over her heart. "It's surreal."

"Did you stay in touch with Maggie?"

"Off and on. Facebook and the occasional emails. We were never all that close."

"I know Dana and Maggie had a difficult relationship."

Carrie sighed. "That's putting it mildly. Maggie was never very accepting of Dana, even when their mother was pregnant. She was used to being the only child. And she didn't want to share anything."

"Even as a kid?"

"Oh yes. Her father worked twelve-hour days and her mother worked two jobs for a long time. I think they felt bad about having to work so much, so Maggie spent a lot of time by herself. She didn't like babysitters, so she was staying home alone by the time she was eight."

"Wow," Nikki replied. "I know things have changed, but that's young to be staying by yourself."

"Well, it was a different time," Carrie said. "I don't mean to speak so negatively about her. After my aunt cut down to one job, Maggie seemed to be better. She and her mom were close for years."

"Dana coming along changed that?"

"Partially, but Maggie found out that my uncle Stan wasn't her real father around the same time. She was so angry."

Nikki couldn't hide her surprise. "I wasn't aware."

"She refused to talk to anyone about it. She just got angry and held it in."

"Was her biological father ever in the picture?"

Carrie shook her head. "He basically abandoned them. Maggie was a year old when my aunt and Stan met. He raised her as his own. Then Dana came along, and I guess Maggie thought she was less important to him. But Stan was a good man. I can't imagine he treated her any differently."

Nikki could understand Maggie's fear, especially when she was just a teenager and trying to figure life out. It sounded like she'd never been able to let those feelings go, and they manifested into anger and jealousy at Dana.

"This is a little delicate, but were your mother and her sister close?"

"They spoke at least twice a week."

"Did Dana's mother ever talk about why Dana ended up addicted? Was there some traumatic event?"

"Her father dying was difficult, I know that."

"Her college roommate said she came back changed after their winter break during senior year," Nikki explained. "She always wondered if something bad had happened to Dana."

"It's possible, but if my mother knew, she never said anything. I do know Dana's drug use put another wedge between Maggie and her parents because she felt like they were too focused on Dana to be there for her. She and Joe tried for a baby for a long time, and Maggie had two miscarriages that I know of."

Things were starting to make more sense. Nikki could see why Maggie felt the way she did, at least to an extent. "Carrie, thank you so much for your time. You've been a big help."

"I don't feel like I have," she said. "Please find out who did this to them."

"I intend to."

Nikki thanked Carrie and promised to tell Maggie to call her and then quickly packed up her laptop before heading out to meet Liam.

Kellan's friend Lindsey lived in the last house on a dead-end street. The blue bungalow was older and relatively small. A yellow sign posted on the black chain-link fence warned trespassers to stay off the property.

"Kim's the mother's name, and she isn't going to be happy we're here," Nikki said to Liam. "So be prepared."

She rang the doorbell several times before she heard the sound of locks being sprung, and the door opened a few inches. "Can I help you?"

Nikki held up her badge. "I spoke with you yesterday. I think Lindsey—"

"I don't care what you think." The woman slammed the door.

Nikki wrinkled her nose. "Did you smell that when she opened the door?"

Liam had been standing at the bottom of the steps. He shook his head. "What did you smell?"

"Dirt," Nikki said. "Mildew."

"Maybe the house has mold."

The blinds on the front window blocked her view inside, but it looked like they had been pushed flat against the windows. Nikki pointed to her left, where the chain-link fence opened to a narrow pathway that led to the back of the house. The fence was padlocked. A line of pine trees blocked the yard from the neighbor's view.

"Look over the fence. How far back can you see?"

Liam walked over to the fence. "All the way back. There's a big blue tarp covering what looks like a pile of junk."

"Terrible smell, a pile of junk in the back, and a mother who doesn't want anyone in the house. What does that tell you?"

"You think she's a hoarder?"

"We're going to find out. I can't ignore that smell when there's a child living here. I've been in houses like this before, and social services takes it really seriously. It's not the environment you want a child growing up in." Nikki rang the doorbell again.

Lindsey's mother cracked the door open again. "I told you—"

"Kim, you understand that as an FBI agent, I'm a mandatory reporter, right?"

"What does that mean?"

"It means that if I think your child is in a dangerous situation, I'm obligated to report to CPS. And I have to tell you, things move a lot more quickly if it's an FBI agent making the report."

Kim's eyes widened. "I don't know what you're talking about."

"I can spot hoarding, Kim. As long as there are pathways and Lindsey has her own space, I won't report you."

"You have no reason—" Kim sputtered.

"Please," Nikki interrupted. "I'm trying to solve a child's murder, and Lindsey knew Kellan best. Her teacher said Lindsey seemed to feel like something was her fault. I think Kellan might have told her something that we need to know."

"Mom, it's OK." A small voice came from somewhere behind the door. "I'll come outside to talk to her."

"Put your shoes and coat on first." Kim looked at Nikki. "She'll be out in a minute."

"Thank you."

A minute later, Lindsey stepped out and quickly shut the door. Nikki's heart hurt for the child, but she seemed cared for. Her mother might not have been looking after her house but perhaps she was taking care of her child.

Kim appeared behind Lindsey a second later, closing the door tightly behind them.

Nikki smiled down at the little girl. "Hi, Lindsey. I'm Agent Hunt. Thank you for talking to me."

Lindsey nodded. She seemed small for a third-grader. "I'm so sad about Kellan," she said softly.

"It's pretty awful." Nikki sat down on the top step. "I know you two were friends. Want to sit next to me?"

Lindsey nodded and sat down. Her mother hovered behind them, but Nikki focused on the girl.

"I'm trying to figure out exactly what happened to him... Your teachers are worried about you," Nikki said. "You mentioned something about not helping Kellan when you should have."

Lindsey's eyes watered, and she nodded.

"Let's get one thing very clear," Nikki said. "Absolutely none of this is your fault. If Kellan told you a secret and you kept it, that's OK. Friends do that. But now that he's gone, I need to know all of his secrets so I can bring the person who hurt him to justice. Does that make sense?"

"Yes."

"Go ahead, Lins," her mother said softly. "You'll feel better after you tell her."

Lindsey took a deep breath. "Kellan's mom got an apartment here. He said he knew where it was and how to take a bus to see her."

"Did he ever do that?"

"I don't know. He said he was going to, because he missed her. His aunt was making him call her 'mom,' and Kellan didn't like that."

"I can understand that," Nikki empathized. "When did his mom tell him about her new place?"

"The day she came to school. She talked to him through the fence at recess before a teacher told her to go away."

"Did Kellan tell you anything else about Joe and Maggie?"

Lindsey shrugged. "Not really. He liked them. But his aunt really didn't like his mom."

"That happens in families sometimes," Nikki said. "Is this what you've been feeling bad about keeping secret?"

Lindsey hesitated and then shook her head. "Kellan said his mom was scared of something. She told him he shouldn't trust anyone but her."

"Did she only come to the school that one time?" Nikki asked.

"I think so."

"Lindsey, you're still not telling her everything. Go on. It's cold out here," her mother prompted.

"Kellan said that his mom came to his aunt and uncle's a while ago. There was a big fight. His mom was yelling at his aunt about some secret, and then his aunt slapped his mom, hard. She called his aunt a bad name, and his aunt said if she ever opened her mouth again, she'd wish she hadn't."

"Did they know Kellan saw?"

"I don't know. But he heard his mom say she wasn't going to stop until his aunt told the truth."

"And that's everything," her mother said. "Lindsey, go back inside."

"Yes, go in and get warm," Nikki said. "Thank you for being brave and talking to me."

Lindsey flushed and then slipped inside the house.

Her mother promptly rounded on Nikki. "Agent Hunt, I know what you're thinking about me, but you can't report me to CPS. I don't have family around here. She'll go into foster care."

Nikki stood. "I understand. Lindsay looks fine and I trust you to do what's best with her, but we can't just leave now and pretend we haven't seen the state of this place. You have one week to clear it up. I'll make sure a deputy comes to check."

Adrenaline rushed through Nikki as she and Liam headed back to their cars.

"It's time for Maggie Anderson to tell the truth."

CHAPTER EIGHTEEN

Nikki parked in the circular drive in front of the Anderson home. She'd brought Liam up to speed about things on the way. "Maggie's involved in this mess somehow. I'm sure of it. And I'm not leaving here without finding out why they waited to call the police and if she knew about Dana possibly talking to a private investigator."

Nikki killed the engine and she and Liam exited, both of them squinting against the bright sun. The ice on the sidewalk had melted, and Nikki could hear the snow dripping from the gutters.

"Spring is coming."

Liam scoffed. "My bet's on ten more inches of snow before May."

Nikki knew better than to take that bet. Snow in April was practically an annual event in Minnesota.

Joe answered the door. "Do you have news?"

"Something like that," Nikki said. "We also have more questions. Is Maggie available to talk as well?"

Joe ran a hand over his bald head. "She's napping, and she really hasn't been sleeping well."

"I'm sorry," Nikki said. "But these questions need to be answered so that we can move forward."

Joe's eyebrows knitted together. "All right then. Go on in and have a seat in the family room. I'll get Maggie."

The Andersons' open concept home had a country log-cabin feel, like something a person might see in *Midwest Living* or a similar magazine. Nikki was drawn to the big bay window that overlooked the backyard. The shades had been drawn when they came by last time, but the window was in full view today. Nikki imagined the view in the summer was lovely, especially with the trees in bloom.

"What's going on?" Maggie entered the room and sat down in the nearest chair. "Joe mentioned that you had news."

"We have some leads," Nikki said. "I know you're exhausted, so I will get right to the point. Did you know Dana was living in an apartment in Stillwater so that she could be close to Kellan?" Nikki could tell by their shocked reactions they hadn't known. "Kellan knew the address and how to get there by bus."

"That means she had been planning this for a while," Maggie said. "Did you search her apartment? Or find her car? You've got to be able to get some kind of evidence to find out who helped her."

"Yes to both those questions," Nikki replied. "Our lab is running tests as we speak. In the meantime, we've talked to several people in Dana's life, and I just need to clarify some things with you to make sure I'm seeing the full picture."

"I can't imagine the caliber of people in her life." Maggie looked disgusted.

"Her drug counselor has worked with her since her final rehab stay. She also had a couple of friends at Gateway." Nikki leaned forward, as though she were letting Maggie in on a secret. "They said Dana was convinced that you somehow had her drug test altered so that she would lose custody of Kellan."

"That's ridiculous," Joe said. "Damn near slander."

Maggie's expression seemed too perfectly arranged and controlled. "I can't imagine why she would say such a thing, but it doesn't surprise me. Meth always made her paranoid and aggressive."

Nikki recounted the sequence of events that Cam and both women at Gateway had told her and then pretended to check her notes, even though she had them memorized. She'd learned from experience that letting someone stew usually produced results. "The custody hearing was on a Friday, which meant Dana had to take the test on Tuesday so the lab had time to fully process it. She took it Tuesday morning"—Nikki checked the notes again—"at 9:07 a.m."

"And?" Maggie said.

"Gateway's bimonthly test taken two days before was negative. Every person who interacted with her in the two days between that test and the court's insists that she exhibited no signs of being on any kind of drug."

"Dana was a long-time user," Maggie said. "She probably managed to hide it."

"Why use so close to the court test, though?" Nikki asked. "She wanted Kellan back so badly."

"Maybe she couldn't handle the reality of being an actual parent. She couldn't care for Kellan after Mom was gone. Maybe she was afraid something would happen and this time he'd end up seriously hurt instead of just left alone at home and starving."

Joe's sheepish look made it clear his wife's bitterness bothered him. "Maybe she thought it wouldn't show up in the court-ordered test and convinced herself it was a one-time thing."

Liam shook his head. "Dana knew the system and how the tests work. She was way too experienced to think the court test would still come back negative—or believe that one hit wouldn't put her right back on the wagon. And by all accounts from those in Dana's life, she was fully prepared to get Kellan back because she'd done everything required of her by the judge."

"Except stay off drugs," Maggie spat.

"Mrs. Anderson, I'm sure you know what a powerful drug meth is," Nikki said evenly. "Dana was clean for the entire year she was at Gateway, and before that, three months in rebab. If she did use between that last test and the court test, it would have been the first time in nine months."

"She's lucky she didn't overdose," Joe said.

"How did she act that morning?" Nikki looked at Joe, hoping he would be able to answer impartially.

"Um… fine, I guess."

"She wasn't fidgety? Unable to sit still? Did she talk fast?"

"No."

"Nothing in her behavior looked alarming?" Nikki asked.

"She was upbeat," he said sadly. "I think I told you that we expected her to get custody. Everyone was shocked."

"Especially Dana." Nikki looked directly at Maggie. "The other thing bothering us is the timing of your call to the bank."

Maggie crossed her arms over her chest. "What call?"

"The judge made his ruling shortly after ten, right around the same time you called the bank and told them the trust payments would need changing. And you came in that day and signed the paperwork."

"There's nothing wrong with that," Maggie said. "I didn't want her to get any more of Kellan's money."

"But that's one of the first things you thought of," Nikki said. "It's almost as if you had a plan."

Joe seemed to finally catch on. "Are you suggesting Maggie did something to the test? That's crazy. She wouldn't have any idea how to do that, let alone be that cruel."

"Maybe you're right. But Dana intended to speak to her about finding proof of the falsified test. She had an appointment Monday with a private investigator." Nikki paused, giving Maggie a final chance to come clean, but she remained silent.

"What Agent Hunt is getting at is that we have enough evidence to procure a warrant for your financial records. If someone was paid to change the test, we'll find out. Telling us now will save a lot of work and give you a shot at leniency with the prosecutor's office."

"Why are you doing this?" Maggie burst out. "Dana's dead. Kellan's dead because of her. How does this possibly help you find out who killed them?"

"I told you to do whatever you needed to," Joe said. "Check our records. You won't find anything. Maggie wouldn't do anything like that."

Nikki looked at him. "Were you here the last time Dana showed up? Maggie called the police, but Dana had left by the time they arrived."

Joe shook his head. "I'd gone to see a client."

"Maggie, we know that Dana said something that made you so angry you slapped her," Liam said.

Maggie's face paled. "You couldn't possibly know that because it didn't happen."

"Kellan saw it and he told his friend. You made it clear to Dana that bringing up that particular subject would cause more harm than good."

"Mags, you didn't tell me that." Joe turned to his wife. "What did she say?"

Maggie shook her head. "It doesn't matter."

"I'm afraid it does," Nikki said. "We know you're hiding something. And we have a strong enough case of circumstantial evidence to get search warrants for your home and grounds."

"Search for what?" Maggie demanded.

"I think you knew Dana was digging about the drug test, and you weren't going to let her find proof. We have to consider the idea Dana might have come to confront you again and things went wrong."

"I wasn't even here," Maggie said.

"Until Joe called your cell," Liam reminded her. "We don't know what he said. You had time to get home before the police were called."

"This is preposterous." Joe finally snapped. "My wife is a good person. She would never do any of this."

Nikki ignored him. "Maggie, we need the truth. I don't have to tell you that if the media gets wind of this—"

"Don't threaten her," Joe said. "I won't have it."

"Stop, all of you." Maggie stood, tears streaming down her face. "Yes, I paid someone to switch the samples at the lab, all right? I did it for Kellan. Even if Dana was sober, she wouldn't stay that way. Kellan deserved better than being on that roller coaster."

Joe stared at his wife. "How?"

"A couple of months before the final hearing, we had a meeting with the judge about Dana's request for unsupervised visits." Now that Maggie had finally admitted the truth, she seemed desperate to purge information. "I insisted she couldn't be trusted, but based on her compliance over the past year, he granted them. She was allowed to have Kellan at Gateway twice a week after school. I had to make sure he was there on time and picked up on time." Maggie shook her head. "I wasn't happy about the decision."

"Why not?" Liam asked. "There were parameters in place. It would have been hard for her to try to disappear with him."

"That wasn't the issue," Maggie said. "I just didn't want her filling Kellan's head about this perfect life with her when I knew she wouldn't be able to stay on track. He'd been through enough."

Nikki guessed that Maggie's issue was more about control and keeping Kellan from trusting his mother, but she kept that to herself. "What did you do?"

"Nothing at first. But then I received a call from a man who said he worked with family court. He wouldn't give me his name, but he had so much detailed information about Dana's case that I knew he must be telling the truth. He said he knew someone at the lab that might be able to help me. We arranged a meeting at a coffee shop not far from the courthouse. He had her test results and the name of the lab doing the court-ordered testing. We talked about how the statistics show that the majority of addicts relapse, and he very much believes that our system gives drug-addicted parents way too much leeway. He said he worked with someone at the lab who felt the same way and was willing to assist in certain cases."

"For how much?" Nikki asked.

"Five thousand." Maggie hung her head. "I paid him in cash."

"My God, Maggie." Joe stared at her. "That's illegal."

"I was willing to take the risk. For Kellan." Maggie's voice was barely audible.

"We need a name," Nikki said flatly.

"He never gave me one," she replied. "He said he worked in the family court."

"What did he look like?" Liam asked.

"Average height, a little stocky, dark hair. He had some acne scars on his cheeks. There was something familiar about him, but I couldn't place it."

Nikki and Liam looked at each other. The pock-marked guy who'd hit Dana had been afraid of her telling the truth.

Joe dragged his hand down his face. "Jesus Christ, Mags. Do you realize Dana and Kellan would be alive right now if you hadn't done that?"

"Of course I do." Maggie's face had turned red and splotchy from crying. "Dana wouldn't have teamed up with someone to take him away. She'd be happy and get everything she wanted, like always." Maggie pointed her finger at Nikki. "I admit to paying that guy, but I swear on my own life that nothing happened to Kellan here. Everything we've told you is true."

"You understand why that might be hard for us to believe," Liam said.

She nodded. "I'll take a polygraph. You can test for blood anywhere on the property. Or anything else you need to."

"Do you have contact information for this man?" Nikki asked.

"No," Maggie said. "We just arranged the next meeting."

Nikki wasn't sure she believed her, but she was confident they could track the man down. If he had that much access to Dana's records, he likely worked closely with the judge handling her case.

Maggie put her head into her hands and sobbed.

"I think it's time you two left." Joe walked them to the door. "What's going to happen to her?"

"I don't know," Nikki said. "We'll tell the district attorney she cooperated. If we can bring down everyone involved, that will hopefully go a long way with the judge."

By the time they got back to the sheriff's office, Liam had a name. "Eddie Nelson. He's the court reporter for the judge assigned to the case. That's probably why Maggie thought he looked familiar."

Nikki was glad to see Miller's SUV in the lot. They found him in his office, trying to catch up on paperwork.

"How's your daughter?" Nikki asked.

"Cranky and mean," he said. "Anesthesia did not sit well with her. She was in so much pain and so confused when she woke up, she pinched the hell out of my wife. I would have laughed if my girl wasn't hurting so badly."

"Thank God she didn't hit her head," Nikki said.

"I know. I saw her fall and almost had a heart attack. Her feet went out from under her and she just went down." He sighed. "But we'll count our blessings. I'm sorry to leave you two hanging today."

"Don't be," Liam said. "We have big news. Dana's test was falsified. And Maggie Anderson paid to have it done."

"Holy shit," Miller said. "How'd she pull it off?"

"She says the guy approached her with all of Dana's information and told her he knew someone at the lab."

"Does this guy have a name?"

"He didn't give it to her, but it wasn't hard to figure out. His name is Eddie Nelson and he's the court reporter. He's stocky and has acne scars."

"The guy who beat up Dana?" Miller asked.

"The very same. Liam, show him the Facebook account."

Liam swiped right on his tablet and handed it to Miller. "That's Eddie's Facebook account. He doesn't post a lot, but his sister, Ava, works at HPH Labs."

"It was that easy?"

"They didn't think they'd get caught," Liam said. "Eddie doesn't do much online except share memes, but scroll down to the pro-life one he shared and read the comments."

"*If she has to make a decision between keeping a kid she doesn't want or an abortion, the baby ain't the problem*," Miller read the comment out loud. "*It's her lack of morals.*"

"That sparked a bigger argument, but Eddie didn't bother to engage. But that single sentence makes me wonder how deeply his hatred for perceived unfit mothers goes."

"What about his sister's account? Does she share the same views?"

"Not that she posted," Liam said. "She's more active on Instagram, but it's all selfies and cat pictures."

"We haven't notified the district attorney," Nikki added. "I'll leave that up to you. But Liam's going to get warrants for HPH tomorrow. I want to hit Ava and Eddie at the same time."

CHAPTER NINETEEN

Caitlin Newport stood in Rory's entryway looking as unkempt as Nikki had ever seen her. A fuzzy cardigan hung to her knees, and she wore an old army T-shirt and worn leggings. Her usually perfectly arranged blond hair was pulled back in a crooked ponytail, and she looked pale and tired, with mascara smudges under her eyes. Fresh tears ran down her face, and Nikki could smell the alcohol on her breath when Caitlin gripped Nikki's shoulders. "Please listen to me. My son is alive."

Nikki removed Caitlin's hands. "Come in and sit down." Caitlin's skin felt ice cold as Nikki led her upstairs to the couch. "Do you want some coffee or water?"

Caitlin shook her head and sat down in Rory's usual spot. "No thanks. I just want to find my son."

Nikki had dealt with enough grieving families to realize that Caitlin wouldn't be able to accept Zach's death until his body had been recovered. "Start from the beginning. Why are you so sure he's alive?"

"Ben told you that Zach is terrified of the water," she said. "He'd never ride on that lake."

"The K-9 tracked him," Nikki said. "Plus the hat—"

"That hat was his father's." Caitlin's voice shook. "Zach loves that thing. He'd never leave it behind, and the hat wasn't wet. The dog tracked Zach to the end of the water, but could they tell if he was in the water? Because I know those K-9s aren't cadaver dogs trained to scent in the water."

"I'm honestly not sure," Nikki said. "And the handler may not have wanted to take the dog on the lake since the ice is so patchy."

"There's a witness," Caitlin said. "She lives down the road from Ben and Helen. When she heard the police were searching, she told Helen that she saw Zach on the snowmobile with another man. They were headed south, just like the dog tracked."

"I thought the witness saw Zach out riding alone, near the river, in the morning?" Nikki asked. "Is this the evidence you have?"

"That's a different neighbor, and Zach had to have been at least a quarter of a mile away from the river in order for her to see him."

"Is Braintree aware of this?"

"He said he knew the woman and that she's made false tips before. That might be, but she knows what she saw."

"What did the man look like?" Nikki asked.

"They were out in the field," Caitlin replied. "She basically saw two heads and body mass. The man was riding behind him. She said it looked like there was some kind of brown blanket or something with them. Braintree sent one of his deputies over to talk to her, and they said she had been drinking and her story wasn't reliable." Caitlin rummaged around in her designer bag and then held up a dog-eared letter. "I found this in Zach's room, hidden under his mattress. Ben and Helen don't know I took it."

Nikki started reading the typed letter, and her stomach immediately began to turn. The writer began by pointing out how happy they'd been to spend time with Zach and then pointed out how lousy it was that Zach didn't have a father.

I grew up without a dad, too. I didn't have anyone around to act like a father figure. I'm happy to do that for you.

"Someone was grooming him?" Nikki said. She'd read words like these before; it was exactly what grooming looked like. One of her first cases as a junior FBI agent had involved a child predator, and during the investigation, she'd gathered dozens of communications similar to the letter sent to Zach.

"By someone who knew how to stay off the radar," Caitlin said. "That's why the letter is typed, on plain paper. There's no visible trace. Read all of it."

The letter went on to talk about "watching videos" together and that it was part of "things a father should teach his son." It appeared that the writer was trying to convince Zach to watch adult videos with him, which was a typical trick of pedophiles, especially the ones who went after boys. It was an easy route to talking about various sex acts in an effort to normalize them before the pedophile made his physical assault.

"This is Zach's computer." Caitlin held up a slim Chromebook. "It's not password-protected. I've skimmed through it, and yes, he's visited porn sites. But nothing like what's on the videos the sender is talking about. If you want to go through it—"

Nikki took in a breath. "Zach lives with his grandparents, right?"

"Yes, but I'm his mother," Caitlin replied, looking confused.

The Caitlin that she knew was fully aware of police procedure and the law, but the desperate mother sitting next to her wasn't thinking clearly. "Technically, you don't have the right to give me permission to look at this. You told me you don't have custody of Zach."

"He's missing," Caitlin said, shocked.

"We have these rules for a reason. You know how defense lawyers can find every loophole. If someone did take him, any information from his computer could be deemed inadmissible because we didn't have permission to look through it."

"But you believe me," Caitlin said. "Right? Some creep targeted my son and then took him. It could be the same person who took Kellan and killed his mother."

"I can't talk about that case, but I have no evidence to suggest this is a similarity," Nikki said, forcefully. She needed Caitlin to understand that just because she wanted her son's disappearance taken seriously didn't mean that it was related to another boy's case. As popular as serial crimes were on television, they were statistically rare in the real world.

"Why not?" Caitlin held up her phone and pointed to the picture of a shyly smiling Zach. "Don't they look alike? Dark hair, dark eyes? And both of them experienced custody issues, meaning they were especially vulnerable."

"How old was Zach when his grandparents were granted custody?"

"Young," Caitlin said quietly. "He doesn't remember any of it, but he accidentally discovered it last month. He's been acting out."

"Um, hey." Rory's voice came out of nowhere. "I didn't know we'd have company."

Nikki was so engrossed in Caitlin that she hadn't even heard him come home. "Caitlin came to talk to me about Zach." She could tell that Rory was as shocked by Caitlin's unkempt appearance as she had been.

"He's my son," Caitlin said softly. "Don't tell anyone, please. But I know your family secrets, so it's only fair."

Nikki glanced at Rory, who watched Caitlin with a look of pity on his face. He cleared his throat. "Well, you look like you haven't eaten in a while." He held up a bag of groceries. "I was going to make pasta if you want to stay."

His kindness continuously overwhelmed Nikki. "That's a great idea."

"It doesn't feel right to do normal things," Caitlin said.

"You have to keep your strength up," Nikki said. "And having dinner with us isn't really normal."

Caitlin tried to smile, but her eyes filled with fresh tears. "I know it in my heart that he's alive, but every minute we don't find him…"

"Miller has deputies looking beyond the river. I'll call tonight and tell him everything you've told me so that he knows to keep searching. But Rory's right. You're exhausted, and you've been drinking. I think you should eat and then get a few hours of sleep."

"You can crash on the couch," Rory said. "I would say guest room, but it's more of a storage room right now."

"I won't be able to sleep unless I know you're going to help. You don't have to believe me right now. Just talk to Ben and Helen. Get the permission to look at his computer. If you just dig a little deeper, you'll find the truth. I know you will. And you can have this letter fingerprinted, right? Maybe this pervert's in the system."

"Yes, we'll have it printed as soon as we can." Nikki glanced at Rory. "I'll help you put away groceries." She followed him into the kitchen and threw her arms around his waist, burying her head between his shoulder blades. "You're a good man."

He pivoted in her arms and hugged her back. "She's so career-driven and single-minded. I can't imagine her as a mother," he said. "Do you think she's right about Zach?"

"About his being targeted, definitely. There's no doubt that this is significant evidence of that. Once Braintree finds out about it, he'll be forced to widen his investigation and consider the possibility that Zach has been taken. And he's already wasted a lot of time. If Zach was taken alive, the chance that he's still alive gets slimmer and slimmer with every passing second. I need to speak with him and Miller now."

CHAPTER TWENTY

It was still dark when Nikki woke up. She rolled over and searched for her phone. Nikki had left Braintree a message the previous evening, asking him to call her urgently. Then she'd called Miller and filled him in. "I didn't tell him what evidence we had in the message. He may not call me back."

"I'll call him, too," Miller had said. He'd promised to have his deputies ramp up their own search, and they arranged to meet at the Chisago sheriff's station in the morning, regardless of Braintree's response.

There were no messages from Braintree, but Miller had texted that his guys were on it.

Rory snored softly beside her, but she could hear Caitlin in the kitchen. Nikki slipped out of bed and walked quietly into the kitchen. She found Caitlin searching the cabinets.

"Did you sleep at all?" Nikki asked.

"Christ." She jumped. "I didn't hear you. Where does he keep the coffee?"

"Sit down and I'll make it."

Caitlin paced the kitchen while they waited for the coffee to brew. Nikki's eyelids felt heavy with sleep. Today was going to be another long day.

"How do you take your coffee?" she asked when it was finally ready.

"Black."

Nikki filled two cups and added cream and sugar to her own, and then placed one down in front of Caitlin before sitting in the chair Rory usually occupied. If she was going to help Caitlin, she wanted the truth from her, every single word of it. "So, start from the beginning," she said.

"Of what?" Caitlin replied. "Zach's life or mine?"

"Whichever you prefer," Nikki said. "If I'm going to investigate this case, I need to know everything."

Caitlin sighed. "I met Zach's father Teddy when I was sixteen. We both went to Chisago Lakes High School. He played football, and I was a cheerleader. He was a year older than me. It was love at first sight. He enlisted in the army before we found out I was pregnant. My parents were mad as hell, even though they didn't kick me out." She stared into her untouched coffee. "Teddy died a month after he was deployed to Afghanistan. Friendly fire. Zach wasn't even a year old."

"I'm so sorry." Nikki was finally beginning to understand Caitlin's near obsession with her journalism career. Like Nikki had done after her parents' murders, Caitlin had latched on to something she could control and blocked out everything else. Her drive came from bitter loss. The two of them weren't all that different after all.

"Thanks." She finally took a small sip of coffee. "My parents tried to help me, but they barely had enough money to support themselves. I worked a part-time job after Zach was born and took some community college classes, but I didn't have the time or money to get a real education. Zach's parents were devastated by his death. He was their only son." She sighed. "I was no good as a mom, Nikki. He was only six months old, and I didn't know anything about babies. And I was selfish. I hated Teddy for leaving me, and I just wanted to put it all behind me. When they asked to adopt him and raise him as theirs, I agreed. It was better for both of us, and I still believe that. I'm not mom material." She sounded like she was trying to convince herself as much as Nikki.

"That had to be an incredibly difficult decision." Nikki didn't point out that Zach's story didn't sound like a custody battle. It would only upset Caitlin and probably make her shut Nikki out. "How much were you in his life?"

"At first, as much as I could be, but then I found full-time work and started taking more classes. And my career took off. I saw him less and less. Up until a couple of months ago, he thought I was the cool family friend who brought him presents whenever she visited."

"How did he find out the truth?"

"He sent in his DNA to one of those sites. His grandfather—Ben—has Native American ancestry, and Zach's always been interested in genealogy and that sort of thing. But he also wanted to find out who his mother really was, so he took an autosomal test."

"Those are the kind that provide you with DNA within a few generations of your biological parents' sides of the family, right?" Nikki asked.

Caitlin nodded. "He'd been saving the money for the tests for two years. The results came back and matched him with my cousin and half my other family. My aunt's trying to trace our family history The match to my family members led him to me."

"His grandparents didn't know he sent in the kit?"

Caitlin shook her head. "The results came back, and then all hell broke loose. We tried to explain it to him, and he said he understood the choice to have them raise me, but not to keep it a secret. Why couldn't I have still been in his life as his mom, even if I had to come and go? We told him that it was because we decided it wouldn't be healthy for him to have a mom that wasn't there all the time. He believed his grandparents, but not me. He thinks I didn't want him, and that wasn't true at all. It *isn't* true. I love him, but I was so young and afraid. And selfish."

"Zach's been acting out ever since?"

"He's been angry all the time, according to Helen. Talks back, that sort of thing."

Nikki tried to think of a nice way to bring the topic up, but she couldn't. There was nothing nice about it. "I think we have to consider that it's possible he was mad and took the snowmobile without permission. He wouldn't be the first twelve-year-old to do so."

"No, but he doesn't like upsetting his grandfather. If he did take that snowmobile, it was because someone manipulated him into doing it. And there's no damn way he went on that river," Caitlin said. "He never learned how to swim. He likes to fish, but he won't go out on the boat. And he won't even consider going ice fishing with Ben, no matter how thick the ice cover is."

"I understand that." Nikki still thought all the stress Zach had been under could have affected his choices, but given the letter, it made sense that someone had talked him into taking the snowmobile and most likely meeting up with them. "I just want you to be prepared. If Zach was being abused amid all the other stuff, he might have made a rash decision about going on the river."

She could tell by Caitlin's expression that she hadn't considered something like that.

"Not the ice," Caitlin said. "Stealing the snowmobile for a joyride? Yes. But not over the ice."

"Have you told Liam that Zach is your son yet?"

Caitlin shook her head. "We're not serious. I don't even know if there is a real 'us.' I stay at his place sometimes, and he's been to my apartment once or twice. We haven't really discussed where things are going. I don't even know if I want them to go anywhere."

Nikki was struck by the similarities to her relationship with Rory. In that moment, she realized that she desperately wanted her own relationship to go somewhere. She wanted the real thing.

"If that man has him right now and is—" Caitlin shook her head. "I can't even say the word. Will you sit down with Ben and Helen?"

Braintree wasn't going to like it, but Nikki didn't have the heart to say no. "As soon as I'm back from the Cities."

"Why can't you do it sooner?" Caitlin asked.

Nikki sighed. "I'm still investigating a double homicide, Caitlin. I can ask Miller if he has time to go see them."

"No," Caitlin said. "I want you to do it."

"Why?"

"Because you're the best. You're the only person I trust—you know what law enforcement is like around here. What they did to you, the evidence they suppress just to solve a case as quickly as possible. I know you won't stop until you find my son."

CHAPTER TWENTY-ONE

Armed with a thermos of coffee, Nikki left Rory's house early to beat the rush-hour traffic into the metro area while Caitlin went to update the Reeves on the situation. The drive still seemed to take forever, and the morning radio shows were either over-the-top goofy or filled with political commentary. She turned on her classic rock playlist and tried to focus on her day ahead. Nikki would drop off the letter with Court and then meet Liam at the drug-testing facility where Ava Roe worked. Miller's guys were going to bring her brother Eddie into the station to question him about hitting Dana and his involvement in Maggie's forging the test results. Nikki had debated going to Eddie first, but if her hunch about his distrust of women was right, she needed to speak with Ava first. If she turned on Eddie, there was a good chance he'd crack when Nikki questioned him.

She glanced at the evidence bag sitting on the passenger seat. She flushed with shame. If she'd set her personal issues with Caitlin aside, she might have read her better and realized that she was a mother begging for help. She felt terrible that it had taken her this long to take her seriously.

Nikki didn't want to push the issue with Caitlin, but the family needed to understand that even if Zach had been targeted, he still could have drowned in the river. If he was being groomed, he might have made a rash decision and gone out on the ice himself. The letters she had read were manipulative, and Zach was so young. With her blinders off, Nikki had to admit there were similarities between Zach and Kellan, and child predators usually had a type.

Nikki had never heard of a single pedophile taking two boys in the same day, but it wasn't impossible. Still, Blanchard hadn't found any sign of sexual assault during Kellan's autopsy. They had to be dealing with two unrelated tragic events, but Nikki was determined to help Caitlin—the person grooming Zach could be a risk to more kids.

Nikki was so deep in thought, she almost missed her exit off the interstate into downtown Minneapolis and the FBI's main building. She flashed her credentials to the gate security and headed to the parking garage. As the head of her unit, Nikki had an assigned parking spot. Naturally, it was on the other side of the building from both the profiling offices and the lab.

Minnesota's FBI lab was every bit as impressive as anything Nikki had seen at Quantico. It spanned an entire floor and employed analysts capable of testing anything from DNA to code breaking. Ballistics had a wing to themselves, with the necessary soundproofed shooting range to run their tests. As the forensic program manager, Courtney was in charge of violent crime investigations in the lab and the primary evidence examiner. She ruled the division with an iron fist, making sure every person on her team followed the rules with precision. As a result, she'd never had evidence thrown out in court. She'd also earned the nickname Napoleon, but it was always apparent that everyone who worked under Courtney respected her.

Nikki scanned her badge to enter the lab. The sterile yet chemical smell always made her feel a little queasy, so she was glad she hadn't eaten that morning. Most of the stations in the forensic section were empty, and Nikki quickly learned why. Courtney was perched on a tall step stool conducting a morning meeting. She saw Nikki and motioned for her to wait in her office.

Courtney's tiny office was full of various equipment and research books, and its lack of windows made Nikki feel claustrophobic. She spied today's *Star-Tribune* and grabbed the paper to read while she waited.

Paper in hand, she sat in Courtney's comfortable desk chair. As usual, politics dominated the front page. Nikki skipped those articles and looked for local news. Miller had told her that Dana and Kellan's murders had been in Tuesday's paper, after Blanchard ruled both homicides. She didn't see any mention in today's edition, but there was a blurb about a twelve-year-old disappearing "on the St. Croix, presumed dead. Recovery mission ongoing." Nothing about the headline was wrong, but seeing Braintree's name irritated Nikki. He was exactly the sort of sheriff that made people distrust law enforcement.

She read another article.

On the twenty-five-year anniversary of his disappearance, David Webster is still missing, and police have no leads.

Nikki remembered eleven-year-old David Webster had been kidnapped in 1996. He'd been riding his bike on the way home from school. A friend had seen him turn the corner onto his street, but David never came home.

His parents had given a new interview about the loss of their son. All these years later, it still seemed as if he'd vanished into thin air. They still held out hope he was alive, and the article detailed their determination not to give up on him. The second part of the article included the age-progressed photo, along with David's last school picture.

He was slender, on the edge of puberty, with dark hair that fell into his eyes. He smirked more than smiled at the camera, clearly thinking he was too cool for a school picture. The age-progression photo mirrored the expression, but his face was generic enough that any number of men could have been considered a match.

"Sorry." Courtney entered the room. "We just upgraded our computer system, and it's a pain in the ass. I'm surrounded by brilliant people who can't figure out how to manage privacy settings. I see you're in my chair, again."

Nikki put the newspaper on the desk. She pointed to the chair meant for visitors. "That thing gives me a backache."

Courtney rolled her eyes. "I don't have great news for you. We aren't getting a decent print off the clothes. It's a partial. If I had something else to compare it to, we might make it work. But I don't think that's going to happen."

"Thanks for trying." Nikki stood, giving Courtney her chair. "I'm actually here about something else. Can you shut the door?"

Courtney's eyes lit up. She quickly shut the door. "What's up?"

"You've heard about the boy they think drowned on the river, right?"

Courtney nodded. "It's awful. I hope they find him for his family's sake."

"His grandfather called me yesterday because they think something else happened, and they have little faith in the Chisago sheriff. Miller and I went out to the dive sight, and as much as I don't like that sheriff, I didn't think he was wrong."

Courtney arched an eyebrow. "But you do now?"

"I don't know. Caitlin Newport showed up at Rory's last night with this." She handed her the evidence bag. "It's a letter from an adult who appears to be grooming Zach. Caitlin thinks he might have been taken by this person, and the police won't listen to her."

"Why is she involved?" Courtney said. "Is this her new crusade now that Mark's free?"

"Because she's Zach's mother."

Courtney's jaw dropped. "Say that again."

Nikki quickly explained what happened between Zach's parents and Caitlin's decision to let his grandparents raise him. "I can't imagine being in that situation. She's been in his life as a family friend, but he's a smart kid. Very into science. He used his Christmas money to purchase one of those DNA kits from a genealogy site. That's how he found out. He's been acting up ever since."

"Dang," Courtney said. "Caitlin isn't my favorite person, but that's awful."

"Could you rush fingerprints for me? I've told Braintree and Miller, but we've got to find the person who gave Zach this letter. He sounds experienced enough to be this brazen, so I'm hoping he's in the system somewhere."

"I'll have it today." Courtney eyed her. "Who knows about this?"

"Me, Rory, Caitlin, and Miller. She didn't tell the grandparents that she took it. She also took Zach's laptop, but I wouldn't let her open it in front of me. It's not password-protected, but I obviously can't just go snooping."

"You know the Chisago people are going to be mad as hell."

"Braintree already is," Nikki said. "Zach's grandfather was so upset, I couldn't tell him no. The sheriff made it clear he didn't appreciate or want me there. I didn't push the issue because Miller and I both agreed Zach probably drowned. Then Caitlin showed up with this. She didn't take it to the Chisago guys because she thinks Braintree will blow her off. He hasn't even returned my call."

"She's probably right," Courtney said. "I'll take care of this myself, today. No one else needs to know until after we get the results."

"Thanks. I promised Caitlin I'd follow through."

"I still can't believe she's a mother," Courtney said. "She must be going crazy right now."

"She's a mess. We had a good talk." Nikki checked her watch. "Don't say anything about her being Zach's mother, either. That's her story to tell. I've got to meet Liam at HPH and deal with the lab tech who falsified Dana's results. Call me as soon as you know anything."

CHAPTER TWENTY-TWO

HPH was located in an upscale business center in a picturesque part of the city. Nikki wouldn't have guessed that it was a lab if she didn't already know it. She parked next to Liam and they walked in together, the fatigue that had been weighing her down the past couple of days transformed into adrenaline. She wasn't going to leave here without answers.

The small lobby looked like any other, with gray carpet and several thriving house plants. Nikki admired a beautiful pink hibiscus next to the welcome counter. She'd never had much luck wintering perennials.

The thirty-something brunette behind the counter smiled warmly. "Can I help you?"

Nikki and Liam showed her their FBI badges and introduced themselves. "Is the associate director available?" he asked. "I spoke with her the other day."

"No, I'm afraid she's away at a conference. I can get our lab supervisor for you."

"Do they have access to office records?" Nikki asked.

"I believe so."

"That's fine."

The receptionist called down to the lab, speaking in tones so low that Nikki only caught part of her conversation. She pointed toward the locked double doors that must be the main lab entrance. "Sara's on her way."

Minutes later, a portly woman in a white lab coat emerged from the locked doors. She was attractive, if not a little plain. A black headband held her dark hair away from her face. "I'm Sara, the lab supervisor. May I help you?"

Nikki introduced herself and Liam. "Is there a place we can speak privately?"

"Yes, of course. What's this all about?"

"It's a sensitive matter." Nikki glanced at the receptionist, who was doing a poor job of pretending not to listen.

"All right, then. Come with me." Sara ushered them through the locked doors into a long corridor. A wall of windows to the right allowed a full view of the busy lab. She opened the second door on the left and led them into a small conference room and closed the door. "Now, please, what is going on?"

"I'll get straight to the point," Nikki said. "We think one of your employees in the lab is falsifying test results."

Sara stared at them as though they'd just presented her with evidence of aliens. "Excuse me?"

Nikki explained Maggie Anderson's confession about Ava and her brother.

"I just can't believe it. There's got to be another explanation."

Liam showed her the warrant. "We need to see Ava's records, starting with Dana Rhodes."

"You're really serious." Sara took the warrant. "I have to notify our medical director. My job is the nuts and bolts of the lab. He handles the big stuff."

"Take us to him."

They followed her to the end of the corridor to an open office door. Sara knocked softly, and the small man with incredible white hair and dark skin looked up in surprise. "Sara, is something wrong?"

"I'm afraid so, Dr. Bahri. These are FBI agents. They have a warrant for records." Sara wrung her hands together. "I'm sorry not to assist you, sir, but I've got the call with the state lab that I can't reschedule."

"Of course," he said. "Go on."

"Thank you."

Nikki touched Sara's shoulder. "The information can't leave this room."

"Of course not." She checked the Apple Watch on her left wrist. "Excuse me. I'm late for the meeting."

Liam shut the door behind her, and Dr. Bahri motioned for them to sit.

"I'm afraid I need you to start from the beginning."

"Ava Roe still works here, right?"

Dr. Bahri nodded. "She's one of my best technicians. Always willing to work overtime."

"We think she's falsifying test results." Nikki repeated the information she'd already given to the lab supervisor.

"No, no. You must be mistaken. Ava would never do something like that."

"With all due respect, Doctor," Liam said, "Maggie Anderson had no reason to lie about this and risk going to jail. We know the court reporter assigned to the judge who oversaw Kellan's custody case is related to Ava." He explained how they'd tracked Ava through Eddie's social media profile.

Dr. Bahri sat back in his chair, shellshocked. "I just can't believe she would do such a thing."

"You have access to the patient records, I assume?"

"Yes, yes." He took the reading glasses out of his pocket and slipped them on. He sat up straight to access the computer. "What's the name in question?"

"Dana Rhodes."

His fingers flew across the keyboard. Nikki knew the moment he found the record.

"Ava was the lab tech who performed the test?" she asked.

"Yes." He took his glasses off and tossed them onto the desk. "There has to be some other explanation. I would like to ask Ava myself."

"Would it be possible for you to bring her into your office without telling her why or that we're here?"

"Why?"

"Agent Hunt believes the best way to get the truth out of the suspect is the element of surprise," Liam said. "She's usually right."

Bahri nodded and reached for his phone. "Could you please send Ava to my office? Thank you."

A few minutes later, a stocky, dark-haired woman knocked on the door. Nikki immediately saw the resemblance to her brother. Ava had a round face with dark eyes that made her look deceptively innocent. "Dr. Bahri, you wanted to see me?"

"Please come in and close the door."

Ava did as he asked, sitting down in the seat Liam had vacated. She primly crossed her legs, folding her hands in her lap. "What did you need?"

Bahri's grave expression had to have tipped her off that something bad was going to happen, but she barely seemed aware of him. Her gaze flashed between Nikki and Liam, who'd moved to stand against the wall.

"Do I know you?" Ava looked at Nikki. "You seem familiar?"

Nikki held up her badge. "Special Agent Nikki Hunt."

Ava's voice was steady as she snapped her fingers, but the sweat on her hairline betrayed her nerves. "That's it. I've seen you on TV. What's going on?"

"Agent Wilson and I are working a murder case," Nikki said. "Dana Rhodes and her son, Kellan. You might have heard about them on the news."

"I try not to watch much news," Ava said. "It's too depressing."

"Well, Dana Rhodes had a court-ordered drug test performed in this lab several weeks ago. According to Dr. Bahri's records, you were the technician."

"OK." Ava stiffened. "I'm sure you know we do a lot of tests here. I don't remember that one specifically."

"Are you sure?" Nikki asked. "Because Maggie Anderson told us your brother Eddie arranged for her to pay you $5000 to make sure Dana's test results came out positive."

Ava choked out a laugh. "You're kidding, right?"

Nikki reminded her of the date that Dana gave the sample. "You performed the test. Dr. Bahri confirmed that."

"I'm not saying I didn't perform the test, but I don't know any Maggie Anderson, and I would never do such a thing."

"We know Eddie does the legwork," Nikki said. "He's with police right now telling his side of the story."

Ava remained stone-faced. "I don't know what you're talking about. If Eddie's into something—"

"We have a warrant for every test result you've signed off on in the time you've been here," Liam said. "It won't be hard to find out if others make the same accusation."

"If you cooperate with us, we can ask the district attorney to consider that when the charges are brought," Nikki added. "And rest assured, you and your brother will be charged."

Ava looked at Dr. Bahri. "Please, sir. I would never do such a thing."

Dr. Bahri spoke sternly. "These are incredibly serious accusations. And these agents wouldn't be wasting their time if they didn't believe they were true. I suggest you cooperate in any way possible."

She stared at him, shaking her head. "This is preposterous. I want a lawyer."

"You aren't under arrest. Yet," Liam said.

"I know my rights. I'm not saying anything else without a lawyer. HPH has to provide me with one, because I work for them. You're accusing them as well."

Nikki didn't miss the challenge in the woman's tone. "That's fine. But you're going to sit right here with Agent Wilson while my forensic people come in here and tear your life apart in front of your colleagues. That means every test you've done and anything else in this lab you may have been a part of. Then we move on to your apartment."

"You can't do that."

Nikki slapped the signed warrant onto the desk. "We can, and we will. I'm heading to speak with your brother right now. I'll tell him you said hello."

Nikki rose to leave. "Liam, call me when you're ready to arrest her."

"Wait." Sweat beaded across Ava's forehead. "If I wanted to talk about… anything… the district attorney would go easy on me?"

"I can't guarantee it," Nikki said. "But this is your only chance at any sort of leniency. You committed fraud and forgery at the very least. Not to mention the inevitable civil lawsuits from people you screwed. Then there's the murder charge."

"Murder?" Ava stared at them in horror. "I'm not a violent person."

"People don't realize what they're capable of until their freedom's on the line," Nikki said. "We know that Dana Rhodes was going to hire a private investigator to prove the drug test had been falsified. Her sister warned Eddie about the accusation. Now Dana and her son are dead. You're the one who works at the lab and has the most to lose. See where I'm going with this?"

Ava's eyes were wide, her olive skin ashy. "I didn't hurt anyone. I'm just trying to fix a screwed-up system. Eddie's the dangerous one."

Nikki sat back down and opened the voice memo app on her phone, gesturing to Ava to continue. She was finally cracking.

"Eddie and I are half-siblings," Ava said. "Same mom, different dads. Our mother was an addict and the state took us away. But we kept going back because she'd get clean for the court. Then it started all over again. She prostituted herself for drug money. The only reason we had food is because a couple of her 'clients' felt sorry for us. When Eddie was seventeen, he got a job and moved out. I went with him. Finished school and got a scholarship. We vowed to help kids like us. That's why Eddie went into the legal system. He wanted to be an attorney, but school was never his strong suit."

"When did the test tampering start?"

"About a year ago," Ava said. "Eddie worked in family court, and he just kept seeing the same kids come through and bounce between foster parents and their real parents who couldn't stay clean. It's not right."

"The system isn't perfect," Nikki agreed. "But that doesn't mean you can play God with people's lives. How did you guys come up with the idea?"

"It was Eddie's idea. I didn't want to, but he wouldn't stop pushing. I finally gave in, but he had to make sure the person was a repeat offender with lousy odds to stay clean. I wasn't going to do it unless the case was extreme. But Eddie kept making me do more and more."

"He made you?" Liam asked.

Ava pulled a tissue out of her lab coat pocket. "He's so bitter. And he's scary when he's angry."

"He threatened you?" Nikki asked.

Ava nodded. "Not at first, but then it kind of became an obsession with him. One night we got in a huge fight and he grabbed my arms. He shook me so hard, I messed up my neck and had bad bruises."

Nikki studied the woman. Her crossed arms and legs made her look defensive, and she looked everywhere but at Nikki. "Eddie couldn't exactly come into the lab and hold a gun to your head."

"That's what I thought, so I decided not to go through with one test. That's when the fight happened." Ava rubbed at her mascara. "Eddie's not all bad, though. He just suffered so much when we were kids. He wants to make sure other kids don't experience the same thing. He begged me to forgive him and keep helping, so I did."

"If you're doing this to help kids, why charge five grand?" Liam asked.

"We don't. At least I don't. He said he brought me the worst cases only. He never said he was taking money."

"What did he tell you about Dana Rhodes?"

"That she was one of the worst he'd seen. Constantly in and out of rehab and being pitied by the judge."

"He lied, then," Nikki said. "She was clean for twelve months until you forged her test. Her sister paid Eddie, and Dana lost custody for good. Now she and her little boy are dead."

"I swear I had nothing to do with that," Ava insisted, sweat glistening on her forehead. "I thought I remembered her name when I saw it on the news. That happened last Friday, right? At least that's when the kid went missing?"

Nikki nodded. "I suppose you have an alibi."

"I do," Ava said fervently. "I was in Michigan at a toxicology conference. HPH sent me."

"That is true." Dr. Bahri finally spoke. He'd been sitting in quiet disgust for the past several minutes. "Ava attended all the sessions. She flew home Monday morning and turned in the receipts to human resources."

"Convenient weekend to be away at a conference," Liam said. "I guess Eddie wanted to handle the dirty work on his own."

"That's not true." Ava looked at the doctor. "I didn't want to go to the conference. Dr. Bahri said I had to."

"Again, that's true." The doctor nodded. "Ava was very resistant."

"Fine, you have an alibi. That doesn't mean you didn't know what your brother was going to do."

"No way. Eddie wouldn't hurt a child. He's not like that. He cares too much."

"Even if that means spending years in prison for fraud and other felonies?"

Ava nodded emphatically. "He'd go to jail before he hurt a kid."

"Do you know where your brother was last weekend?"

"Home. He just moved into a new place not far from his work."

Nikki double-checked the address. "The Bryer Lofts. Expensive place. Guess we know how he paid for it. Does he own any weapons?"

"I don't know," Ava said. "He collects stuff, but nothing that could really hurt anyone. He does have one of those kickboxing kits, but that's just for exercising."

Liam cleared his throat. "Agent Hunt, can I talk to you for a second?"

Nikki grabbed her bag. "We'll be right back."

She and Liam walked out into the hall.

"What's up?"

"Courtney's going crazy trying to call you. She says it's urgent, about the thing from this morning."

Nikki dug into her bag. Sure enough, there were four missed calls from Courtney and a text saying, *Results huge. Call back.* "I didn't realize it was on silent."

Courtney answered immediately. "Finally."

Nikki's pulse raced. She could tell by the tone of her voice that Courtney was amped up by her results. "Did you get a hit in AFIS?"

"You're never going to believe it." Courtney talked so fast, Nikki barely understood her. "Nikki, the prints from that letter to Zach match the ones police managed to get from a cold case. David Webster. The prints were found on his bike after he was taken."

Nikki braced against the wall for support. "You're absolutely certain?"

"I ran it three times," she said. "David rode a ten-speed bike. The print was on the bar that extends from underneath the seat down to the back wheel. Police believe David must not have been riding fast and his kidnapper snuck up on him from behind, grabbed the bike and then snatched him somehow."

"Email me everything. Miller and I will deal with the Chisago guys. And keep this between us for now." She ended the call, her legs weak.

"What's going on?" Liam asked.

Nikki told him about Caitlin's visit and the letter. "I honestly didn't think we'd get a hit. I've been so focused on talking to Ava, I didn't get a chance to tell you before."

"So you're telling me that whoever gave Zach this letter is the same person who snatched David Webster? The kid who vanished without a trace twenty-five years ago?"

Nikki nodded. "Suddenly staging Zach's drowning in the river doesn't seem so far-fetched, does it? Who knows what this person has been doing all of these years? Probably hurting dozens of kids." Jesus, had Nikki's refusal to listen to Caitlin cost Zach his life? Was he being held somewhere, hurt and terrified, because of Nikki?

"Listen, I need to tell you something about Caitlin."

Nikki realized that Liam still didn't know Caitlin was Zach's mother. "I already know the two of you are seeing each other," Nikki said. "You need to talk to her as soon as possible."

A grunt came from behind her, followed by a look of horror on Liam's face. "Jesus, Dr. Bahri."

Nikki turned to see Dr. Bahri in the hallway with a small switchblade stuck in his neck, blood running down his shirt.

Liam reached the doctor first, putting pressure on the wound.

"Out the window," Dr. Bahri gasped. "She's out the window."

"Christ." Nikki grabbed her gun out of her bag and raced toward the doctor's office. "Liam, call an ambulance and then get some backup here."

CHAPTER TWENTY-THREE

Heart pounding, Nikki leaned out of the open window as far as possible. The doctor's office was in the back of the building, and there was about half an acre of open land between this building and the next. Between the snow and the wide space, Ava should have been easy to find, but she was nowhere in sight.

Had she gone into one of the other buildings? And then what? Pretended she needed to use the phone? Given Dr. Bahri's injury, Ava had to have blood on her. Would she risk being stopped by security?

Nikki could hear Liam talking to the police and went back into the hall. A dark-haired man in a lab coat and an office worker were frantically trying to stop the bleeding.

"Where's the employee parking?" Nikki asked the woman closest to her. "And what kind of car does Ava drive?"

"It's the west side of the lot. I don't know exactly. It's blue and has a bunch of things dangling from the rearview mirror."

"Liam, tell the police I'm going to check the car right now." She looked at the woman. "We need access to all security videos from today."

Nikki tucked her gun into the back of her pants and ran past the locked lab and the front office. Outside the main entrance, she paused to get her bearings and then raced to the west parking lot. The trinkets on the rearview mirror made Ava's car easy to spot. She didn't see Ava anywhere, but she could be hiding behind one of the vehicles. Nikki retrieved her gun and slowly approached. She wished she'd worn a vest. If Ava kept a gun in the car, she'd had enough time to get it and find a place to hide. Nikki crouched low, looking beneath the cars. She didn't see anyone hiding, but she still had to clear Ava's car. Gun ready, she stayed low and slowly approached.

Her cell vibrated from her back pocket. She ducked behind another car and checked the message.

Her keys are here.

Nikki's shoulders sagged in relief, but she wasn't going to fully drop her guard. Ava's Nissan was a newer model and could have keyless entry. She crept forward and peeked in the window. Ava wasn't in the car, and the heavy winter coat and boots in the back made Nikki think she'd not made it this far.

She crossed the parking lot and circled the building. Bahri's window was still open, and the open area behind the building had no real places to hide. Nikki walked over to the window, trying to see if Ava had left any sort of tracks, but the sun had burned off any precipitation on the frozen ground.

Her phone vibrated, this time with a call from Miller.

"We've got a problem."

"No shit." Nikki cradled the phone against her shoulder. "Ava attacked her boss and took off. She doesn't have her car keys or bag, so she can't be far."

"Eddie had the day off," Miller said. "By the time my guys got to his apartment, he was gone. Could she have tipped him off?"

"I don't know when. She didn't have her cell phone, and the only people Liam and I told were the medical director and the lab supervisor." She stopped cold. "Damnit. I'll call you back."

She immediately called Liam and told him about Eddie's disappearing act. "We need everything you have on Sara. She had to have tipped Ava off before she even came into the room." Nikki scanned the parking lot. "What does she drive?"

Liam's voice was muffled for a few seconds. "A red minivan."

"It's not here. She must have picked Ava up, damnit. Make sure we get all of the security videos, and I want to talk to everyone in the lab. How's the doctor?"

"We have the bleeding stopped, but the ambulance needs to get here now."

"I'm going to circle the building one more time and then I'll be back inside."

She shoved her phone in her pocket and started walking. Uneasiness shivered down her spine. The area seemed strangely quiet, as though much of the nearby traffic had come to a halt. The sun had started to peek out from the heavy cloud cover, but Nikki didn't register the shadow until it was too late. She started to raise her gun, but a hard object hit her in the back, and an electric current locked her muscles in place. She hit the soft ground with a thud, the gun slamming her diaphragm. Her bones felt like they'd been lit on fire, and her legs and arms refused to move. A man chuckled, and then a pair of thick hiking boots were in front of her. Nikki tried to block the kick, but her arms wouldn't cooperate. Pain shot through her head and down her spine. She heard another laugh and then the sound of someone walking away.

"Stop," Nikki gasped. Assuming who it was, she made an attempt to distract them. "Eddie, your sister told me this was all your idea, that you bullied her into it."

Nikki heard him moving back toward her, his boots sloshing in the wet snow. A large hand grabbed her hair and pulled her head up from the ground.

"My sister would never do that."

"She did." Nikki's vision was still hazy, but she could see Eddie's hulking form hovering over her. "She also said you talked about taking care of Dana Rhodes."

His boot slammed into her ribs. "You're a liar, just like every other person with a shred of authority."

Her arm muscles started to relax, and then her legs. He kicked her head again, and Nikki's head swam. She tried to get her wits, shifting to see him walking away. He was average height and wore a black hoodie just as Dana's neighbor had described. Dazed, she could make out some kind of car parked on the street.

Nikki caught her breath and rolled over, fighting not to cry out from the pain. She had a clear shot, but her vision was still blurry. She shook her head, trying to see straight enough to shoot without hitting an innocent person.

Finally, her vision cleared for a second. She aimed and fired. The man's legs buckled, but he was able to drag himself to the waiting car. He got into the passenger seat and the car sped off before he shut the door.

Nikki managed to get on all fours and then find her cell phone. Her ears were ringing, but she could hear the ambulance wailing down the street.

Someone ran toward her, moving quickly. Nikki saw only a smear of colors. She raised her gun. "Stop or I'll shoot."

"It's me." Liam knelt beside her, his hand on her back. "Where are you hurt?"

"Fine. Black Mustang. They left in a black Mustang. It looked like the ones from high school." Her tongue felt thick, and her stomach rolled. "Nineties model. Six cylinder, not an eight."

"How do you know that?"

"Only one exhaust pipe. Eight cylinders always have two exhaust pipes. My dad taught me that."

CHAPTER TWENTY-FOUR

Nikki winced as she pressed the ice pack on her head. The ambulance had just left with Dr. Bahri, and she'd managed to regain normal vision. She and Liam were sitting in the lobby of HPH, with Liam barking orders to both the Minneapolis and Saint Paul police. He'd already called the state troopers and put out an APB for the Mustang and Sara's red minivan.

"Police are getting all the traffic camera footage they can and setting up roadblocks. They won't get far."

Nikki drained the cup of water someone had given her. "Send a unit to both Ava's and Eddie's apartments. I want our forensic people on it. What do we know about Sara?"

"Just relax." Liam handed her another cup of water. "The paramedics said you could have a concussion. I want you to go to the hospital."

"Give me some aspirin and I'll be fine." Every muscle in her body ached, but Nikki wasn't about to sit around with three suspects on the run.

"Nikki—"

"Please," she said. "I promise you if I feel worse or throw up, I will go. I'm not leaving right now."

"You're not driving, either."

"Let's argue about that later. Do we have HPH's security videos pulled up?"

Liam sighed. "Yes."

Nikki got to her feet and willed herself not to sway. "Let's go." She glanced at the lab as they passed. The secured door had been propped open, and two uniformed police officers had corralled everyone inside. The employees were white-faced and talking over each other. "Make sure you interview those people. I want firsthand, not filtered."

They passed a woman in a neat suit talking frantically on a phone. "They said Dr. Bahri should be fine. But we need you back here."

Liam answered Nikki's question before she could ask it. "That's the lab's administrative director. She worked under Sara, I guess. She's talking to the associate medical director. This is human resources." He held the door open for Nikki.

She could see the small staff looked as shaken as everyone else.

Nikki tried to sound like she didn't feel like a Mack truck had run her over. "We need to see the security videos."

A young woman waved from the corner. "I already have them pulled up."

Nikki had intended to stand, but Liam pulled out an office chair and looked pointedly at it. She hurt too much to remind him that she was the boss.

"Thank you for getting these so quickly," Liam said.

"No problem. I'm just glad I could help. I can't believe this."

Nikki could see several videos cued up. "Could you play them in order, please?"

"Absolutely."

They watched in silence as a video from the lab camera showed Ava picking up the phone and then going still. She nodded twice and then said something Nikki couldn't make out. She unlocked her top desk drawer and casually glanced around before slipping the switchblade into her lab pocket. She started to bring her cell phone and then changed her mind, grabbing some cash from her large bag.

"She intended to run," Liam said. "She didn't take her cell so we couldn't track her."

"Where's that bag?" Nikki asked.

"We have it," Liam replied. "I had the front desk clerk put everything of Ava's in the safe."

Nikki gave him a thumbs up. Her jaw hurt every time she opened her mouth.

"We checked the parking lot security video." A slim woman with dark glasses looked up from her computer. "Sara's minivan left about five minutes after you two arrived."

Nikki ground her teeth and immediately regretted it as a new round of pain rippled across her shoulders. "We just let her take off."

"This is the hallway by Dr. Bahri's office," the tech girl said.

Ava seemed to steel herself before she entered Bahri's office.

The tech clicked on another video. "This is outside, to our left. You can see her ditch her lab coat and run."

"To her brother, who was waiting," Liam said. "How close does he live?"

"At least forty-five minutes away this time of day." Nikki checked her watch. "Ava and Sara wouldn't have had time to tip him off."

A throat cleared behind them. Nikki realized the entire human resources staff was watching in fascination.

The front desk clerk stepped forward.

"I heard Agent Wilson mention 'Eddie.' Sara's dating a man named Eddie. No one's met him, but she talks about him a lot."

"How far away does she live?"

"Uhh…" Liam checked his notes. "About ten minutes from here. I've got police heading there now. Sara tipped him off, just like she did Ava. They probably had some kind of contingency plan," Liam said.

"Did you check on the Mustang?" Nikki asked.

"It's Eddie's," Liam said. "And it stands out like a sore thumb. Every cop in town has the information. They'll stop them."

"Did you see how Ava started to take her cell and then changed her mind?" Nikki asked.

"Yep. She didn't want us tracking her. Ava lives in Eden Prairie. I have a unit heading there, and Miller's guys are at Eddie's place."

"Good. You and I need to talk to everyone in the lab, and I want to get a look inside Ava's bag."

She also needed to find out who was currently handling the David Webster case—if it wasn't completely cold—and let them know about the print match.

Nikki and Liam spent the next two hours scouring Ava's records and personal life. Police had been dispatched to all three apartments. Eddie's appeared untouched, but it was obvious that someone went through both women's apartments, likely snatching up all the cash and anything valuable. It had to have been Eddie. He'd probably been staying at Sara's when she called and warned him. Her red minivan had been found in Sara's usual spot at her apartment complex, but there was no sign of Sara and no indication of where she'd gone.

Liam and Miller both wanted Nikki to stay off the road for the night, but she insisted that her head was fine. She couldn't just go home and pretend their two best suspects weren't on the run.

Her cell phone rang with Tyler's number.

Nikki sighed and answered impatiently. "Hey, this isn't a good time."

"Are you in town? Or close?"

Nikki's heart skipped a beat. "Why? Is Lacey OK?"

"She's fine, but she got into a fight at school," Tyler said. "She's been crying and asking for you. I can't get her to come out of her room."

Nikki sagged against the seat. She didn't want to leave the case, and she needed to talk to Braintree. And Lacey would be upset when she saw that Nikki was hurt. But she would be even more upset if Nikki didn't come see her.

"Tell her I'm on my way." Nikki searched the small office for her bag. "Lacey needs me. I'll meet up with you later. Text me if anything changes."

Tyler lived in a two-bedroom townhouse not far from Nikki's place, but the drive from HPH took more than thirty minutes thanks to rush-hour traffic. Even though she knew that Lacey was physically fine, the thought of her locked in her room, crying for her mom, made Nikki's heart ache. She should have stayed in town the other night instead of going back to Rory's and spent time with Lacey, and she felt terrible for that.

Nikki parked on the street and searched the back seat for the change of clothes and toiletries she kept in the jeep in case she ended up stuck in the office or on a case. She grabbed the bag and hurried up the sidewalk.

"Ouch." Her right side ached from the kick to the ribs. She probably had a lovely bruise by now, but at least nothing was broken.

"Mommy!' Lacey's screech filled the air. She waved furiously at Nikki from the second-floor balcony. "Daddy, Mommy's here."

"Hi, baby. Daddy said you were missing me, so I came right over."

Lacey disappeared, and a second later, the front door flew open. Lacey raced to Nikki and threw her arms around her waist.

Nikki gritted her teeth in pain but held her daughter close. Lacey smiled up at her, a fresh Kool-Aid stain on her mouth.

Nikki searched her face for signs of a crying fit, but her skin was as porcelain as ever. Her eyes sparkled with their usual excitement, and she certainly didn't sound like she'd been crying. "Where's Daddy?"

"Right here." Tyler leaned against the doorframe, still in his suit, his tie loose. "Thanks for coming."

Nikki worked to keep her expression and tone neutral for Lacey's sake. "I'm glad to see she's out of her room."

Tyler looked down at his shoes and rubbed the back of his neck, his tell-tale sign that he'd been caught in a lie.

Lacey grabbed her hand. "Mommy, come see my new drawing. It's a unicorn with butterflies. We're still doing the butterfly garden, right?"

"Yes." Nikki leaned down and kissed the top of her daughter's head. "Why don't you go on inside and get your art supplies, and we'll draw a picture together. I just need to talk to Daddy for a minute."

"OK." Lacey skipped off, singing something off-key.

Tyler shut the door behind Lacey. "Are you all right? You're walking like you're in pain."

"I am." Nikki rolled her neck from side to side. "Getting tased really sucks."

"Jesus, Nik. What the hell happened?"

"I'm fine. We need to talk."

He sighed. "Listen, Nik, about yesterday. I was out of line. I'm sorry."

"Yes, you were, and I accept your apology. But calling me and saying that Lacey is upset just to get me over here is way over the line."

Tyler looked surprised. "I know, but it wasn't a lie," he said. "She did get in a fight at school. She has to spend recess inside for three days. I told her we couldn't go ice skating tonight because she'd got in trouble, and she went into her room, crying. She did ask for you."

Nikki crossed her arms over her chest. "That's a little different than what you told me over the phone."

"I was afraid you wouldn't come."

"And disappoint Lacey, or you?"

"Both." Tyler flushed. "I guess the idea of you seeing someone else has really thrown me for a loop."

"That's fair," Nikki said. "But you and I have always been honest with each other, especially about Lacey. You can't do this again. And you need to accept that I'm going to see other people, and that you should, too. Before you ask, I don't know how serious it is, and I probably wouldn't tell you if I did. I haven't introduced Lacey yet, and when I decide to do so, I will be sure to tell you."

"Guess that's all I can ask for." He gestured toward her bag. "Are you staying?"

"No," she said. "I've got to get back to the team. We have two suspects on the run. I won't leave straight away, it will be too hard for Lacey, but I can't stay long."

Nikki found Lacey in her room, art supplies spread over her big desk and most of the floor. "What's this about you getting into a fight at school, bug?"

"Gavin said that my butterfly garden was stupid and that he hoped all of them died before they came out of the cocoon. I knocked him down and told him to mind his own business." She said it so matter-of-factly that Nikki almost laughed.

"He wasn't very nice to say that, but you can't go around fighting with people who say mean things. You have to be better than that and not let them bother you."

"But why are people so mean? I don't say mean things to people."

Nikki ruffled her wavy hair. "You're a happy little girl. But some kids aren't very happy, and they take it out on other kids."

"Why aren't they happy?"

"Lots of reasons. Just remember that everyone is going through something, and we don't always know what it is. The best thing to do is be compassionate. Can you do that?"

Lacey nodded. "I think so. As long as Gavin doesn't say anything about my bugs."

An hour later, Nikki and Lacey had filled half her sketchbook with unicorns, butterflies, and letters. Lacey was an advanced reader and writer, and she loved making up her own stories. Tyler made spaghetti, and Lacey begged her to stay and eat. Nikki's stomach growled with hunger, so she relented. Lacey dominated the conversation, chattering about her day and kids at school. Nikki was happy to listen and not worry about saying the wrong thing to Tyler.

"Mommy, your phone's blinking."

Nikki went to the counter, her stomach dropping. She'd forgotten to call Rory. "I have to take this call. I'll be right back."

By the time she reached Lacey's room, the phone had stopped ringing. Nikki called Rory back, anxiety rolling through her.

"Hey," he said. "I texted you a couple of times to see when you'd be home. I'm thinking about firing up the grill and making steaks."

"Isn't your grill covered with snow?"

"I'll clean it off and then pull it up to the deck door. We can finally sit down and talk about everything. When do you think you'll be home?"

Fresh butterflies erupted in her stomach at the word "home." Rory's house definitely felt more like home than Tyler's, and she missed him on the nights they were apart. But after the last few days, she hadn't expected him to sound so eager to see her.

She cleared her throat. "Actually, I need to stay in Saint Paul tonight."

"Oh. Everything OK?"

"Yes," she said. "Things got a little crazy today and we had two suspects run on us. I… uh… one of them tased me—"

"What?" Worry filled his voice. "Are you all right?"

"I'm fine. Just sore. Tyler called in the middle of it and said Lacey needed me, so I rushed over here."

There was a beat of silence. "You're at his place, then?"

"Well, yes. Lacey's staying with him while I'm working this case."

"Are you going to sleep there?"

The hurt in his voice made Nikki feel like a jerk. "I'm going back to the office as soon as I finish eating."

"OK." His voice sounded strained. "I'll put these steaks back in the refrigerator then."

"Are you OK?"

"Sure," he said. "I wish you would have kept me in the loop."

"It was hectic. We've got three people on the run, and there's a good chance one of them killed Dana and Kellan. I also have a lead on Caitlin's information."

"Right, I know. You gotta do your job."

"I'm sorry I didn't think to call you."

"It's cool." He didn't sound like he thought it was cool. His voice sounded strained. "You have to put other people first."

"I know that's part of our issue, and we do need to talk about things. I'm back in town in the morning," Nikki said. "I'll check in as soon as I can. Maybe I can stop by your job site—"

"Not tomorrow. It's going to be too hectic." He emphasized the last word.

Nikki sighed. A beep signaled Rory had hung up and a lump formed in Nikki's throat. She understood why he would be hurt that she'd forgotten to call, but he was being petty.

Nikki checked in with Liam, who told her they had roadblocks set up on all the major intersections and interstates. Minneapolis and Saint Paul had joined the search effort, along with the state police. Liam also had the name of the agent in charge of the unsolved Webster case and had left him a message to call Nikki as soon as possible.

"Seriously, boss," Liam said. "Rest. I'll call you when things start moving."

CHAPTER TWENTY-FIVE

Someone was shaking her shoulder. Nikki had been sleeping hard, caught in a montage of inexplicable dreams. Dana's face in death haunted Nikki, as though she were reaching out and trying to tell her something vital. What was she missing?

She pushed away the hand. "Rory, I need to sleep."

The hand stilled. "Nikki. Wake up."

Was that Tyler? She peeled her eyes open and found herself staring up at her ex-husband. For a second, she had no idea how she'd gotten to his place or wound up snuggled against her sleeping daughter.

"What time is it?"

"Almost 5 a.m. Liam's been trying to call you. He says it's urgent." Tyler's voice was tight with hurt. "Rory? That's Mark Todd's brother, right?"

It took her a few seconds to figure out why she was at Tyler's house and why he was asking about Rory. Tyler stood next to the bed, staring down at her with hurt and disappointment in his eyes.

Nikki slipped her arm from underneath Lacey's and carefully eased out of the bed so she didn't wake her daughter. Her head ached. "I'm not doing this right now, Tyler."

"Fine, but when this case is over, we need to talk." He turned on his heel and walked out.

Nikki swallowed back her retort and reached for her cell. She'd left it charging in the kitchen. Miller had texted her that Braintree wasn't responding to calls and they'd have to deal with him in person. Liam had called four times in the last fifteen minutes.

Mustang found. Call me.

Nikki hoped that Eddie and the others hadn't managed to ditch the vehicle and find a way into Canada.

"I'm sorry to wake you up," Liam said as soon as Nikki answered the phone. "But this can't wait."

"Please tell me you found at least one of them with the car?" she asked.

"They're holed up in a motel northeast of the Cities, right off the I-10. We've had eyes on them for the past hour, and they haven't left the room. I have a SWAT team ready, but I knew you'd want to be here."

Nikki was already on her feet. "I can be there in thirty minutes, but if something changes and you think you need to go in, don't wait for me."

She hung up and then tiptoed around Lacey's room, grabbing her overnight bag and shoes. Nikki took a couple of aspirin for her head and then quickly brushed her teeth and yanked on the jeans and sweatshirt she kept in the bag. She found Tyler in the kitchen, making coffee.

"Let Lacey sleep," Nikki said. "Tell her I got called in and I will talk to her later. And tell her I love her."

He handed her a travel coffee cup without looking at her. "I will. You'll need this. Be careful."

"Thank you." Nikki didn't want to leave things like this between them, but she wanted to help Liam. And destroy Eddie. "I'll text you later."

The melting that had begun yesterday had frozen overnight, leaving everything crystallized. Nikki plugged the address into her GPS and left without bothering to let the jeep's engine warm up. The leather seats were still cold, and she could see her breath in the air. At least she would beat the worst of the rush-hour traffic.

Nikki drank the coffee quickly, feeling a pang of sadness. Tyler still knew how to make her coffee exactly how she liked it. Rory teased her about the sugar.

"Focus on this raid," she said out loud. "Deal with everything else later."

The I-10 wasn't as empty as she'd hoped, but she still managed to make good time. She spied her exit and signaled to get in the right lane. Traffic backed up on the exit ramp. From her vantage point, Nikki could see the dentist's office on one side of the intersection where Liam had set up the briefing area, out of sight from the motel across the street. Nikki looked for the Mustang, but the morning sun glinting off the snow made it impossible to distinguish between vehicles.

Suddenly, a woman raced through the motel parking lot, dodging parked cars, chased by a large figure Nikki recognized as Eddie. They were running straight for the busy intersection.

Nikki laid on her horn, trying to get Liam and his team's attention, and then took her badge and gun out of the glove compartment. She jammed the magazine in, turned on her flashers and got out of the car. She held up her badge, motioning for traffic to stop, but rush hour had arrived and drivers were so caught up in their morning commute that most still sped by.

Ava had made it to the intersection. She looked frantically between Nikki and Eddie, who was less than ten yards from her. Ava quickly glanced at the slowing traffic and then darted into the road. She made it across the southbound. Nikki had managed to get the northbound traffic to stop and motioned for Ava to run now.

She didn't see the man who dipped onto the shoulder until it was too late. His car struck Ava's body, and she hit the windshield before tumbling down the hood onto the road. The driver stared with wide eyes, cell phone in his hand. Another driver was out of his car. He waved at Nikki. "I called 9-1-1."

Nikki hurried toward Ava, who was bleeding. In her peripheral vision, she saw Liam and the SWAT team racing toward them. Nikki reached Ava first, but Eddie was only seconds behind her.

Ava's eyelids fluttered, and her pulse was weak. Nikki could tell that her leg was broken, and she likely had internal injuries. Her face also had a bruise tinged with yellow that hadn't been there yesterday.

"Ava?" Eddie started to grab her shoulders, but Nikki caught his arm.

"We don't know how badly she's injured. Don't try to move her."

Eddie's gaze shifted to hers. "Don't tell me what to do with my sister."

Before Nikki could respond, Eddie was yanked to his feet by Liam and cuffed. He started resisting, and two SWAT officers jumped in to help, while the others surrounded Ava and took care of traffic. One of them said something about medical training, and Nikki moved out of the way to let him work on Ava, who had started to move around.

"Ava?" Nikki knelt down and pressed her hands to either side of the woman's head. "Try not to move. You might have a spinal injury."

Ava's eyes fluttered open. She stared at Nikki for a moment. "You're the FBI."

"Yes, and there's an ambulance on the way. We just need you to stay still."

"Where's Eddie?"

Nikki glanced at the median. Eddie lay face down, hands cuffed behind his back. He looked like he was crying.

"He's OK." Ava tried to move her head, but Nikki held firm. "Stay still."

She coughed, blood leaking out of her mouth. "I lied. But he killed her."

"Who? Did Eddie kill Dana?" Nikki still couldn't put her finger on a real motive. A terrible thought raced through her mind: what if Maggie Anderson had paid Eddie to take care of her sister? But how did Kellan become involved?

Ava closed her eyes, and Nikki couldn't tell if she was trying to nod or fighting to stay awake.

"Ava, who did Eddie kill?"

"In the motel. She's in the motel. She broke his heart."

CHAPTER TWENTY-SIX

"He strangled her a few hours ago, at least."

Liam and his team found Sara face-up on the shoddy motel room carpet, deep red marks on her neck. Her expression was fixed in place, and her body had already started to go into rigor. The smell of death mixed with stale sheets and old furniture made Nikki want to gag. The lone nightstand with the phone had been tipped over, the phone jack yanked out of the wall.

Nikki and Liam had gone through the hotel room and found a duffle bag of cash. A baggie of cocaine and a pipe had been left on a small table in the corner, along with what looked like spreadsheets. "Ironic that a group trying to save kids from addicted parents is doing coke," Nikki said. "At least one is."

"My bet's on Eddie," Liam said. "He was acting like he was on something. SWAT tased him."

Nikki raised an eyebrow and Liam held up his hands. "They didn't know what he'd done to you, and I didn't tell them to do it. He was resisting."

"What about the spreadsheets?" she asked.

"They're in some kind of bizarre code," Liam said. "But we found a laptop in Sara's big bag. I bagged it and the spreadsheets. I'll take them to the cryptos at the lab."

"You know they hate it when we call them that." The FBI cryptanalysts were able to break just about any sort of code, and Nikki was always in awe of them. She'd never been good at puzzles, let alone something like that.

"It's a compliment."

"Ava?"

"Going into surgery," Liam said. "Broken leg, internal injuries, head injury. Doesn't look good. What's so hard to understand about the damned hands-free law?"

"People don't think they'll make a mistake." The driver would live the rest of his life haunted by the image of hitting Ava, and since Minnesota had a hands-free law and he'd been on his phone, he was looking at a hefty fine and possible criminal charges.

"How are you this morning?" Liam asked. "'Cause you don't look great."

"I'm fine. Just sore. Seeing Lacey helped." Nikki couldn't get Tyler out of her mind. He'd looked so hurt finding out about Rory, and she had no idea how to make him feel better. She needed to talk to Courtney about everything, but now wasn't the right time. "Is Courtney bringing her team?"

"It'll be a while. Bad traffic and she drives like an old lady."

"Where's Eddie?"

"One of Miller's guys picked him up a few minutes ago. They're waiting for you at the station."

Nikki rolled her neck from side to side. "Are you OK with me heading that way?"

He nodded. "We'll process this place and I'll make sure everything gets to the lab. You deal with Eddie and I'll check on Ava." He sighed. "We need to track down Sara's family."

"Have the police make the notification. Will you tell the lab and also check on Dr. Bahri?"

"You got it, boss. Give Eddie hell for yesterday."

Nikki's adrenaline was still pumping when she arrived in Stillwater. She hoped the code guys at the lab got the information quickly. She had a feeling that Ava had been responsible for more than a few false test results. There was a good chance she wouldn't make it through surgery, and Nikki didn't expect Eddie to share much information. She had bigger things to focus on anyway. Braintree needed to be informed about the letter and the fingerprint print match to the Webster case.

She glanced at her phone. With everything going on, it would have been nice if Rory and she weren't fighting. She waited for the beep. "It's me, but I guess you know that since you're sending me to voicemail. I'm sorry if I hurt you last night. It was just a really bad day. Please call me when you get a chance. Today's going to be crazy, but if I miss your call, I will call you back."

She switched back to her navigation system and tried to focus on the day ahead. Ava had said that she lied, but about what? She'd obviously been terrified of her brother, but had she exaggerated his abuse yesterday?

A call boomed through her Bluetooth, and a glimmer of hope went through Nikki until a different number showed on the caller ID.

"This is Agent Hunt."

"Agent, I'm sorry not to return your call last night. My name is Ron Bryant with the Minnesota Bureau of Investigation. Someone from your team mentioned information about David Webster."

"Right, yes. Thank you for calling me back."

"The voicemail shocked the hell out of me," Bryant said. "You really have new information?"

"Yes." Nikki briefed him on Zach's disappearance and his family's belief that he had been taken, and the evidence they had found in Zach's room. "I took it to the FBI lab for fingerprint analysis. The prints match the ones taken from David Webster's bike."

Bryant was quiet for so long Nikki wondered if she'd lost him. "Are you still there?"

"Your lab is certain?" he asked.

"They ran it multiple times," Nikki said.

"Holy God." Bryant sounded choked up. "You know I was the original agent on the case? David's part of the reason I went to the cold case unit. He's my responsibility."

"I understand," Nikki said. "Right now, only a few people know about the prints. After I talk to Eddie, I'll go to the Chisago County Sheriff to see how they're getting on with their investigation now this evidence has come to light. There are a lot of years between David Webster's disappearance and Zach's. You and I both know that if this person was involved with both boys, they've likely assaulted dozens of others, too."

"Damnit," Bryant said. "I'm in California at a forensics conference. I can't get back to town for a few days."

"Obviously this is your call, but I could work the case until you're able to arrive?" Nikki asked. It wasn't ideal, and she was reluctant to take over, but it sounded like Bryant needed the help. She didn't want Caitlin to be let down again; she felt like Zach was her responsibility now.

"Thank you. Is there any chance we can keep this low profile until we know more? The last thing I want to do is give the Websters false hope."

"Absolutely. It stays in our circle until you choose to tell them."

Bryant thanked her, and she promised to keep him updated.

Miller's desk sergeant told Nikki that Eddie was already in an interview room, but Miller was waiting for Nikki. She stopped in the restroom and splashed cold water on her face. She found Miller pacing the hall outside the room like an impatient tiger. He stopped walking when he saw Nikki.

"You OK?" he asked.

"Stiff. Is he talking?"

"I haven't tried," Miller said. "Figured I'd let him stew. You deserve first crack anyway. You think he's good for Dana's murder?"

"I think there's a damned good chance. I don't know how Kellan became involved, but my guess is that Eddie decided to take care of Dana when he heard that she hadn't heeded his warning." One thing bothered her, though. How did Eddie know Dana had defied him? Had Maggie Anderson called him after something happened Friday and asked him to take care of Dana? "You want to go in with me?"

Miller shook his head. "I'll be out here if you think you need me."

Eddie was still handcuffed, his chin against his chest. Nikki shut the interview room door hard, and he jerked. The dark circles under his glassy eyes made her wonder how long it had been since he used.

"Napping while your sister's in surgery fighting for her life?"

"Wasn't napping. I was praying."

"Good," Nikki said. "She needs all the help possible." She sat down stiffly, determined not to show Eddie how sore she was from yesterday. "You want to tell me your side of the story?"

His jaw was tight, moisture in the corner of his eyes. "I never meant to hurt anyone. When I found out what Ava said and that Sara was backing her up, I lost it. I grabbed Sara and couldn't stop choking her."

"Being hopped up on cocaine doesn't help."

He shrugged noncommittally.

"Maggie Anderson told you that Dana was looking into hiring a private investigator to find out who falsified the tests. Is that why you went to Dana's apartment and beat her up?"

His shoulders tensed. "I didn't."

Nikki left that one alone for now. "How did this whole thing get started? Because according to Ava—"

"I know what she said, and it's a lie. She and Sara came up with the idea one night after drinks. They both have bills hanging over their heads and they thought it was a way to make money and help kids. Ava knew it wouldn't be hard to convince me. I hate the damn system."

"So I've heard. When did this start?"

"About a year ago."

Nikki stared at him with disgust. "How many people?"

He shrugged. "Ten? Fifteen? I did screen them and find out what their chances of rebounding were."

"Then you did a lousy job," Nikki replied. "Dana Rhodes had been sober for nearly a year. She had a good chance of making it. Regardless, you didn't have the right to do any of this."

Eddie looked down at the table. "Her sister said that didn't matter. She said that Dana had been sober for months before and always relapsed."

"Not nearly as long as she'd been this time," Nikki noted. "As the court reporter, you knew her test results were constantly negative. Why did you let Maggie convince you that Dana wouldn't stay sober?"

"She offered me double what we charge. I'm not proud of it, but I wanted to buy Sara an engagement ring. A really big one that she could show off. And I needed the deposit for my new place."

"Maggie said she gave you five thousand."

He shook his head. "She had ten thousand in cash and offered all of it to me. I took it."

Maggie had lied about the money, but why? To lessen the blow of Joe finding out? "But Dana was out to prove her innocence. She had the support system to do it, too. Did Maggie pay you to go to Dana's apartment and threaten her?"

"I never went to her apartment," he said shortly.

Nikki leaned across the table. "We have your prints in her apartment, Eddie."

He stared at her, and she waited for him to call her bluff. But his shoulders sagged. "Maggie didn't need to tell me. I went to talk to Dana and things got out of hand."

"She still didn't stop, so you had to get rid of her," Nikki said. "Who knew how to cut her wrists so efficiently? And why Kellan? Did he see something?"

Eddie paled and leaned forward, his big hands balled into fists. "I didn't kill her. Ava said she told you that I would never do something like that."

"Actually, she said that you had bad anger issues, and if you killed them, she had nothing to do with it," Nikki explained. "And considering what happened this morning, I think we can rule out you never doing something like that. Where were you last weekend?"

Eddie ground his teeth, hate burning in his eyes. "Home."

"All weekend? Can anyone corroborate?"

He looked down at the table. "Sara could have."

"Well, that's not going to happen now," Nikki said. "Did Maggie Anderson call you any time on the weekend? Did she ask you to take care of her sister?"

"No," Eddie said. "I haven't talked to her since she told me about her sister's plan to get a private investigator."

Nikki stared into his small eyes, trying to decide if she believed him. If he'd agreed to dispose of Dana along with Kellan's body, Maggie must have given him a chunk of change in order for him to get involved.

"Were you following Dana?" Nikki tried another route. "You saw her go to the Andersons' and realized she was going to take Kellan and eventually expose you all, so you attacked? Kellan's death was an accident, right?"

His nostrils flared. "You've got nothing on me, and you won't get anything. I'm done talking to you."

CHAPTER TWENTY-SEVEN

Miller drove them to the Chisago County Sheriff's office while Nikki went through all of her notes and tried to make sense of the most recent events. Eddie would be charged with murdering Sara and assault on a police officer, and he was currently waiting to go before the judge about bail. If the judge set bail, it would be high since Eddie tried to run. Today was Saturday, which meant he wouldn't go in front of the judge until Monday morning, so they had some time to find enough physical evidence to charge him with Dana's and Kellan's deaths.

"We know Eddie's capable of killing in the heat of the moment," Nikki said. "But I'm not sure he would have been able to keep his head and arrange the crime scene. His sister and girlfriend came up with the idea about the tests over drinks, which means he's the worker bee. Ava was away at the conference, but that doesn't mean she wasn't aware of a plan to eliminate Dana. Unfortunately, she may not regain consciousness. Sara's dead, and Eddie's not talking."

"So the women planned it and Eddie was the goon?"

Nikki shrugged. "I don't know. He's definitely a creep and obviously has temper issues. But his denial about Dana and Kellan seemed sincere. He won't talk, but he also didn't ask for a lawyer. He either doesn't care since he knows he's going down for Sara's murder, or he really wasn't involved. Liam's looking into all of their finances and so far nothing useful."

"They kept the cash. Much harder to trace. Maggie also said she paid Eddie five thousand," Miller explained. "He claims it was ten."

"My guess is he was keeping some for himself," Nikki said. "And I don't think Joe had any clue about what she's done. She may not have wanted to admit to the ten thousand."

Miller sighed. "I met with the D.A. this morning. It's a jurisdictional nightmare. Ava and Eddie live in Hennepin County. Sara's in Ramsey along with the lab. They're arguing over charging Maggie Anderson. The Washington County D.A. wants to make a deal and give her a break considering the circumstances and her leading us to Eddie. He's not sure the others are on board yet."

Nikki wasn't convinced that her nephew's welfare had been Maggie's only motivation in having the test falsified. She had so much resentment toward her sister, and it seemed that she relished the control of Dana's life. Finding out that Dana wasn't going away without a fight and had planned to prove Maggie's deceit could have set her off. "If Eddie killed Dana, I think Maggie paid him to do it. I'll have Liam search for offshore accounts or see if there's any way she could have tapped into Kellan's trust. Still, what she did is pretty callous, even if it did come from concern about Kellan. But if Eddie is the killer, what's the real motive?" Nikki looked at Miller. "He threatened Dana and hit her, we know that. But what does he care if she takes her son? He works in the system. He's got to know that her doing that takes away any chance of her accusations about the test having any validity with the judge."

Miller nodded. "I've been wondering the same thing. Seems like money's the only thing he's motivated by, which brings us back to Maggie, damnit."

Nikki drained her lukewarm coffee as Miller pulled into the Chisago sheriff's parking lot. It was barely 10 a.m., and Nikki was on her third cup. "I really dread talking to this man."

She spotted Caitlin's vehicle, and before Miller had the chance to park, Caitlin was out of her car and pacing.

"I don't want to give her false hope," Nikki said.

"Neither do I. But I'm not sure it matters. She's convinced herself that Zach is still alive."

Caitlin rushed to Nikki as soon as she exited the SUV. She was still pale and tired, but there was a gleam of hope in her eyes. "It's true?"

"Yes, the prints match, but listen to me. As of now, there's nothing to change the fact that Zach is probably gone. I don't want you to get your hopes up."

"He was being groomed by a killer," Caitlin said. "The way his hat was left in plain sight. Can't you see it's all a cover-up? That man has my son."

"Caitlin, you need to calm down. I believe you, and we're going to do everything we can to get to the bottom of things, but I need you to let us handle Braintree."

"Fine," Caitlin said. "But I want to go in with you."

"Absolutely not. You can wait outside. And if you say anything about David Webster to anyone—"

"I won't tell anyone about the link to David Webster. All I care about is my son."

"Good," Nikki said. "I'm sure you know that if word about the print match gets out, we'll lose our shot at finding this guy."

The Chisago sheriff office looked similar to Washington County's, although the building was newer, and the desk sergeant seemed more like a private secretary for Braintree than anything else.

Braintree made Nikki and Miller wait twenty minutes before bringing them into his office, and Nikki had to silence her phone because of Caitlin's endless stream of impatient texts.

Braintree sat at the edge of his desk and looked down at the two of them, arms crossed over his chest. His bullishness reminded Nikki so much of Hardin in the moment that she had to tell herself this man hadn't done anything to wrong her.

"If this is about the Reeves kid, I don't want to hear it." He pointed to the large window in his office that overlooked the parking lot. Nikki followed his gaze and gritted her teeth. Caitlin was pacing in front of the building. "Why is she here?

"Zach Reeves is her son."

Nikki watched Braintree's expression shift from irritation to pity. "Well, that explains a lot. I wish she'd have told me from the beginning."

"Would it have made any difference?" Nikki asked.

"In my investigation, no. But in my treatment of her, yes. I just saw her as a bloodthirsty reporter."

"I know the feeling, but she's not imagining things."

"Zach is gone," Braintree said tightly. "We're doing everything we can to find his body and bring closure."

"Until now, I've agreed with you," Nikki said. "But we have new information." Nikki handed him the evidence bag containing the letter. "Caitlin took this from Zach's room. It was tucked under his mattress."

Braintree closed his eyes. "And brought it to you. Fantastic."

"Read it." Nikki handed him the letter, enclosed in a plastic sleeve to protect it against evidence contamination.

Braintree rubbed his temples, but he opened the letter and started reading. "Christ. The world is full of perverts. Do you or his grandparents have any idea who might have given this to Zach?"

Nikki glanced at Miller, and he motioned for her to go keep going. He'd already told her that she had the honor of breaking the news to Braintree since she'd been the one to have the letter fingerprinted. "His family isn't aware of anyone, but you know as well as I do how these guys operate," Nikki said. "I took the letter to the FBI forensic lab for fingerprinting. The prints are a match with prints found on David Webster's bike in 1996."

Braintree sank into his chair. "You're certain?

"Yes," Nikki said. "My lab was very thorough. I notified the cold case agent from the BCA."

"This is my jurisdiction." Braintree held the letter between them, clearly debating whether or not to give it back to Nikki. He finally sighed and handed it to her. "Technically, this is my evidence. You should have told me about this."

Nikki slipped the evidence bag into her purse. "This isn't about whose case it is, and I did try to call you. I assume it's your ego that stopped you from accepting my call."

"Zach lives in my county. The letter came from my county," Braintree said.

"Danny, I don't know why we're having this discussion," Miller said. "The victims and their families are the priority. And Nikki has jurisdiction. She's FBI for God's sake."

"Says the man who got his job by helping to ruin a man's career," snapped Braintree. He glared at Nikki. "I'm not going to let you bring me down like you did Hardin. And you aren't going to walk in here and take control of my case because you like being in the spotlight."

"No one here wants this in the news," Miller said. "This guy's kept his head down for twenty-five years. He knows how to hide."

"I came here with every intention of keeping you involved." Nikki barely managed to keep her tone even. "Agent Bryant at the BCA has worked the David Webster case from the beginning and moved to the cold case unit in order to keep working it. Unfortunately, he's in California at a conference and won't be able to get here for a few days. He asked me to handle things until then."

"I don't care," Braintree said. "Zach's the key to finding out who killed David Webster, and he lives here. Why wouldn't I work the case?"

"No one's asking you not to work the case," Nikki said evenly. "But the BCA and the FBI have a lot of resources you don't. We need to put aside differences and jurisdictional bickering."

"Fine," Braintree said. "But I'm not wasting officers on something I don't agree with. I believe we're doing the right thing by searching the river." A muscle in Braintree's jaw twitched. "Ben Reeves is a vet. Served in the army during the Gulf War and then the Minnesota National Guard. Shouldn't be too hard for your lab to access his prints."

"Thank you." Nikki quickly texted Courtney with the information. She didn't suspect Ben, but his prints would clear the way to investigate real suspects. "I'll be sure to let you know about any new information."

Braintree grunted and sat down behind the desk. He waved dismissively. "Shut the door on your way out."

Caitlin pounced the moment they were outside. "That's a waste of time," she half-shouted. "Ben can be a hard-ass, but he's also a good man. He and Zach's father were very close, and losing Teddy nearly killed Ben. I think taking care of Zach saved his life. Ben isn't the guy."

"I'm sure he isn't." Nikki spoke calmly. "This is just routine."

"Don't talk to me like I don't know how things work." Caitlin glared at her. "I know the stats on abused kids. It's usually someone close to them. I know why you're looking at him and I'm telling you Ben would never do that. You're wasting your time."

"It's not going to take Courtney very long to check the prints. It's not a waste of time." Nikki looked directly at Caitlin. "I've kept you in the loop because you brought us the letter and you know how an investigation works. But I think you need to step aside now and let us do our jobs."

"I'm not the type of person who can sit on the sidelines," Caitlin said.

Nikki wasn't going to press the issue right now, but she had no intention of allowing Caitlin to tag along much longer. "Let's go and talk to the Reeves."

CHAPTER TWENTY-EIGHT

Ben and Helen lived on the outskirts of Shafer Township, just a few miles from the St. Croix River. Their home wasn't as rural as the Andersons', but Zach did have a few minutes' walk from the bus stop. Caitlin must have called ahead because Helen Reeves opened the front door before anyone could exit their vehicles.

Shivering in an oversized sweater, Helen ushered them into the eighties-style ranch house. Pictures of Zach and a man Nikki assumed was his late father lined the walls. "There's room for everyone in the kitchen. And I have fresh coffee," Helen told them.

Ben Reeves sat at the table, his shoulders hunched, staring at his coffee. He stood when Nikki introduced herself and then sat back down as though the movement had taken every effort. Caitlin rubbed his shoulder, and he patted her hand.

Helen set four cups of coffee on the table along with a little basket of sugar packets. "Does anyone take cream?"

"Nikki does," Caitlin replied. "She likes her coffee not to look like actual coffee."

"It's more about the taste," Nikki said wryly.

Helen handed her a small ceramic pitcher of cream. "Take as much as you need. I'm just so grateful you're willing to listen to us. The sheriff thinks we're crazy."

"Sheriff Braintree is still in charge of the case," Nikki said gently. "He's following a logical trail of evidence. But we've had a new development and I've agreed to step in and help." More like Braintree didn't have much choice in the matter. "I want to be clear that as of now, the most logical explanation is that Zach drowned,"

Nikki said gently, "but because we now know about the letter, we're re-evaluating things."

The four of them had agreed not to mention the print match until the BCA informed Webster's family in a few days, but Nikki hoped that Ben and Helen would be able to give them enough information about Zach's life that they'd have a chance at finding the person who left the prints.

Ben turned red with anger and looked at the table, but Helen nodded emphatically. "We had no idea. Is there any way to find out who sent the letter?"

"My guess is that it was hand-delivered," Nikki said. "If it's all right, I'd like to have our tech people look at Zach's laptop. You'd be amazed at the way information can be hidden. If this person tried to contact Zach on the internet, we have a shot at getting a name and possibly a location."

"Take whatever you need." Ben's weathered face flushed with color. "He's alive."

"We know there's been upheaval in Zach's life the past few months and that he's lashed out." Nikki didn't address Ben's optimism, but she privately had little hope that Zach was still alive if he'd actually been kidnapped. Too much time had passed. "Has he been spending more time away from home? Coming home later after school?"

"Some days," Ben said. "I don't get home from work until dinner time. Helen works at the high school, so she's home earlier. He missed the bus a few times. He'd say he was hanging out a friend's or doing homework. We tried to give some space. He's so mad at all of us."

"How did he get home on those days?" Nikki asked.

"I picked him up a couple of times," Helen said. "But he also told us his friend's parents gave him a ride. I guess we should have confirmed with the parents, but we just didn't think about him lying."

"Are there any family friends or relatives he would have reached out to?" They needed to talk to anyone with access to Zach and cross-reference prints if at all possible.

Both grandparents shook their heads, but Ben answered. "We're both only children. Don't really keep in touch with cousins. Zach's not the type to reach out, either. He's a shy kid."

"What about his friends?"

"There are a couple of boys he spends time with," Helen said. "He used to spend more time with them, but lately he's been less social."

"Could you make us a list of the adults in Zach's life? Parents of friends, teachers?" Nikki asked.

Helen nodded. "And you'll talk to all of them? You'll do a real investigation?"

"Sheriff Braintree will have units continuing to search the river. Sheriff Miller and I will talk to Zach's friends and teachers."

Helen grabbed Nikki's hands. "Thank you. I assume you want to search his room?"

Nikki was happy to see the relief on Helen's face, but she worried about giving false hope to the family. Even if Zach hadn't drowned, chances were slim that he was still alive. "That would be great, thank you."

"It's just down this hall," Helen said. "Caitlin, why don't you come with us?"

Caitlin looked surprised, and her eyes were suspiciously wet. The invitation obviously meant a lot to her. Nikki hadn't been sure of the dynamic between the family, but so far, it appeared the Reeves considered Caitlin a part of Zach's life.

Zach's room was cluttered with various collectibles from Marvel superheroes, along with a plethora of comic books. He'd left his math book lying open on his bed as though he'd intended to come back and finish his homework.

"He's a little messy." Helen looked embarrassed. "I was going to straighten up, but Caitlin said you'd want to see it this way."

"She's right," Nikki said. "And it's pretty much what I'd expect from a boy his age." Nikki pointed to the chest of drawers. "OK if I look in this?"

"Of course. Whatever you need."

Nikki slipped on latex gloves and started looking through the room. Zach wasn't the tidiest kid, most of his clothes dumped haphazardly in the drawers, but Nikki didn't find anything unusual. His closet was standard size and predictably full.

"I went through his clothes and checked the pockets of all his coats and pants," Caitlin said. "I didn't find anything."

Nikki didn't want to chide Caitlin in front of Helen, but she should have known better than to go touching things that could be used for fingerprinting. Nikki knelt down and focused on the mess of shoes and gear at the bottom of his closet. Several pairs of well-used sneakers had been discarded, along with some potent football cleats. A shoebox in the back corner caught Nikki's eye. She wriggled it free from the mess.

"Air Jordans," Caitlin said. "I bought them for him last Christmas. He only wears them on special occasions because they're retro, a limited edition."

While Nikki was familiar with the shoe brand, she had no clue what Caitlin meant. "Retro?"

Caitlin nodded. "These are red and black, like the ones Michael Jordan wore early in his career. Nike put out a retro edition a few years ago, and Zach loved them. Helen and Ben didn't want to spend the money—which I completely understand." She looked around at Helen and Helen smiled. "I bought them as a special gift."

Nikki opened the box and removed the tissue paper. A roll of cash was tucked into the left sneaker. "Did Zach earn an allowance?"

"Yes, but it's only ten dollars a week," Helen said. "But he always spends it quickly. We put half of it into a savings account."

Nikki carefully removed the cash. "I'd say there's at least two hundred dollars here."

"Why would he hide it in his shoes?" Helen said. "And where did he get the money? He spent his savings on the DNA test. I know we haven't given him that much allowance since then."

Nikki looked at Caitlin's face; it seemed that she had come to the same conclusion as Nikki had, her face ashen. Pedophiles often used cash and gifts to earn kids' trust; it was something Nikki knew Caitlin had reported about when she covered a famous criminal Nikki had caught a couple of years back.

Caitlin reached past her and took out the right shoe. "There's a stain."

Nikki took the shoe and examined it. A quarter-sized dark stain was easily visible on the red fabric between the toe and the laces.

"Is that blood?" Caitlin asked.

"It could be, or it could be plenty of other things. The fabric is porous and the color makes it hard to figure out what the stain actually is. I'll need to take this as evidence." Hiding the cash in these shoes might be completely unrelated to the cause of the stain, but Nikki's gut told her that wasn't the case. She put the lid back on the shoes. She'd have Liam get these to the lab this afternoon.

They finished in Zach's room and promised to keep the Reeves updated.

Caitlin moved to follow Nikki outside, but Nikki stopped her. "Is there any way you could stay here? Miller and I need to discuss things with Braintree, and you can't be involved. If things are awkward between—"

"I'll stay," Caitlin said. "Just please call me the minute something new happens."

"I'll do my best. But you need to remember what I said."

She joined Miller outside.

"What have you got there?" Miller asked.

Nikki showed them the shoe. "It's impossible to know what this is without testing. I need to get it to my lab ASAP."

The idea of driving back to the Cities tonight wasn't appealing. Nikki's entire body hurt, and the drive would just make it worse. She also hoped to see Rory, but she couldn't allow that to be a factor in the investigation.

"The Reeves have security cameras," Miller said. "I'll email Braintree and have him send it to me. Our tech people can go through the last few days before Zach's disappearance and see if anything sticks out."

Miller held up the list of Zach's friends and teachers. "I'll handle these."

"We need phone records," Nikki said.

"Zach didn't have a phone," Braintree. "Grandparents are old-school."

"Then how did Zach communicate with this guy?" Nikki asked. "I'll have our techs search the laptop, but I really don't think this guy is dumb enough to send anything electronically."

"I'll ask the school if they've ever noticed Zach meeting anyone." Miller shook his head. "I just hope we don't spook this bastard."

Nikki checked in with Liam on the way back to Stillwater. Ava had made it through surgery but was in a medically induced coma because of brain swelling. The surgeon didn't sound very optimistic. Liam hadn't been able to find out anything more about Sara other than she was a respected employee. Dr. Bahri was recovering in the hospital, and the associate director had rushed back to HPH to handle the chaos in his place. The lab had hundreds of Ava's cases to investigate. If the operation involved as many people as Nikki suspected, they were in for one hell of a civil suit and possibly negligence charges. He hadn't found any other bank accounts tied to Maggie or Joe Anderson, but Maggie could have them under another name or even keep cash stored at the house.

"Liam's almost to Stillwater," Nikki said. "He went to the hospital and saw Ava. He's hoping he'll be able to convince Eddie to talk for the opportunity to see her. He'll get Zach's shoes to Courtney this afternoon."

"Good." Miller worried his lower lip. "That's a long drive for you to make when you're obviously miserable sitting down very long."

"It's just my muscles trying to crush my lungs." Nikki forced a smile. "No biggie. I still want to look at the Reeves' phone records."

"You mean the landline?" Miller asked.

"It's a long shot, but it's worth taking the time. I'm hoping we can bypass the phone company." She fired off a text to Caitlin and told her to ask the Reeves for three months' worth of phone bills. Even if they received paperless bills, most phone companies still included a call record on the digital statements.

Nikki's stomach growled, and she realized she'd yet to eat today. They stopped at a sandwich shop and Nikki ordered the biggest one on the menu. She wasn't sure if Liam had eaten, but he never turned down a meal, so she ordered him a turkey club and his favorite greasy potato chips.

Liam was waiting outside Miller's office when they returned. He leaned against the wall, eyes closed. Nikki waved the sandwich under his nose. He groaned and gave her an appreciative look. "You know me so well."

They took the food into the room Miller had set up as a command center when Kellan first disappeared.

"Eddie's not budging," Liam said. "The guy confessed to one murder and assaulted a cop. He's not getting out of jail, and the state isn't going to go easy on him. But he doesn't seem to care about leveraging anything."

"Even when it involves his sister?"

Liam shook his head. "He said she's dead to him after betraying him. I think he's banking on her dying, which isn't a bad bet. She's pretty messed up."

"He cares about her," Nikki said. "But he feels like she betrayed him and is clinging to that anger."

"I told him he had until tomorrow to change his mind. We have no physical evidence to tie him to Dana's and Kellan's murders."

"Courtney's still working on the men's clothes we found mixed in with Dana's," Nikki said. "But she didn't sound very hopeful about getting an actual print."

"What about those black fibers under Dana's nails?" Liam asked. "It's a long shot, but Eddie seems to favor that black hoodie. We can have Courtney test it. She can also search his apartment to see if there's anything else they might have come from."

Nikki shrugged. "It's worth a try."

"What about Dana's car?" Miller asked. "Did we get any hits from the prints there?"

"Nothing we could use. Whoever drove wore gloves and didn't touch anything."

"Where are you with Zach's case?" Liam asked quietly.

Nikki brought him up to speed. "I'm hoping Miller will get something from the school or Zach's friends that points us in the right direction. I don't think his grandparents have been very strict with Zach, especially since he found out about Caitlin. He's come home late after school multiple times, and we don't know what he was doing or where he was. Unfortunately, their leniency means we don't have much to go on."

"What about comparing Ben Reeves' prints to the ones taken from the letter?"

"Still waiting on Courtney to get back to me, but I don't think we'll get anything. I am expecting something from Caitlin." Nikki checked her phone, and sure enough, Caitlin had texted her back with copies of the Reeves' phone bill.

Nikki forwarded the messages to her email and brought the images up on her laptop. As thorough as ever, Caitlin had outlined several numbers on the second page of the most recent bill. Nikki didn't recognize any specific number, but the Reeves had an incoming call every weekday around 4 p.m. Zach would have been the only one home at that time. The call only lasted ten minutes or so and came from a different number each day. Nikki wondered if the caller was using one of the burner phone apps like Eddie had done when he sent Dana the warning texts.

"Those burner apps are really popular, too." Nikki shifted in her seat, trying to get some form of comfort. "I suppose plenty of people use them."

Liam eyed her. "You don't seem all that convinced."

She shrugged. "Something bugs me about the situation. I just can't put my finger on it."

"The whole situation bugs me," Miller said. "I don't like Braintree knowing about the letter and the link to David Webster."

"You don't trust he'll stay quiet?" Nikki asked.

"I don't know," Miller replied. "I guess the idea that the person who took David Webster has been under our noses for months and no one knew it has me on edge."

"That's what these guys do," Nikki said. "But he made a mistake giving that letter to Zach. We'll get him this time."

CHAPTER TWENTY-NINE

Nikki pulled into Rory's driveway and killed the lights. She felt as nervous and out of place as the first time she'd showed up at his house almost two months ago. She'd just come from talking to Mark in prison and had finally realized that he was innocent and that she'd helped put him there. The actual killer, her childhood sweetheart John, had been someone she'd trusted for her entire life, and the sense of betrayal had been overwhelming. And now she had to deal with Braintree. She wasn't sure if she could trust him yet. He struck her as the type who would put his own interests first, but maybe everything that had happened with Hardin had made her too biased.

And what about Caitlin? She fully believed Caitlin was devastated about Zach, but the case would be over at some point, and then what? Would she go back to being career-hungry and stepping on toes to get what she wanted?

Then there was Maggie Anderson, who had done such a horrible thing to her sister.

Nikki took a deep breath and got out of the jeep. She walked slowly to Rory's front door, afraid of going through the garage and being told… she didn't know exactly. The motion-sensor lights came on, and before Nikki could knock, the door flew open.

Rory looked at her with frustration, but once he saw the state she was in, that quickly turned to shock. "You said you got tased. Not beat up," he said, taking her face in his hands.

She'd forgotten about the bruises on her forehead and jaw. "It all happened at once," she said.

"Who did this?"

The reality of the past few days suddenly crashed down on Nikki, her legs weak. "That's not why I'm here. I wasn't even sure if you'd want me here, but I didn't want to sleep at the station. You have a guest room."

"Why would I want you to be anywhere else?"

"I don't know."

Rory grabbed her hand and pulled her to his chest. "I thought you might not want to come back here. I acted like a jealous ass." He buried his face in her hair. "You've told me that Tyler still has feelings for you, and he's the father of your child. The thought of you going to him instead of me…"

"I went there because of Lacey, not him. But you're right. I should have remembered to call. And I shouldn't have avoided talking to you about so many things." She shifted so that she could look into his eyes. "I realized something this morning when Caitlin and I talked. This is the first real relationship I've had since Tyler, so yes, I'm taking things one day at a time and trying to live in the present without worrying about whether or not things will work out for us. But that doesn't mean I expect it to fail, or that I want it to. I want us to work, but I'm scared."

Emotion flickered through his green eyes. "Of what?"

"Of getting too close and getting hurt. Of Lacey not handling it very well. I'm afraid of screwing things up, because I'm not exactly the best at letting people in or allowing myself to be vulnerable. Then you come along and I can't stop talking."

His lips twitched, and she could tell he was fighting a smile. "I'm glad."

He led her inside the house and shut the door. Nikki's leg felt ready to give out, and she leaned against Rory on the way to the bedroom. His lips met hers, and she sighed into the kiss. Rory's grip around her waist tightened, and she couldn't stop the gasp of pain.

"What?"

"Sore ribs," she said. "They're bruised, too. Same guy who tased me added some kicks for good measure."

Rory loosened his grip, but Nikki could feel the tension in his arms.

"I don't like that part of your job." His voice trembled with anger, and something primal came over Nikki. She pulled his face down to hers and kissed him hard. She slid her hands into his running pants.

"Are you sure this is a good idea?" Rory groaned.

"Yes," Nikki said. "I need you."

Nikki woke to the smell of bacon and fresh coffee and smiled. Rory always made bacon and pancakes on Sundays. She got out of bed gingerly, her ribs still sore from being kicked. Last night's activities hadn't exactly helped. Rory had tried to go slow, but Nikki had blocked out the pain and taken control. And it had definitely been worth the pain she was currently experiencing.

She found her slippers and then brushed her teeth and hair before going into the kitchen.

Rory stood in front of the stove in athletic shorts and nothing else, cooking the pancakes and watching the local morning news on the small flatscreen television in the corner. Nikki quietly sat her phone on the table and then tiptoed up to him. She wrapped her arms around his narrow waist and nuzzled her chin in between his shoulder blades.

He leaned against her. "Did you get a good night's sleep?"

"Yes," she said. "I passed out from satisfaction. And exhaustion."

He laughed. "How are your ribs?"

"Sore."

He moved the pan off the burner and then turned around to kiss her. "I told you to take it easy."

"I didn't want to."

Rory's hands wandered down her back and underneath her shirt, his lips still on hers. Nikki was debating between the kitchen table and the living-room sofa when she heard the morning news anchor mention a shocking new update in the David Webster case.

She pulled away and moved to turn up the television, her blood pressure skyrocketing.

"Breaking news: A fingerprint taken from a letter found in a missing local boy's room is a match for a twenty-five-year-old cold case. An anonymous source told Channel 11 that FBI Special Agent Nikki Hunt obtained the letter and the fingerprint match. It's unclear at this time how the missing boy, Zach Reeves, came to possess the evidence. We have reached out to the Webster family and learned that Agent Hunt is yet to notify them."

"Oh my God." Nikki couldn't think straight for a few seconds. Who had done this? Who would leak this information? It didn't benefit anybody to give this false hope to David's family, and Bryant was still at his conference; he hadn't spoken to them yet. "It had to be Braintree," she said.

"Why would he do something like that to the Webster family?" Rory asked.

"He was territorial over the investigation. The BCA guy is going to be livid. I promised him he would be able to sit down with the Webster family before this broke." Nikki grabbed her phone. "I've got to talk to Miller. He'll go ballistic on Braintree."

She knew she shouldn't have trusted him. Braintree was as greedy as Hardin. Unless Caitlin had called, and surely she wouldn't have been so selfish.

Nikki could see that Rory was disappointed that she was half out of the door. "Will you at least eat something before you go on the warpath?"

Nikki inhaled a pancake and a couple pieces of bacon before hightailing it to Chisago County. She spent the entire drive dealing with the fallout from Braintree's selfish decision. Her boss called to reprimand her, and she promised to make things right with the Webster family. The only way she knew how to do that was to find the person who killed their son.

She pulled into a parking spot too fast, her tires bouncing off the concrete median. She didn't see Miller's SUV, but by now she wasn't in the mood to wait for him or to play nice with Braintree.

The desk sergeant didn't put up a fight when she stormed into the sheriff's office. She marched past the cubicles, ignoring the whispering deputies. Braintree's door was already open, but Nikki still pounded her fist on the wood as she shut it.

"What the hell were you thinking?" she said.

Braintree had been sitting at his desk with his head resting on his hands. He jerked up in surprise at Nikki's outburst. Instead of the cocky smirk she'd prepared for, he looked pale and nervous.

"I swear to God, I didn't talk to the press," he replied.

"Right." Nikki waited for him to blame Caitlin. She had to admit the thought had crossed her mind, but Caitlin believed her son was alive and this news getting out put him in jeopardy. "Who did?"

"My bet's on a lieutenant who wants my job," Braintree said. "He's undermined me before, and he was one of the few people who had any information about the matching print."

"No one else was supposed to have that information."

"My guys wanted to know why we were doing anything other than looking for Zach Reeves' body. I admit, when they razzed me about letting some female FBI agent walk all over me, I lost my cool and told them we had a good reason. I didn't think about any of them going to the media."

"And I'm supposed to believe that?"

He glared at her. "I don't care what you believe. I'm dealing with a public relations shitstorm right now. Unless you have something other than an ass-chewing to discuss with me, you can leave."

CHAPTER THIRTY

The Websters lived almost an hour northeast of Stillwater, and Nikki didn't think this was an occasion to show up uninvited. She'd received an angry call from Agent Bryant demanding to know why the news had leaked. She'd managed to pacify him, but he'd told her that he expected her to talk to the Websters. He'd only given her their home number, however, and no one answered.

Nikki had a couple of missed calls from Caitlin. Knowing she would likely be at the Reeves', Nikki drove over there while she continued trying to reach the Websters, but they were probably screening calls because of the media coverage. Nikki left a message asking to stop by and update them on what they'd found out. They had to be absolutely livid to learn about the break from the news. Nikki wanted to make sure she spoke with them and explained their decision to wait.

The Reeves' driveway was a sheet of solid ice from the snow melting during the day and then freezing again at night. Nikki doubted anyone had even thought about putting ice melt down.

A minivan Nikki didn't recognize was parked in the Reeves' driveway. Nikki debated whether or not to knock on the door. She didn't want to interrupt if they had visitors, and she definitely didn't want to encounter the media. But she was already here, and Caitlin would keep demanding an update, so Nikki might as well go inside. Since she'd taken on the case, she felt like it was her responsibility to deal with the family while Liam chased leads and Courtney worked her lab magic.

Caitlin answered the door. "What did the phone bills show?" she asked. Nikki was surprised that this was her first question, but she was glad that Caitlin's focus was on something that could help find Zach.

"What I suspected they would show. Calls to the home phone when only Zach was home."

"I can do you one better." She glanced over her shoulder. "The Websters showed up here about ten minutes ago."

"You're kidding. I've been trying to get hold of them for the past hour."

"They're asking questions none of us have the answers to, so you've got perfect timing. I already told them you're here."

Nikki didn't need to introduce herself when she entered the kitchen. Both of David's parents jumped out of their chairs. They looked older than Nikki expected. Mr. Webster was thin and white-haired, and his wife used a cane. They couldn't be much older than their early seventies, but stress took an enormous toll on the body.

"Why didn't you call us?" Mr. Webster demanded. "Some reporter rang us this morning right before the news aired. My wife fainted in shock."

"I'm so sorry," Nikki said. "I don't know if you've spoken with Agent Bryant—"

"After the reporter," he said. "Agent Bryant explained that he'd asked you to let him tell us. I appreciate that, but I don't understand why you changed your mind and went to the media."

"Sir, I promise you I didn't. I spoke with the Chisago County Sheriff, and he's confident the leak came from someone in his department. He's determined to get to the bottom of it, and I am very sorry about the way you found out. I've actually called your home a couple of times this morning. I'm glad to be able to speak to you face-to-face."

She offered her hand. He sighed and shook it. "Tom Webster. This is my wife, Betsy."

Betsy leaned on her cane as she spoke. "Do you know who took our son and Zach?"

"At this moment, we don't. Sheriff's deputies are talking to everyone in Zach's life to figure out who he might have been in contact with."

Betsy held up a thick binder. "This is a list of all David's friends and their immediate family members. A couple of them had brothers in their early twenties. One was quite disturbed. The police never looked at him closely enough."

Nikki understood why they had scoured every aspect of their son's life; it was clear that they questioned how David's disappearance had been handled. The binder would come in handy, as long as she was able to weed through everything. They could cross-reference the names against those they had listed as being in contact with Zach.

Nikki sat down next to Caitlin and opened the binder. As she expected, there were a lot of news articles that may or may not have the right information, along with handwritten lists of every lead the Websters had followed.

"Did you find anything on our phone bills?" Helen asked. Nikki hadn't noticed her in the room; she looked even more worried than she had yesterday.

"Sort of. I think Zach had a regular scheduled phone call with someone." She explained the timing of the calls and how they'd likely come from a burner app.

"What's a burner app?" Betsy asked.

Nikki pulled her phone out of her pocket and then opened the application. "Basically, they can buy one-time-use phone numbers that are pretty much untraceable. Some of these applications charge a monthly fee for so many numbers, while others charge per number. They're easy to use and a goldmine for creeps."

"Are they all a one-time use?" Caitlin asked.

"As far as I know," Nikki said. "But there are several different ones, and I haven't had the time to mess with each one."

She went back to the binder. Her throat tightened when she got to the picture section. David's parents had included several color photographs of him in happier times, and seeing them made the pain of their loss even more real.

Nikki cleared her throat. "Tell me about David. It looks like he enjoyed 4H." A lot of her friends had been in the 4H, but Nikki had never been interested in science projects or raising animals, and she'd always hated sewing. She wanted to get a little background. Any detail could help.

"He did," Tom said. "I used to be a dairy farmer, so we had cows and other livestock. David raised prize-winning Guernsey calves, but he only showed the one born at our dairy. The other was a runt David and I saw for sale at the old Anderson dairy, and damned if David didn't fall in love with that calf. Named her Starlight." Tom's eyes misted. "My boy's life was precious; he didn't deserve what happened to him."

Betsy took her husband's hand, while Ben patted his shoulder. Helen was quiet, lost in her thoughts.

Caitlin squeezed Nikki's elbow. "Could we talk privately for a minute?"

Nikki started to say no because she didn't want to be rude to the Websters, but she couldn't ignore the fierce look in Caitlin's eyes.

"Sure." Nikki closed the binder. "We'll be right back."

Caitlin practically dragged her down the hall into a large bedroom Nikki assumed belonged to Ben and Helen. "Did you hear what he said about the calf?"

"You've lost me," Nikki said.

"Anderson Dairy. David got the cow from Anderson Dairy. Didn't Joe Anderson sell his family dairy farm a while ago?"

"That's a stretch. I bet there was more than one Anderson Dairy."

"Not around here," Caitlin said. "I know because I was working at the paper at the time, and it was big news because they were one of the last locally owned dairies in the state. Joe would have been in his early twenties in 1996, right?"

"He and Maggie were married by then, but..." A jolt of electricity shot through Nikki.

"What is it?"

Nikki shook her head.

Caitlin popped her on the arm. "Don't do that. Don't cut me out. I'm not your average grieving family member. We've gotten this far because of me."

"All right," Nikki said. "Just keep your voice down. It's probably nothing, but do you have your phone?"

Caitlin took the phone out of her pocket. "Right here."

"Look up what year *Fargo* was released."

"Uh, okay." Caitlin's hand shook as she typed on her phone. "1996. That's the same year David disappeared."

"When in 1996?"

"March." Caitlin's eyes were wide. "David disappeared at the end of March."

"I know." Nikki felt like her entire body was vibrating. Dana's therapist had told her that she'd had a panic attack when she mentioned her parents going to see the movie. The movie itself hadn't caused a panic attack, but rather the discussion about her parents going to see it.

"1996. Dana probably wouldn't have been allowed to stay home alone." Hadn't Joe mentioned that he and Maggie had lived within walking distance when Dana was young? If she went somewhere else while her parents went to see the movie, it might have been their house. Nikki knew she shouldn't say anything to Caitlin, but her adrenaline took over.

"If Joe is involved in all of this, there's just one thing that doesn't make sense," Nikki insisted. "How does this connect to Dana's and

Kellan's deaths? Kellan was almost nine; he lived with Joe all this time and nothing happened to him."

It hit Nikki as soon as the words escaped her mouth. Dana had struggled for a long time to get clean, but she'd had a breakthrough and fought to stay sober after the Andersons were given temporary custody of Kellan more than a year ago. She'd become determined to get Kellan back. Had she been afraid of what Joe might do to her son? "I have to go," Nikki said.

"That's it, isn't it?" Caitlin said, desperation in her eyes. "Joe Anderson has my son. I'm going with you."

Nikki grabbed her shoulders. "You stay here and don't say anything. I might be way off, and we can't go barging in. You know that. If Zach's alive—and that's still a big if—we have to do this right. The leak about the print match has to have spooked Joe. If it's him. And it might not be."

"You don't believe that," Caitlin said.

"I don't know. I'm going to bring in Miller and Liam, and we'll figure this out. You don't say anything until you hear from me. And you don't go anywhere near the Andersons. I can't be worrying about protecting you right now."

Caitlin shook her head. "It goes against my every nature to keep quiet and to sit and do nothing."

"I know," Nikki said. "That's why you need to do exactly that."

Nikki told both families that something with another case had come up and she had to leave. She promised to keep them updated and tried not to race outside to her jeep. She called Liam as she barreled away from the house. Were all three of these cases connected? Had Caitlin been right all this time?

"I was just about to call you," he said. "What—"

"Listen to me." Nikki cut him off. "What I'm about to tell you might sound crazy, but I just need you to hear me out." She quickly walked him through what she'd realized, hushing him every time he tried to interrupt. "Joe's gas receipt from Friday was a cash receipt. There's no name. How easy would it have been for him to backtrack some time that day when they were supposedly searching and dig that receipt out of the trash?"

"That's what I've been trying to tell you," Liam said. "Courtney just called me. Remember Dana's car mats that had a few stains on them? Courtney tested them, and they're a common chemical used to stain wood. She's running tests on the stain you found on Zach's shoes, but I'm betting it's going to be a similar result."

Nikki's heart raced. "Please tell me you're getting the search warrant."

"Miller's on it," Liam said. "He's having trouble trying to track a judge down. You know how hard that is to do on a Sunday."

"Damnit. We can't wait. Joe's got to have heard about the print match."

"We don't have a choice."

"Yes, we do. I'm on the road right now. I'll go to the Andersons and tell them I wanted to update them on what happened yesterday. I'll talk about that and see if I can get a feel for Joe's reaction. You come with Miller and the warrant as soon as you can."

"Let me meet you there," Liam said. "Miller can bring the warrant."

"Fine, but if I'm already inside, don't come in. You'll be able to park out of sight in the driveway and wait for Miller." She ended the call and pulled up her navigation system.

CHAPTER THIRTY-ONE

Nikki took a deep breath as she drove slowly down the Andersons' driveway. If she was right about this, why had Joe killed Dana and Kellan after being so careful all these years? Had Dana caught him trying to do something to her son?

The sight of Rory's work truck sent a wave of fear through Nikki. She'd forgotten that Joe was working on a custom build for Rory's new construction project. She dug through her bag for her phone and texted Rory that he needed to make an excuse to leave without mentioning that Nikki was here or that she'd asked him to leave. She prayed that he would see it before Liam and Miller arrived with the warrant. She had a feeling Joe wouldn't go without a fight.

Nikki didn't see Joe's truck, but the garage door was open and Maggie's car in its spot. Nikki parked in front of the garage and looked inside. Everything seemed to be in order, but the idea of Rory being somewhere on this property with Joe terrified her.

The blue tarp at the back of the garage covering the snowmobiles caught her eye. She crept inside the garage, hoping Joe didn't have cameras set up inside. She was pushing her luck without a search warrant, but the garage door had been left open. Nikki didn't need to lift the tarp to see there was only one snowmobile. There had been two the other day.

The other snowmobile must have been Zach's, and Joe had disposed of it after Nikki and Liam's visit the other day.

Nikki longed to go to the wood shop, but she didn't want to press her luck any further. And she wanted to make sure Rory was all right. She left the garage and walked to the front door, searching for any sign of being watched along the way.

Maggie answered the door. She was still in her robe and pajamas and looked like she hadn't slept in days. "Agent Hunt. I didn't expect you," she said.

"I'm sorry to drop by without calling, but I was in the area, and I wanted to let you know what happened with Eddie and the lab."

"The district attorney has made me aware," Maggie said.

Nikki had forgotten about that. "Not all of the details. May I come in?"

Maggie smoothed her tangled hair. "I look a mess."

"Don't worry about it. It's Sunday."

Maggie smiled slightly. "Of course. Come in."

Nikki waited for her to offer tea or coffee, but Maggie went into the living room and sat down on the couch. Nikki followed her and sat in the recliner that faced the open-floor plan.

"Where's Joe?" Nikki tried to keep her tone light.

"In the shop with a client. I don't want to disturb him." Maggie's eyes seemed glazed over as she looked up at Nikki. "Did Eddie confess to killing Dana?"

"Not exactly." Nikki watched for any reaction from Maggie, but she appeared to be numb. "Eddie was working with his sister and his girlfriend." Nikki told her how the siblings had been part of the system and believed that it didn't work. "Eddie really has anger issues for mothers who can't stay sober. His mother never could."

"It makes sense." Maggie sighed. "I'm not sure if I should be talking to you anymore, now that I think of it. Our lawyer said to let everything go through him."

"Well, I'm not here to bring you in or anything like that," Nikki said. "I understand why you did it. Past behavior is the best indicator of future behavior, after all. You had every reason to believe Dana wouldn't stay sober."

"I underestimated her," Maggie said. "I should have listened to her. She tried to tell me, after all." Maggie's eyes had a glazed look. Nikki wondered if she were medicated or just lost in her own misery.

"What do you mean?"

Maggie's chin trembled. "It doesn't matter now. Kellan's gone."

The sound of the back door banging open sent a wave of anxiety through Nikki. Was Rory leaving? Or coming inside to find out what was going on?

Joe came in from the kitchen, looking huge in his heavy flannel shirt. "Agent Hunt. I didn't realize you were here. Did you come to see Rory? He's in the shop."

"She stopped by to update me on yesterday's events," Maggie said flatly.

"I heard you have someone in custody," Joe said. "I'm praying this will all be over soon."

Was Nikki imaging the undercurrent in his voice? If Joe had watched the news this morning, he had to know about David Webster. Murderers were at their most dangerous when they were cornered. She didn't want to panic him.

"You're welcome to join me and Rory in the shop, but I'm afraid you'll find our conversation pretty boring."

Nikki forced a smile. Why hadn't Rory texted her back? "I need to get going, but thanks."

Joe nodded and headed back to the kitchen.

Nikki walked to the large bay window that overlooked the back of the Andersons' property. Beneath the window, several heavy stained-glass vases and sculptures rested on a beautiful side table. Joe was already halfway to the shop, and Rory was inside, at Joe's mercy.

"Can I walk you out, Agent?" Maggie asked.

Nikki's heart raced. Walking out now meant having to drive away from Rory. She couldn't do much without the warrant unless she had probable cause, and busting into the wood shop because of a gut feeling could ruin the entire investigation. It could mean Joe would walk free no matter what evidence was there.

Turning away from the window, she started to tell Maggie no. But something about the look on the woman's face stopped Nikki in her tracks. She wasn't scared or angry. She was resigned to the situation. How many years had she looked the other way?

She'd said Dana "tried to tell her" for years.

Nikki's phone vibrated.

He found a judge. Stand by.

She slipped the phone back into her pocket and sat down.

"When did Dana tell you that she saw Joe with David Webster?"

CHAPTER THIRTY-TWO

Maggie stared at Nikki with dull eyes. Seconds clicked away on the grandfather clock in the hall that Joe had surely built. Maggie sighed and folded her hands in her lap. "The night he disappeared," she said.

"And you didn't believe her?" Nikki replied.

Maggie made a face. "Would you?"

"I wouldn't have threatened her into silence," Nikki said.

Maggie looked out the window again. "I didn't. She looked up to me back then. I convinced her that Joe and the boy she saw were just wrestling. Joe was a wrestler in high school. I told her he gave private lessons. But she couldn't say anything because Joe would be a suspect and get in trouble for something he didn't do. Our lives would be ruined all because of her. She believed me, at least for a while. She was really too young to understand what she saw, anyway."

"What do you mean 'something he didn't do'?"

She shook her head. "I told myself that I'd told Dana the truth. And if I hadn't, it was a one-time thing. Joe would never do something like that. He would never take advantage of a child..." She looked completely defeated. "But Agent Hunt, you of all people should know that a person can convince themselves of anything if they try hard enough."

Nikki shook her head. She knew what Maggie was referring to. "This isn't the same situation I was in. This is nothing like my parents' murders. Nor is it about them. It's about you and what you've been hiding for almost thirty years."

"He's not a bad person," Maggie said.

"Dana never brought it up again?"

"Not until she came home for winter break. She was taking a psychology class and they were learning about traumatic events. It triggered her memory somehow. We got into a big fight. I knew she was using speed to study because she had such a big course load. I told her she'd better keep her crazy mouth shut, or I would tell Mom and Dad. I guess she believed me. Or decided it was in her best interests to pretend she did. It was all in the past, anyway."

"Until Kellan came along."

Maggie stilled. "Joe never put a hand on him."

"Because he was too young. But at some point during her journey to sobriety, Dana remembered everything. She struggled to deal with it, but she knew her son would eventually be at risk. She lived the last year of her life for him. To save him from Joe. And you knew what your husband was capable of and still paid to have the tests results altered. You couldn't let Dana win, could you?"

"Kellan was all I had," Maggie said. "My parents are gone. Dana was never going to be family. She wouldn't have stayed sober. I know that in my heart."

"Like you know in your heart that Joe wouldn't touch your nephew?" Nikki said angrily. "That goes against everything we know about serial predators. Kellan would have been the right age, not to mention easy to manipulate. You gave Joe endless opportunities. How many boys has Joe hurt over the years? Are Kellan and David the only two he's killed? What about Zach Reeves?"

"Stop it," Maggie shouted. "Kellan's death is all Dana's fault. She should have stayed away."

"Zach Reeves went missing that same Friday," Nikki said. "Joe had put the time in grooming him. He might have felt safe enough to let Zach go. But he forgot Kellan got home early that day. He saw them and called his mother, didn't he? He must have called from a cell phone with a burner app. I'm assuming the same one Joe used to communicate with Zach the past few months. Dana shows up and all hell breaks loose."

Maggie's lips were pressed so tightly together they'd gone white.

"Was your sister still alive when you got home, Maggie? Did you help him cover both murders up?"

"No," she burst out. "I had no idea until I heard about Zach going missing, even when you said that Dana was murdered. Zach had been here before, working in the woodshed with Joe. He was supposed to come Friday morning and work since they didn't have school. That's when I started to wonder. Even then, I kept telling myself I was going crazy. Joe wouldn't kill anyone. But this morning's news said that a print from something of Zach's matched the Webster case. I couldn't believe it."

"The print was from a letter your husband sent to Zach as part of his efforts to groom him. He's likely done the same thing with other boys. How many opportunities did you have to stop him?"

She rocked back and forth. "I didn't know about any others, I swear. Joe spends so much time in the shop. He has apprentices in sometimes. Wanting to learn about woodworking."

"You didn't want to know," Nikki said. "You're partly to blame for Kellan's and Dana's murders. Zach's death, too."

Maggie looked blankly at her. "Zach's not dead. I heard him last night."

Nikki stared at her. "What?"

"I crushed sleeping pills into Joe's drink last night and went to the shop to search. I called out for him, thinking I was nuts. He answered me. It sounded like he was beating against a wall."

Nikki swiftly walked over and grabbed her shoulders. "Where in the wood shop?"

"I don't know. I went to bed."

The woman had lost her sense of reality. Had she even heard Zach? And if she had, was he in there with Rory right now?

Nikki pulled her cell out of her pocket and stopped the recording she'd started after getting Liam's text.

"Put that away."

The familiar click of a trigger being cocked sent a wave of fear through Nikki. She looked up in time to see Maggie take aim.

Nikki hit the floor, her ears ringing. She stared across the room at what used to be Maggie Anderson. The shot to her mouth had snapped Maggie's head back. Teeth and brain matter spilled out from the exit wound. The bullet must have gone through and embedded into the chair.

Nikki's head was still ringing from the gunshot. She heard the back door slam open and barely had time hit "call" on her cell before shoving it under the couch.

Joe barreled into the room, calling his wife's name. He sagged against the wall when he saw her. "Mags?"

Nikki inched toward the side table sitting beneath the big bay window. If she could get to one of the heavy glass bowls, she could use it as a weapon. Joe seemed paralyzed with grief. She raised her arm, her fingers brushing against one of the bowls. She grabbed it and started to get up.

Joe turned, staring at her as though he'd just now realized she was there. "You did this."

"Maggie shot herself because she spent her life protecting you. She couldn't take it anymore."

Shaking with rage, he advanced on her. If he got his hands on her, Nikki might not be able to get free. She backed away, trying not to get caught on the table. "My team knows I'm here. You better think twice about doing something stupid."

"Something stupid? Woman, you don't know who you're dealing with. I've lived life my way long before that accident with that kid."

"His name was David Webster," Nikki replied angrily. "The boy you're hiding right now is named Zach Reeves. And I'm not the only one who knows he's here."

Joe lunged at her, moving surprisingly fast for such a big man. Nikki swung as hard as she could, slamming the bowl against his skull, the glass cracking from the impact. Joe staggered back, and Nikki bolted for the door. Her boots slipped on the hardwood floor and she went down hard, smacking her head on the floor, her ribs throbbing. Dazed, she rolled over and started to crawl to the front entry. Meaty hands grabbed her ankles and yanked her backwards. Nikki twisted, trying to find the advantage, but Joe's grip was too strong.

He grabbed her head and slammed it on the floor. Nikki spit blood, and her vision blurred. She tried to get up, but he straddled her, his knees on either side of her waist. He pinned her wrists to the floor.

"All Maggie and I wanted to do was raise Kellan in peace. But Dana couldn't just let things go. It's her fault that Kellan got hurt. Then she shows up and goes crazy. I didn't have a choice." He pressed his heavy chest against her back. "I didn't have a choice. Now Maggie's gone. Even in death, she manages to ruin Maggie's life."

Nikki tried to control her breathing and conserve energy while her mind raced. Joe was too heavy, his full weight bearing down on her.

"Here's what I'm going to do," he said. "You and I are going to go to the shop where your little boyfriend is probably wondering what's going on, and you're going to watch me kill him."

Nikki couldn't control the cry that escaped her mouth. She couldn't let Rory die. Where was he? Why hadn't he run in the house when he heard the gunshot like Joe? Had Joe already done something to him?

"I'll kill you," Nikki managed to choke out. "If you hurt him, I swear to God I'll kill you."

Joe's big belly laugh sent a new round of pain through her body. He stood and yanked Nikki to her feet. Her ribs felt like they were on fire as he dragged her through the house and outside. A freezing fog had moved in. Nikki could feel the tiny bits of ice as he marched her through the snow.

Liam had to be on his way. Even if he didn't pick up the call, at least part of the struggle had to have ended up in his voicemail. Miller probably knew she'd come to the Andersons', too. Where were they? Had the stupid ice fog caused the delay?

"When I heard the shot," Joe said, "I knew things had gone bad. I made sure Rory couldn't follow me. But don't worry. You'll get to watch me finish him off. Open the door."

Nikki couldn't stop her hands from shaking. Joe had so many tools in the shop that could be used as deadly weapons. She held her breath, afraid of seeing Rory bleeding out on the floor.

Joe pushed her inside, his hand still around her neck.

She immediately looked at the main shop area, terrified of what she'd see. But she saw only a small pool of fresh blood and no other sign of Rory.

"Don't get too excited," Joe said. "His hands are tied real tight. He's not going to save you."

Nikki's mind raced. Could she get away from Joe? Her neck hurt from his grip, but maybe if she could sweep his feet out from beneath him, she could reach one of the tools. He didn't have a gun on him or he would have used it by now.

"Look, he left us a bread trail."

It took Nikki a few seconds to register the trail of blood leading to the back of the shop. The lounge area, utility room and bathroom were in the back. Liam had checked both the furnace room and the bathroom. She hobbled toward the back of the big building. Had Zach been hidden somewhere else? Had Maggie really heard him?

"Rory." Nikki's heart lodged in her throat when she saw him curled on the floor. Joe laughed and released her. She ran to him, praying she'd find a pulse. He was alive. Unconscious and bleeding from what looked like a hard blow to the head. Nikki cradled his head in her lap. "Rory, wake up. I'm here."

He groaned in pain, but his eyes fluttered open. Nikki brushed his hair back off his face, and he tried to smile. "Where did he go?"

"Don't worry about Joe," Nikki said. "You're going to be just fine."

Joe sneered. "She's lying to you, Rory. I'm sorry you got involved in all of this. You're a good man. But she killed Maggie."

"She killed herself," Nikki shot back. "But you might as well have pulled the trigger."

"Not him," Rory mumbled. "The kid. Where'd he go?"

Nikki froze, staring at Joe. "What kid?"

"Don't answer him," Nikki said. "Just rest."

"Shut up." Joe stepped toward them, his bear-like arms reaching for Nikki's throat. His body jerked and spasmed. A second blow struck the back of Joe's body. Nikki could see the saw blade in the dim light. Joe grabbed his neck and tried to turn around, but the blade struck a third time, and then a fourth. Joe fell to his knees, begging, blood flowing out of the wounds on his back, but his pleas for mercy went unanswered and he stopped moving.

A dirty, thin boy with a cracked lip clutched the saw, his knuckles white from the grip. Nikki could see the dried blood on his fingers and the deep purple bruises on his arms.

"Zach." Nikki kept her voice as even as possible and the boy took a step forward, recognizing his name. Nikki knew it was him. "Zach, look at me," she said. "My name is Nikki. I know your grandparents and your mom. You're safe now, but I need you to stop." He took another step forward, and despite the dirt and bruises, Nikki could see the resemblance to Caitlin in his fine features. Zach was young, not yet grown into his features, but he would grow into his cheekbones and rosy lips.

"I want him to die," Zach said.

"I know you do," Nikki replied slowly. She knew adrenaline would be pumping through Zach's body, that he needed to calm down. "But that's the easy way out for him. If he lives and goes to prison, his every waking moment will be a living hell. I promise you that."

Zach held the saw blade in mid-air. Joe hadn't moved, but he was breathing.

"Zach, my name is Nikki," she repeated. "I'm an FBI agent."

"Caitlin talked about you," Zach replied. "She said you were the bravest person she'd ever met."

Rory tried to sit up, but Nikki put her hands on his shoulders. "Stay." She maneuvered out from underneath him and slowly stood. "I'd say the same thing about you. Caitlin helped me find you. She refused to give up, even when everyone else thought you were gone. She's waiting for you, and so are your grandparents. Put the blade down."

Zach slowly lowered it, but he never stopped watching Joe. Nikki gave Joe a wide berth, making sure to move slowly as she approached. She could see tears welling in Zach's eyes, but he handed her the blade, and all Nikki could see was relief on his face.

CHAPTER THIRTY-THREE

Nikki found zip ties and secured Joe's hands before calling for paramedics and backup. Rory sat up with a groan, clutching his head. "Asshole hit me from behind," he said to Nikki as she knelt down beside him.

"I'm sure you have a concussion. Just stay there until the paramedics get here, OK?"

Zach still gripped Nikki's hand tightly. She pulled up the familiar number on her phone and hit send, putting the call on speaker.

"Nikki? What's going on?" Caitlin said.

Zach's eyes widened at the sound of her frantic voice. He opened his mouth, but no sound would come out.

Nikki squeezed his hand reassuringly. "I thought you and the Reeves might want to talk to Zach."

Caitlin's guttural sob made Nikki's eyes tear up. She couldn't imagine the mixture of joy and fear that the family had to be feeling. Zach had been through something unthinkable, but Nikki knew that he had three people ready and waiting to do everything in their power to help him move on.

"Zach?" Ben's voice came over the line. "Are you there?"

The sound of his grandfather's voice snapped Zach out of his silence. "I'm here, Grandpa," he said, a tear falling down his face. "I want to come home."

Rory tried to get out of going to the hospital, but Nikki threatened to call his parents and brother, so he relented. Nikki climbed into the ambulance and kissed him. "I'll be there as soon as we get things in some kind of order here."

"OK," he said. "You think Zach will be all right?"

"I hope so," Nikki replied. "He has family who love him, and that's a huge asset."

"So do you," Rory said thickly.

Nikki's pulse quickened. "I know. And I feel the same way about them."

Rory grabbed her shirt and pulled her in for a hard kiss. "I'll see you soon."

She eased down out of the rig, and the paramedic shut the doors.

Zach and Joe had already been taken to the hospital in separate ambulances. Caitlin and the Reeves would meet him there. With Maggie gone, Joe didn't have anybody. Nikki hoped that he survived to endure the loneliness of her death.

Nikki went in search of Liam and Miller, who'd arrived before the paramedics. She found them at the back corner of the shop, where the utility room was. Joe had installed a tornado-safe underground shelter beneath that area of the shop and hidden the entrance with a sliding door similar to the one he'd shown Nikki and Liam the first day they'd visited the shop. Four concrete stairs led down to the in-ground shelter, which looked large enough to hold roughly four people. It reminded Nikki of a burial crypt.

"This had to be where Kellan's body was kept," Liam said when Nikki joined them.

Zach had told her that he'd been with Joe when Dana arrived. Kellan had seen them when he got home from school and called his mother in a panic. Nikki guessed that he used the first phone he saw and used the burner app on Joe's phone without realizing it. That's why they hadn't been able to trace the call.

Zach's account was fuzzy, but Dana had confronted Joe and tried to call the police. Kellan had fallen in the process and hit his head. He died in his mother's arms in the storm shelter while

Zach sat hopelessly by and watched. He wasn't sure when Dana and Kellan left the shelter, and Nikki suspected they would find sedatives in Zach's system.

Zach hadn't told her much about how he and Joe met, but Nikki hoped he would open up to his family in the coming days.

"Once Joe's face is plastered all over the state, I think we'll find out he's hurt a lot more people," Liam said. "Unless he killed all of them like he did David Webster."

It was true that victims often came forward when they knew it was safe. How many lives had Joe ruined? "He's a master manipulator. My guess is he threatened and shamed them into silence or believing it was their fault. I just hope he gives the Websters closure and tells them where he buried their son's body."

"We're going to tear this shop and house apart," Miller said firmly. "If he's hiding anything else, we'll find it."

Dizziness washed over Nikki. She sat down on the steps and looked up at Liam. "I guess Caitlin told you about Zach."

He nodded. "I told her to focus on her family for now. Things between us can wait." He studied her with narrowed eyes. "You should get checked out, too."

"Paramedics cleared me," she said.

"Then go to the hospital and be with Rory," Liam said. "We can handle this."

For once, Nikki didn't argue with him.

Nikki paced nervously in the quiet hospital waiting area reserved for family. The charge nurse had told her that Rory was arguing about spending the night and that his family was in the emergency room with him, waiting for X-ray results.

"Should I tell him you're here?" the nurse asked.

"I'll wait until his family leaves." Nikki sat down in the nearest chair and rested her head against the wall. The aspirin she'd taken on the drive to the hospital was finally starting to help, but she felt like her body had melted from fatigue. She closed her eyes and prayed for sleep.

A warm hand nudged her shoulder. Nikki peeled her eyes open, half-expecting to see Rory. Instead, a disheveled but happy Caitlin Newport was standing over her. Before Nikki could ask how Zach was doing, Caitlin bent down and threw her arms around Nikki's neck, sobbing her thanks.

"I was just doing my job." Nikki patted Caitlin's back.

"I know." Caitlin sniffled. "But you listened when no one else would, and you found him."

"Only because you wouldn't give up," Nikki grumbled. "Your talent for getting your way finally came in handy."

Caitlin snorted with laughter. "I guess so. Is Rory going to be OK?"

"He's got a concussion. His parents are in there right now," she said awkwardly.

"They don't really hate you," Caitlin said. "They just can't let go of that mindset. But hang in there."

Nikki forced a smile. "I always do."

EPILOGUE

A week later, Nikki stood in front of her bedroom mirror, trying to tame her thick hair. The bruises from the fight with Joe were healing, and her skin had regained most of its color after several days of rest. She felt silly at butterflies tearing through her stomach. She and Rory had spent enough time together that she shouldn't be nervous to see him. But for the first time, he was coming to her house and meeting Lacey.

She pulled the brush through her hair one more time and then tossed it on her dresser. "Lacey, what are you doing?"

Her daughter rounded the corner wearing sparkling butterfly wings and a pink eye mask she'd made at school. "Don't I look like a butterfly, Mommy?"

"Absolutely."

Lacey hopped onto Nikki's bed and started bouncing. "I heard your name on the TV earlier."

"You did?"

"You're a hero," Lacey said solemnly.

"I helped." The Websters had held a press conference today to announce that their son's remains had finally been recovered from a shallow grave at the dairy farm that Joe had sold. Joe had agreed to tell the location of David's body in exchange for a lesser sentence, but between the murders of David and Dana, he would spend the rest of his life in prison. He refused to name any other boys, but Liam had managed to locate a few of them from evidence found at the Anderson home.

The doorbell rang, and a fresh jolt of nerves went through Nikki.

Lacey jumped off the bed and ran for the living room. "Is that your new friend, Mommy?"

"Yes, and I can't wait for you to meet him." Heart racing, Nikki walked towards the door.

Getting justice for Caitlin, for the Websters, and for Dana and her son was all that Nikki had wanted, and it was a relief to put their cases to bed and know that they could sleep soundly. She'd fought for justice every day since her parents' deaths, but there had been mistakes and wrong turns. She knew what it felt like to have closure, and now, so did the Websters.

A LETTER FROM STACY

I want to say a huge thank you for choosing to read *One Perfect Grave*. If you did enjoy it, and want to keep up to date with all my latest releases, just sign up at the following link. Your email address will never be shared and you can unsubscribe at any time.

www.bookouture.com/stacy-green

I hope you loved *One Perfect Grave* and if you did I would be very grateful if you could write a review. I'd love to hear what you think, and it makes such a difference helping new readers to discover one of my books for the first time.

I love hearing from my readers—you can get in touch on Facebook, Instagram, Twitter or my website.

Thanks,
Stacy

 StacyGreenAuthor
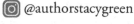 @authorstacygreen
 @StacyGreen26
stacygreenauthor.com

ACKNOWLEDGMENTS

I want to thank my readers for their incredible support of the Nikki Hunt series. She's such a fun character to write, and I am thrilled so many people are enjoying the series. I also want to thank my editor at Bookouture, Jennifer Hunt, for her help in creating the series. Thank you to the entire Bookouture editorial and marketing staff for their hard work and dedication.

To my family, particularly my husband, Rob Whisenand, and my daughter, Grace: I couldn't have finished this book without your support and understanding. Thank you so much for putting up with me.

Special thank you to John Kelly for his input on Minnesota's natural resources, the St. Croix River, and Stillwater. As always, massive thank you to Kristine Kelly for her support and attention to detail.

Maureen Downey, thank you for all you do despite my constant state of disorganization. Many thanks to Theresa and Poised Pen Productions for handling much of my social media so that I can focus on writing.

This book was written during the Covid-19 pandemic, but I chose to leave it out of the series because it's taken up enough of our lives, and fiction is supposed to be an escape. I'm so fortunate that my husband and I are able to work from home, but I want to send a massive thank you to all the essential workers and medical professionals on the frontlines.

One Perfect Grave was partially inspired by the Jacob Wetterling case. Jacob disappeared in 1989, and his killer was finally brought to justice in 2016. There are far too many stories like Jacob's, and too many parents suffering unimaginable loss. Thank you to the National Center for Missing and Exploited Children for their efforts to help these families, and to all law enforcement officers who work so tirelessly to bring closure in these cases.

CPSIA information can be obtained
at www.ICGtesting.com
Printed in the USA
LVHW041632220721
693425LV00007B/1023

9 781800 192744